The Darkest Night

"Wings Of Dawn"

For Melissa and my lovely Grandma Ann.
Our love for you continues to soar high above the heavens,
as our memories of you sparkle like the rays of dawn.

The Darkest Night
"Wings Of Dawn"

Written By
A. LaQuette

Cover Photo By
Brian Zurakowski
*of **Atomic Cat Studio***

Cover Designed By
Sun Child Wind Spirit

Edited By
Mylia Tiye Mal Jaza

The Darkest Night – "Wings Of Dawn"

Copyright © 2018, A. LaQuette
All Rights Reserved.

ISBN 10: 1983546771   ISBN 13: 978-1983546778

Author
A. LaQuette
angel_mylove28@yahoo.com
www.alaquette.org

Imprint of Record
CreateSpace On-Demand Publishing
7290-B Investment Drive
Charleston, SC 29418

Self-Publishing Associate
Dr. Mary M. Jefferson
BePublished.Org - Chicago
(972) 880-8316
www.bepublished.org

Series. Volume 3. First Edition.
Printed in the United States of America.
Recycled Paper Encouraged.

TABLE OF CONTENTS

🕊 🕊 🕊

"Hope deferred makes the heart sick, but when the desire is fulfilled, it is a tree of life."

Proverbs 13:12

CHAPTER 1

Dark skies, gray clouds, and a drizzle of rain that's ever so slight that it feels as if cool soft kisses of comfort were being showered upon the somber crowd. *How appropriate was the weather for such occasions.* I often wondered if it was more than just a coincidence that sometimes, on days such as these, that nature decides to match the mood of others by forecasting an atmosphere of gloom, as a way of paying respect to those that no longer graced the presence of the living. *No,* I don't think it was a coincidence at all. Nature is God and God is nature. Nature loves all of its children and takes no satisfaction in having to accept one of its beloved back into its bosom.

I slowly began to take in all the faces in the crowd. There had to be at least 80 people in attendance. Some of them I knew and some I didn't. Phillip and his dad where standing beside us. I don't think Phillip ever took his eyes off me. Even when I would turn to look at him, he would not avert his eyes. He just held my gaze until I looked away. It was as if, to him at least, I was the only one present; no one mattered at the moment but me.

He had tried to come over to talk to me on several occasions, but someone would turn him away, knowing that I wasn't up for company. I knew that he was concerned about me, but I didn't want him to see me in such a bad state of mind. So much had happened so fast and it was too much for me to handle. I would allow him to comfort me when I was ready and at the moment I wasn't quite sure when that would be.

I recognized several of my school mates, as well as some teachers; white teachers. I shouldn't be that surprised though, because Belinda was very smart and played the part of teacher's pet quite well. And besides, not all the teachers saw the world in white. Some of them were actually pretty decent and it appeared as though all those that came to mind were the ones who made it to show their respect. School had started earlier in the week, but I was not ready to go just yet; to face that place and be the center of everyone's attention.

By now, the news of Dominique's body being discovered had made its way throughout Pearl, MS. My parents said that I can take all the time off I needed before going back to school. Maybe I would return this week, just so I can concentrate on something else beside the turbulence that had consumed my life.

Majority of our neighborhood was in attendance as well. I spotted Big Roy, Charlie Boy and even Douglas. I allowed myself to smile a little as I remembered how he and Belinda were always at each other's throat about something. How honorable of him to come and pay his respect. Funny how death tends to make us forget our detestation of others, allowing us to see just how much time has been wasted on such petty occurrences, leaving us to deal with the days, months and even years ahead which are filled with remorse, knowing that there is nothing we can do to make atonement. The understanding that flowers must be given while their scent can still be enjoyed will have come too late.

There were so many faces. I was trying my best to take them all in. These faces were so different, but yet the same. Every cheek was wet with tears of mourning; mine being the only exception. I haven't cried in days. I wasn't even sure I had any tears left to be shed. All I felt was numbness and a detachment from everyone and everything. It was almost as if nothing seemed real, like a dream I couldn't fully awake from. But if this is what kept me from feeling, I wanted to remain in this state of deadness.

Whenever the police decided to release her body, we would be right back at this same cemetery to lay my sister to rest, a day I was not looking forward to. When I first heard the news about Dominique's body being discovered, it ripped me apart. I don't know why exactly, but that deep sense of loss that I felt before didn't remain the way I thought it would have. I don't know if it's because I have mourned her for so long and now the closure we sought was now made available to us, or was it because I was mentally and physically drained and there was nothing left inside me.

My father went down to identify Dominique's body and when he returned home, he was very hesitant about telling us any of the details, such as the state her body was in. After my mother insisted, he finally told us that he couldn't identify the body with certainty. He said that the body was badly decomposed and appeared to have been a meal for whatever underwater creatures that dwelled in the lake. It looked as though her head and the side of her face had been smashed in. Her hair was so matted and tangled that he couldn't even make out its color.

So, in the end, the only thing we could go by was her dress and ankle bracelet, which were the only things that could be truly and without a doubt identified as hers. After hearing about the horrible state of Dominique's body, and listening to Mama's screams that followed, I allowed myself to envision the pain she must have endured during her final hour and this caused my body, mind and spirit to just completely shut down. I don't feel anything anymore, like I'm not even a human being. I was just an empty shell of the person I once was, *just like Belinda.*

I continued surveying the crowd as the Reverend was reciting the 23 Psalm. My eyes finally fell upon Belinda's mother. They lingered on her for a long while. She was dressed in all black, from head to toe. She wore a wide black hat that held a lace veil that concealed her face. But her heartache could not be hidden behind a piece of cloth. Her pain was apparent and exposed for all to see. Her only child was gone. The look on her face; the glistening on her cheeks and the way she gazed at the brown casket that held her child, told the story of a mother's suffering. Her brother, Benjamin, supported her as she walked slowly over to place two red roses on top of the casket. She stood there a moment with her head hanging low, as she placed her hand on the glossy surface. She stood back as the Reverend began to speak again.

"Before we say our final goodbyes, with heavy hearts, to our beloved sista Belinda, let us rememba what tha word tells us Saints, 'The Lord is near to the brokenhearted and saves the crushed in spirit. Blessed are those who mourn, for they shall be comforted'," he continued as he walked over to place a rose of his own on top of the casket. "From dust we were raised, and to dust we shall return," The Reverend recited as the casket was being lowered into the earth signifying finality.

Belinda's father, Amos, cries could be heard above all others, setting off a chain reaction from the crowd. It seemed like everyone in attendance had begun to cry out. I wanted to just cover my ears to shut them out, but I knew that would be inappropriate of me. I just stood still as if I was a block of stone.

My mother was standing beside me seeming as motionless as I was. She, like all the others, was overcome with tears. But who were her tears truly for? Were they for Belinda or were they for her own child who she would have to lay to rest very soon, were they for them both? She squeezed my hand when she noticed me looking at her. I didn't even feel her touch before now. *How long had she been holding my hand?*

I looked down at Xavier, who stood in front of our father. Something else was holding his interest. He was staring off to his right, looking towards two huge oak trees on the other side of the cemetery. I looked to see if I could see what held his attention so keenly . . . *nothing*. I turned my attention back to Mrs. Kirkland. She was being led back to her seat now. It appeared as though each step she took was harder than the step before. Others in the crowd began to come forward to drop flowers into the ground, adorning the box with a different array of flowers. My family was the last to do so.

As my rose landed among the others, the last gift any of us will be able to bestow, my head became overwhelming filled with so many reminiscences. I thought of Dominique, of Belinda, the three of us, the closeness and comfort we felt with one another. They're both gone now, leaving me behind to mourn their loss. Death was easy for those whose time had come to give up their spirit, but so hard for those left behind to pick up the pieces left in its wake. As I stood there looking down into the grave; I felt a feeling of uncertainty. The girl lying in the ground below was my friend from the beginning, but what was she to me in the end.

The mystery surrounding Dominique could have been solved a long time ago, if only Belinda would have told us what she knew. There are still so many questions that needed answering, and in due time, Claire won't have a choice but to talk. The Monroe's have conveniently pulled a disappearing act. Their somewhere "taking a break" from it all we were told. *How convenient.* They can't hide forever. There is a story that needs to be told; minds that needed putting to ease; hearts that needed mending. I know they're afraid of losing the one child they have left, but if she played a part in Dominique's death, she deserved everything she got coming to her.

My father brought his handkerchief up to my cheeks. *Was I crying?* I brought my hand up to my face and felt the wetness there, tears that had been absent for so long, had suddenly returned. A realization occurred to me in that moment. I had been too angry to cry -- angry at Belinda for taking knowledge about Dominique's death to the grave with her; angry with her for betraying me in ways I have yet to figure out; angry with Dominique for being too kind and trusting of everyone who was undeserving of it; and angry with my mother for not listening to grandmother and insist Dominique stay in that night.

But, I was even more angry with myself for being so useless in it all. I wasn't there for anyone when they needed me the most, not my sister, not Belinda, and ironically enough, not even David. If only I would have talked to him and listened to what he had to say, maybe Belinda would be alive today, and David too, *if only.*

The rain had begun to come down a little harder, blending in with the tears that I now allowed to stream freely. Belinda's family and mine were the only ones that remained at the site as the diggers began to cover the hole that was now Belinda's final resting place. I couldn't take my eyes from the area of the casket that I knew her head laid; prompting me to think about how lovely she had looked inside, as though she were only sleeping.

Mrs. Kirkland had her dressed so nicely in a dark blue dress that looked so good on her. Her long hair flowed on either side of her shoulders with bangs neatly trimmed. The makeup was done in a fashion that I knew Belinda would have hated; subtle colors; not bold enough for her, but appropriate for her life's finale.

"It's time to go honey," my mother said as she grabbed be by the shoulders, turning me away from the casket.

"I just want to stay a little while longer," I heard myself say.

I tried to loosen myself from her hands as I looked back over my shoulder, wanting to focus on that area of the box once again, but my mother wouldn't let me go. I didn't want to leave right now. I don't know why, but I felt like I needed to stay. The grip on my shoulder was firm, but her voice was full of sweetness.

"Baby you can't stay out here. This weather is only gonna get worse," she said as she continued to lead me away. "Let's go on home."

The thought of not having my sister or friend around me anymore sent a chill through me so deep that it caused me to tremor. My father took noticed and quickly removed his jacket and draped it over my shoulders. I wanted to tell him that this chill ran bone deep and his jacket gave me absolutely no comfort at all, but I couldn't form any words at the moment.

As I was being led away, I looked back once more as the men were still at work covering the grave. I realized that no matter how angry I was with Belinda or how betrayed I felt, I didn't want to leave. Even now, I wanted to be there for her until the very end.

CHAPTER 2

The journey home seemed to take hours. No one uttered a solitary word. The ambiance was thick with the sadness that followed loss. I was thankful for my mom sitting in the middle, because I didn't want to be caught between the stares of her and my father. We decided not to go to the repast at the church, because the funeral was enough for us. I was thankful for the decision not to attend. Being around all of Belinda's family and having to sit through all the chitter-chatter I'm sure would be going on about her life, and to gaze upon her mother in her grief stricken state, was a little too much for me.

I laid my head up against the windows cool pane. Home is what I longed for at the moment. And the solitude of my room, I longed for even more. Strange thing is, I could sit in there all day long, but not sleep. Dominique's things seemed to be too overwhelming for me suddenly. Before, I wanted nothing more than to be able to just be amongst her belongings, to feel that sense of closeness to her; waiting for the day to come when she came through the door ready to claim her possessions once again. Now I couldn't even look at them knowing that she would never claim what was hers.

At first, I was sleeping on the sofa in the living room, but I knew it would only be a matter of time before my mother would have a few things to say about that. She couldn't stand for nobody sleeping on her good couch or even sitting on it for that matter, causing it to look sunk in and all worn out she said. Nobody could do that except Grandma, so I knew I only had a pass due to recent events. But lately, I have been sleeping in Xavier's room, which was by far the smallest room in the house. At first I thought Xavier would complain about the invasion of his minute space, but he didn't seem to mind the intrusion at all. He seems to welcome the company. It made me feel remorseful about all the times I kicked him out of mine.

My father added the extra room on after my mother had become pregnant with my brother. He said he wanted to get started building it soon after they found out they were pregnant, but my grandmother told him to wait until after the seventh month, because doing anything before was considered bad luck. After hearing enough spooky tales about Louisiana folks and their beliefs, he took heed to the warning, not wanting to test the validity of the claim. I wish he would have made the room just a little bit bigger though. It was only big enough for a small bed and a chest. Without the window that was added, which gave a perfect view of Phillip's back yard as well as a portion of their back door, I would definitely feel claustrophobic. I felt my mother running her fingers gently through my damp hair.

"You okay, baby?"

I turned to look at her. She looked so exhausted. I know I must look the exact same way to her. Rest didn't come easy for any of us these days.

"No, I'm not," I replied softly, leaning my head against the window again.

She took my hand into hers as I stared out the window, "I don't think I will ever be okay again."

She brought my hand up to her mouth and placed a soft kiss there. With each passing landmark, I felt a sense of longing. A memory could be attached to each of these places. How many times have we gone to Lizzy's Ice Cream Parlor, or hung outside of Willie D's Barbershop waiting on Xavier and Daddy to finish getting their haircut. A walk to Shine's Corner Store was something that we did every other day up until some years back, when Sampson Shine and his wife Daisy Anne were killed in a fire that swept through the store. They were good folk who were still missed round here.

I closed my eyes wishing that blindness would strike me quickly. I didn't want to be faced with so many familiar things that reminded me of what I've lost. They would now and forever be a constant reminder that I was alone and without those who meant so much to me. I could no longer keep my composure. The penned up feelings inside of me were screaming for release. I suddenly broke into tears. I had taken my parents completely by surprise. They hadn't heard or seen me cry this way in days. My mother pulled me close to her. My father wrapped his arm around my mother's shoulder. The only comforting action he could give at the moment.

"We're gonna get through this together," she said through tears of her own.

I needed her more than ever. I needed to feel her embrace and I'm sure she needed mine as well. I'm sure her pain was much deeper than mine, she had lost her child and here I was acting as if it was all about me and my pain. I found myself not even stopping to think about hers. *How selfish of me*. I admired her strength and her ability to come out of that place of darkness and face the fact that she would never see her daughter again.

I wrapped my arms around her neck tightly; burying my face into her hair, the sweet smell of her shampoo filled my nostrils. I took comfort in her embrace.

I desired her strength. It was a much needed necessity in my life right now. I want it to surge through me so that I could finally be permitted to face what's to come without the threat of being mentally destroyed.

✳✳✳

By the time we finally pulled up in front of our house, the rain was coming down heavily. Our neighbors, the Morrison's, had just driven up as well. Xavier and Grandma got of the car quickly, both scampering across the yard trying to escape the rain. They rode to the funeral with the Morrison's since rain had been in the forecast and no one wanted to be caught in a storm on the back of Daddy's pick-up truck.

"It's getting pretty nasty out here," Daddy said, surveying the darkened sky.

He opened the door and quickly jumped out with my mother close behind him. I watched as they ran toward the house. Once he made it to the porch, his shelter from the rain, Daddy turned around and saw that I was still sitting in the truck. I just wanted to sit here by myself. I thought home is where I wanted to be, but now that I am here, I didn't want to go inside. It was not that place of warmth or solace that I always looked forward to once I stepped through the doors. Now it was a place full of constant reminders of things that I will never obtain again.

I watched the rain as it beat against the truck. It was kind of soothing in a way, almost hypnotizing. I closed my eyes; head still pressed against the window. There were no tears at the moment. Only the stinging and swelling of my eyes were the only reminders of those that I recently shed. The soft tap at the window startled me.

"Angelique, you need to come on inside now," Daddy said holding a small umbrella above his head.

It was almost comical to see such a huge man holding such a tiny thing. I climbed out of the truck slowly, not caring about the wind or the rain that was swirling about me swiftly. I suddenly remembered how sometimes when Dominique and I were a lot younger and our mother was in a good mood, she would let us come out and play in the rain, even on messy days like today. Oh how we used to enjoy it. We would be the only ones outside too, that somehow made it even better, knowing that the other kids weren't allowed to do this. I smiled at the memory.

"Can I just sit out here on the porch for a little while, Daddy?" I asked looking up at him.

He hesitated a moment before finally relenting. "Not too long," he said, "you need to be around your family right now; we all in this thang together."

I gave him a faint smile.

"I know."

I watched him walk inside before I took a seat. The wind was blowing the rain onto to the porch, causing the mist to fall upon me. I just sat there, not minding the cool droplets landing on my face. I didn't wipe them away, because this too was somehow soothing. I looked across the street at Belinda's house, looking at the window that I knew was hers. She must have yelled out of that thing a million times. I wonder if I would always remember their voices, Dominique and Belinda's. Would I always remember their laughter? I should, because I heard them almost every day. Surely I wouldn't forget. *Would I?*

I could feel the tears starting to build. *I didn't want to cry again, at least not today.* I quickly removed my shoes and stepped off the porch into the rain. Water seeped through my stockings, engulfing my feet. I held my head back, closed my eyes and with outstretched arms I began to spin around as if I was 6 years old again; spinning faster and faster. I stopped spinning when I heard her voice. It was as clear as the water pounding my body. It sounded like the sweetness that accompanied innocence.

"I'm going faster than you Angie," she giggled.

I opened my eyes. There she was, so beautiful. She had two braids in her hair that hung well passed her shoulder's, boots that were way too big came up to her knees. Mama sure knew how to dress us for the rainy days.

"Don't need y'all to be gett'n sick round here cause y'all wanna go act a fool in the rain," she would say.

"I'm beating you Angie," Dominique sang as she continued to spin.

I knew this was not real, only my imagination in overdrive, but I didn't care. I was seeing my sister again and I wanted to enjoy being with her one last time.

"Oh, no you not," I replied excitedly, closing my eyes again as I began trying to spin as fast as I could.

Both of our eyes shut tight with mouths wide open, letting the water overflow and spill from every angle it could as if it wasn't one of the grossest things ever. I heard the child like giggles again.

"Faster Angie, faster."

I began to laugh loudly, frantically before falling hard to the ground. My head was spinning and Dominique's giggles had faded away. I opened my eyes and searched for her, but she was gone. I was alone. My laughter turned into sobbing. No matter what my experiences were with my sister, they didn't define my current reality and the sadness that comes along with it. I lay down on the soaking ground and curled up on my side, not caring that I was now lying in the muddy puddle.

"Why did you leave me Dominique?" I said, unable to control the tears that mingled with the rain. The sobs turned into a loud scream and I screamed as loud I could as the downpour began to beat against me.

"Please God," I roared to the heavens, "give her back to me! Please send my sister back to me! I will do anything you want me to, anything."

As I screamed into the icy rain, I knew that what I was asking for was not at all possible. God granted us many things, but giving back those we've lost in death is not one of them. In order to see my sister again, I would have to visit that place where she would always be flashing that beautiful dimpled smile, never changing, remaining forever young; a place that was mine and mine alone . . . my memory.

I heard the slamming of the screen door and the quick approach of footsteps behind me.

"Oh baby," my mother said through tears of her own as she tried to pull me from the ground.

The screams wouldn't stop. I wanted them to; telling myself that screaming wouldn't help anything, but I obviously didn't care because I just kept right on

27

screaming. I wanted my screams to reach God's ears, prompting Him to bring me comfort swiftly.

"Please God," I screamed. "Please!"

My mother was sobbing heavily now as well, but I couldn't comfort her. As long as this damaged spirit dwelled within me, I couldn't bring anyone no kind of comfort, only more gloom is what I offered.

I felt myself being lifted from the ground and into the strong arms of my father. He carried me quickly into the house. Instead of taking me straight to the bathroom to get cleaned up, Daddy stopped right inside the front door, dropping to his knees with me still in his arms. He hugged me close to him. I could feel water or tears dropping onto my face from his.

I didn't look up to see which one it was. My screams had stopped, but the tears did not. I buried my face into my father's chest. I was so overwhelmed with grief, wanting to escape this body. Being someone else is what I really wanted. I want to be someone who doesn't understand the depth of pain that comes along with loss, betrayal, loneliness or regret; someone that's was still virginal when it came to the tribulations of life. It wasn't until I felt the towel being draped around me that I realized I was freezing.

"Come on," Mama said pulling me gently from my father's grasp. "Let's get you cleaned up."

Before standing, I glanced at Daddy and saw that his cheeks were covered with tears. I was still not used to seeing him cry.

"I love you, Daddy," I said softly.

"I love you," he said keeping his head hung low.

Sadness draped his tone. I hugged him briefly before finally getting on my feet. Mama led me to the bathroom and was about to close the door behind her after ushering me inside.

"Mama," I said almost in a whisper, "I can clean myself up. Go make sure everyone else is ok."

I began to undress, looking forward to stepping into the tub of water that awaited me. I really wanted to be alone. Her hovering over me is something that I was really not up for. She just stood there as if she didn't hear me. The look on her face told me that she was not real sure about leaving me alone.

"I'm ok, Mama," I assured her.

"Ok," she said with reluctance as I climbed into the warm water, "I will be back to check on you."

Before she closed the door, she turned back to me and said, "Leave the door unlocked."

Now I understood what that concerned look on her face was for. She thought that I was going to harm myself in some way if I was left unattended. "Ok." I answered quickly. *Just go away*, I thought.

"Be back in a minute," she said as she closed the door.

"Please, just leave me alone," is what I wanted to scream at the closed door. I knew she was just trying to be helpful, but help is not what I wanted. I wanted to hear my sister pound loudly on the bathroom door with the threat of coming to get in the tub with me, if I didn't hurry up and get out so she could take her bath. I recalled the numerous times she actually picked the lock and did exactly that.

"That's just disgusting Dominique," I would tell her as she began to bath as if no one else was in the small tub with her. "You're gonna be as dirty as you was before you got in."

She made me so mad. I would rush to get out of the tub then, trying to get done bathing before her, so that she would be left sitting in the extra muck.

"Well, what's mine is yours and what's yours is mine, Angie, dirt included," she'd say, flashing me one those breathtaking smiles.

I remember even trying to get Mama to make her stop doing that, but all I got from her was "I guess you better be done in ten minutes then huh girl."

I finally learned to stick to the allotted bath time, because I got tired of swopping dirt. I sank down a little deeper into the warm water. There was a soft knock on the door.

"It's me," mama said, coming inside. "You ok?" She asked, closing the door.

She sat on the edge of the tub.

"I'm fine," I answered, waving my hands across the warm water.

She began running her fingertip through the water absentmindedly.

"How do you do it Mama?" I asked.

"Do what, baby?"

"Hold it all together like you're doing?

She smiled at me, "But I'm not."

I looked at her a minute, sort of confused by her answer. I guess I expected her to be agonizingly distraught like Belinda's mother.

"I think I mourned for my baby long before any of y'all did. In a sense, the minute she went missing is when my mourning began. I was lost inside my own mind, not wanting to face the *maybe*'s or the *what if*'s, *is she* or *isn't she*, not wanting to deal with anything really and not wanting the answers to the questions that needed answering the most. That wasn't fair to Dominique in any way for me to just shut down like that. So I had to pull myself back and allow myself to feel what I needed to feel."

The tears were starting to flow from her eyes now.

"I grieve for her every second of every day," she continued. "Oh, how I grieve for my child, but I try not to let y'all see that, because I want to be strong for you and Xavier. But what you don't know is how your Daddy got to comfort me every night, because I can't stop crying or how Mere has to pray with me and for me every day because she is afraid that I will find my way back into that dark place again. And sometimes I can feel that darkness trying to surround me, trying to creep back in. Every time I think about Dominique and how she died it's just breaks my heart all over again. She didn't deserve to die like that."

She closed her eyes. I could tell she was trying hard to regain her composure.

"To have one of your children snatched from your life for no reason at all, without a warning, can mess your head up bad, real bad. But I can't lose myself again. I still have more children that need me still. But know that the burden of pain that I carry right here," she placed her hand over her heart, "is so heavy that I wouldn't wish it upon my worst enemy. Just because I don't show it on the outside like a lot of people expect that I should, doesn't make it any lighter. It's just that I am stronger now than I evah been in my entire life."

She looked at me and I saw it clearly then, the pain was planted deep within her eyes.

"Come to me, all you who are weary and burdened, and I will give you rest," I recited quietly.

"I see someone's been reading their Bible," my mother replied, wide-eyed as if she was surprised that I could quote scripture.

I gave her a small, broken smile. It was all I could muster at the moment. I was so tired.

"Keep reading the word of God. I'm 100% sure that there are plenty of scriptures there that can surely offer you some comfort." She stood up and headed for the door, "Lunch will be ready in a few, so finish gett'n cleaned up."

"Mama," I called out to her. "You need to read it too," I said when she turned to look at me.

"I'm way head of you. I read the Bible every single day. I have to or else I would lose my mind. So, I think you're the one who's playing catch up."

She blew me a kiss as she headed out the door.

CHAPTER 3

During lunch, I pushed the food around on my plate, trying my best not to make eye contact with anyone. I got the strangest feeling that everyone was watching me, waiting for me to completely lose my mind again. The few times I did manage to glance away from the food on my plate, my suspicions would be confirmed. I'm sure I'm not the only one that's in agony at this table, just the only one who's showing it outwardly.

I didn't know how to keep what I was feeling locked away on the inside, no matter how hard I tried to restrain my emotions from; they would always get the best of me and begin to boil over. I didn't have the strength of my mother or the spirituality of my grandmother to help me deal with all this. I was grateful for the knock at the front door.

"I'll get it," Daddy said standing up.

"No," I said quickly pushing myself away from the table before anyone could protest, "I got it."

I was out of my chair so fast that they couldn't stop me if they wanted to. I bolted for the front door, needing to get away from the eyes of concern. I saw Phillip standing on the front porch, his back was facing me. I stood there a moment thinking how I could easily slip to my room and let someone else come to the door, but while I was standing trying to my decision, Phillip turned around and saw me before I could make my move. *Why didn't they close the door?* I thought.

I had avoided him long enough, I guess I may as well go ahead and talk to him. It was either that or go back to the kitchen and let everyone stare at me as if I was some kind of freak.

"Hey," he said as I made my way to the door.

"Hey Phillip," I returned stepping out onto the porch, closing the door behind me. It was still raining, but not as bad as it was before, but still bad enough to keep everyone inside. Everyone accept Phillip obviously. "How you been?"

"Been worrying bout you. You d-d-oing ok?" He asked.

"At this moment, but can't guarantee if I will be ok in a minute or two," I answered quietly, really wanting to ask him did I look like I was ok.

My eyes were almost swollen shut and dark from lack of sleep. My hair looks as if birds had made my head their new nest and he had the nerve to ask me if I was ok. *Keep cool Angelique*, I had to tell myself.

"I don't know if y-you know or not but I have been come'n ova to s-see if you was aw'right, but yo folks was s-s-saying that you wasn't really up for company just yet," He explained nervously.

"Yeah, I know," I said, sitting down in one of the chairs. "They was right. Everything just came at us so fast and I couldn't handle it. I just wanted to be left alone."

"And now?" He asked, sitting beside me, gazing at me with those dark eyes in a way that just warms my heart. He was truly concerned for me.

"And now," I looked at him, "I think I could really use a friend."

My eyes began to water as I realized the truth behind those words. I was not liked my many of the kids my own age, black or white, and I know that was my fault. I didn't allow anyone to get close to me. My attitude kept many from approaching me and I liked it that way. I guess I felt like I didn't need friends, Dominique and Belinda was enough for me. And the few kids that did talk to me or sit with me at school was only because of my sister who had tons of friends.

Dominique and I were inseparable, so her friends became mine by default. I have only spoken with a few of them since Dominique's been gone. I could tell how much they loved and admired her by the tone of their conversations, but after a while, they stopped calling. And now, when I really needed a friend, I didn't have one.

Phillip appeared as though he was in deep thought about something before he finally decided to speak.

"I use to be a little jealous of yall's relationship, you and ya s-sistas, and Belinda's, how close y'all were. Even ya family seems to be really close. I w-wish for somethin' like that; you lucky to have that. It's always been j-just me and my daddy for as long as I can rememba. I don't know w-what it's like to have friends, and to be honest, I neva really wanted any, but if you would let me try to be yours, here I am," he said kindly.

I brought my hands up to my face, trying to cover it so that Phillip couldn't see me cry. He pulled me close to him so that my head could rest on his chest. He didn't say a word, just held me close to him and allowed me to weep for those that I loved. He stroked my hair softly. He moved my hands from my face and began to wipe away my relentless tears.

"You don't have to hide your face from me," he whispered as he cradled my hands in one of his.

"My grandmother always say that pain don't last always, and that time is a really good healer," I began, still leaning against him, "But how much time will it take for me to heal? When will all my pain go away?"

"Maybe w-when you don't have no tears left. I thank you should cry all you need to," he said, stroking my hair. "I w-wish I could help you. I can only imagine how you feel."

How I wish that he could too. If only there was a magical pill to help someone forget the unpleasant things that triggered our delicate emotions; to make us forget what real pain and heartache felt like. Life would be so much easier, but would you really be living? The things we go through in life, good and bad make us who we are. These things help define our character and mold us into the person we will ultimately become in life. But I don't see how any of this can shape my character or characterize who I am as a person, nor is it making me stronger, it's doing the exact opposite, weakening me. This is something I would rather do without. I would gladly pop a pill if it would heal my broken heart.

"You are helping me," I said. "You just being here gives me a little comfort."

I raised my eyes so that I could see his face. He was so incredibly handsome. As soon as he looked down at me, I started to divert my eyes. I didn't want him to see me staring at him, but his free hand came to my cheek, forcing my face upward once again so that I was staring at him.

38

"You can look at me," he said. He wrapped his arms around me and squeezed me tightly, "I'm here as long as you need me to be."

I repositioned myself so that I could place my arms around his neck, so that I could give him a hug. *This felt good.* I tried to pull away, but he only pulled me closer to him, but we both parted quickly, when we heard the front door open. I don't know why, but I didn't want anyone to see me and Phillip this way. I didn't want the fifty million questions that would surely follow. Mama stuck her head out of the door.

"Hello Phillip," she said courteously, looking from me to him as if she had just caught us doing something sneaky.

"Hello, Mrs. James," he returned nervously.

"Everything ok out here?" She asked, more so to me than to Phillip.

"Yes ma'am."

It was Phillip who answered, "I just wanted to come and c-check on her."

He turned to look at me.

"That's very kind of you to do so," she said, but I caught something in her tone that he obviously did not.

Her voice betrayed what her expression did not, suspicion. I wanted to tell her to just go back inside and stop embarrassing me. Phillip had been nothing but kind to me and there was no need for her to be treating him like he had done something wrong.

Xavier made his way out onto the porch as well. Phillip put his open palm in front of him "Give me five my man," Xavier quickly slapped it and flipped his hand over waiting for Phillip to slap his in turn. He came over and took the seat next to me.

"Are you done eating?" Mama asked him.

He nodded his head, "And I put my plate in the sink, too."

I could tell he was proud of himself for doing that without being told.

"Thank you, that's less work for me," she said, giving him a huge smile.

"This storm isn't over," she said looking up toward the sky.

It was starting to darken again and I don't think it was even three o'clock yet.

"I think it's gonna get a lot worse," she said, then turned her attention back to me and Phillip. "Y'all don't sit out here too long now."

She looked at Xavier, "And you better not take one step off of this porch mister."

Xavier looked disappointed. I noticed that he had two of his little plastic toys in his hands, no doubt preparing to have a little fun with them in the rain.

"I'm gonna head on home now," Phillip said as he stood to his feet. "I was just mak'n sho you was ok."

I stood up as well.

"Thank you. I'm really glad you came by," I found myself saying and I meant it.

He smiled at me before turning to make his way down the front steps. He turned to face me again.

"I think I want t-to take you up on your offer," he said. He saw the confusion spread quickly across my face, "You s-said you could help me with my problem."

"Which is?" I asked, obviously at a lost to his meaning.

He placed his hands in his pockets and flashed me a crooked smile, "My talking problem."

I had completely forgotten that I had offered to help him with his stuttering problem.

"Oh, your stammering, of course I will help," I replied, "But seems to me it's already getting better."

He smiled.

"Let me know when you w-want to s-start, no hurry," he said.

There was a loud clap of thunder that made us turn our attention towards the sky. It had become dark almost instantly and the rain began to fall just as quickly. The lightening danced across the sky followed by another loud crack. Xavier came to stand beside me and grabbed my hand. I was surprised that he didn't run in the house instead. I knew he wasn't a fan of thunderstorms.

"I thank I'm gon get a lil wet," Phillip sarcastically stated.

I smiled at him.

"I don't think you will," I said mockingly.

He gave a low chuckle.

"I will check on ya soon," he said.

"Thank you," I replied. "Maybe Mama won't give you the evil eye next time."

I was sure he noticed the look she gave him.

"I'm s-sure she don't mean no harm," he touched my face gently and made his way down the steps.

"Later lil man," he told Xavier as he began jogging towards his house.

"Later Phillip," Xavier said without turning in Phillips direction.

He had the same look on his face that he had earlier today at the funeral. He was staring at something straight ahead, something that I could not see. I turn to

42

look in Phillips direction, but he must have made a run for it, because he was nowhere in sight.

The approaching car caused us to turn in curiosity. A dark blue car pulled up in front of Belinda's house. A few moments later a few more cars followed. Benjamin stepped out of the dark blue vehicle and made his way to the passenger side. He grabbed Mrs. Kirkland by the elbow, assisting her to her feet. She moved very slowly as if all of her energy had been drained from her body. She held a few flowers close to her chest as if it was an essential necessity to have them as close to her heart as possible.

The rest of the visitors followed closely behind her. I knew most of them from the neighborhood, but some I didn't. I assumed that these were probably other family members that came down from Memphis, as well as some other family friends that I didn't know.

Xavier quickly spread his toys across the porch and his playtime sound effects began immediately. I took a seat on the bottom step, not caring that it was still wet from the rain which had quickly subsided, just as quick as it had started. The sun was trying to shine through the gray clouds, but I could tell that the rain was not over.

The crowd at Belinda's house had grown. Cars now lined both sided of the street. They had left the front door open and I could hear some of the chatter coming from inside. A part of me wanted to go over to give her a little support, but the other part of me didn't want to blend my grief with hers. I think that somehow it would make us both feel only worse, and I couldn't deal with worse right now.

I saw Belinda's curtains being pulled aside and her window went up. I could see Mrs. Kirkland take a seat on Belinda's bed. I couldn't tell what she was doing, but it looked as though she had her head down looking at something. She did not move. She just sat there with her head low. I stood up and begin making my way across the street towards the window, like I have done a million times before to have a conversation with Belinda. It was always easier to just talk to her that way sometimes rather than going inside the house. The closer I got, I begin to hear music coming from the opened window.

I cried over you, I cried over you
You know that I've always, I've always been true

It was a tune that I knew all too well, and one of Belinda's favorite songs "I Cried" by Tammi Terrell. I remember how she would be lip syncing that song as me, Dominique and sometimes even Xavier, would be standing

44

outside that window; being the audience, cheering her on and getting down outside like we was at a real show.

"Y'all don't know noth'n bout Tammi," she once told me and Dominique after one of her many Tammi performances, and there were many. "She has the best voice I done ever heard. She sang as though she has experienced every thang she sings about in her songs. How many women sangers can sang with so much emotion like Tammi does? Not a one."

I couldn't make myself take another step. I stood there with my eyes closed listening to that song as the tears raced down my cheeks. It brought back so many memories for me. I'm sure it's doing the same for Belinda's mama right now. I felt someone grab my hand. I turned to see Xavier looking up at me. I wiped my face and gave him a little smile as we turned around and headed back home, hand in hand as Tammi's voice faded into the background, telling us how she would never love again. The sky became dark again.

"It's gonna rain again?" Xavier asked, obviously disappointed.

"Yes it is," I answered. "Pick your toys up so we can go in the house."

I turned to face Belinda's house again, wanting to go throw my arms around her mother's neck and give her consolation that I know she needed. I felt Xavier hand tightened around mine. I turn to look at him, but not before noticing that his toys were now on the ground in a puddle of mud.

"Xavier, why did you," I began to scold him for intentionally throwing his things on the ground, but when I looked at him I knew something was terribly wrong.

He looked as though he had gone pale and his eyes were wide with fright. I kneeled down beside him and he threw his tiny arms around my neck and squeezed me so tight that he almost took my breath away,

"What's the matter?" I asked frantically.

The sudden sound of thunder caused me to jump. I look up into the sky to see the dark clouds rolling swiftly.

"Tell her to leave me alone," he screams into my ear.

Feeling his finger nails dig deep into my shoulders caused me to flinch. I could hear the panic in his voice, along with fear. I turned around to see if I saw anyone. No one was there. I looked behind me. There was no one.

"Who? Tell who to leave you alone?" I asked, looking all around us.

The rain had begun again. Without moving his head from the crook of my neck, he pointed to his right and quickly placed his arm back around my neck. I turned to look but still saw nothing.

"No one is there, Xavier," I said soothingly. "No one is here. It's ok."

He slowly raised his head and took a quick peek and then quickly turned it back again.

"Noooo, she right there, she's right there."

His body was so tense underneath my arms. Something was definitely frightening him, *but what or who?*

"Where?" I asked, he was beginning to terrify me. "Who is it, do you see Dominique again? Remember, she loves you and you will make her sad if you made her think she was scaring you?"

"Noooo, it's not Dominique," he said with frustration.

I tried to pull him away from me so that I could look at him, but he would not release his grip. I thought a moment before asking my next question.

"Xavier, is it Belinda?"

"No. I don't know who she is. She sitting right there on the porch," he said loudly. "Why can't you see her? Tell her I don't know how."

There was nothing to see. No one was on the steps. No one was on the porch but me and him. But I knew that something was making him react this way. And I definitely know that it is possible that he is seeing someone. He had never acted this way before. I have never seen him this terrified, not even once. I'm certain, without a doubt in my mind that my little brother is special.

"What don't you know?" I asked still trying to calm him down. "What is she asking you?"

"I don't know how," he screamed, "Leave me alone."

He began to cry out. He was shaking so violently that I had to hold him tighter to make him be still. *What in the hell.* I picked him up in my arms, deciding now was definitely the time to go inside, but just as I was heading for the front door, a strong gust of wind mixed with rain came from out of nowhere and knocked all four of the chairs in front of the door, piling them on top of each other, blocking the way. I began shaking my head swiftly. I did not just see this.

"Oh my God. What the . . ."

This is not possible. This was definitely not the winds doing. The chairs looked as though they were deliberately stacked up against the door. Whatever this thing was didn't want us to go inside. I took a step backwards, losing my footing. The wet porch and a heavy

Xavier caused me to fall flat on my behind. Xavier gave a little yelp as he fell from my arms. I grabbed him again quickly, holding him close to me.

"Mama," I screamed as I begin to look around us. "Mama," I yelled again, lifting Xavier up into my arms again.

I surveyed my surroundings once more. This feeling I had, I couldn't quite explain. Something's standing behind me. I turned around preparing to see some ghostly figure, but there was nothing or no one here. Again, it seemed like something was behind me once again, stalking me. I swung around as the wind and rain thrashed our bodies. Xavier was crying loudly and the wind was still howling; whipping my hair all about my face I could barely see a thing. A cold chill suddenly swept across me, causing me to shudder. I rubbed my brother's back briskly; a poor attempt at trying to warm him. I stopped suddenly, staring at the void before me. Something was standing in front of me, I could smell it.

My heart was pounding so fast, I was afraid. It was so close, directly in front of my face. I could see my breath as I exhaled, realizing that the spot in front of me was the source of the icy coldness. Xavier's arms tighten and legs tightened around me as if he could since the presence at his back. Before I could even attempt to back away, my rain soaked hair was being swept from my face and tucked behind my left ear with swift precision. *The icy phantom touched me.* I screamed, which caused Xavier to wail even louder.

I went towards the door and sat Xavier down. He stayed in front of me with his hands wrapped tightly around my waist, his face buried in my belly. I tried to move the chairs, but it was as though they were glued together this way. They wouldn't budge. I could hear someone on the other side of the door trying to pry it open. Then I heard my grandmother call out to daddy.

"Hurry up," I hollered. "Something is out here with us."

I looked all around me, waiting for something to appear.

"I don't know how," Xavier bellowed again through his tears.

"Open the door," I yelled, banging on the wood as hard as I could.

I don't know what caused Xavier to scream as loud as he did, but he loosened his grip on my waist and I looked down, able to see his face clearly. He looked as though he had seen his worst nightmare come to life. I picked him up and turned around. They were trying to pry the door open on the other side. Something is doing this. I can't see it, but I could sense it. Its presence was so overwhelming that it was suffocating. This was not Dominique. This was someone else. Something ELSE!

I begin to look all around me once again. I was beginning to panic. It felt as though something was closing in on me from all directions attempting to take life from me. Suddenly the wind stopped blowing just as quick as it had started, but my senses are still in overload.

"Shhhhh," I said to Xavier.

I needed him to stop crying. There is too much going on around me at one time.

"Please, calm down, hush."

It was standing so close to me that the hairs on the back of my neck and arms started to prickle. *That sweet smell of flowers.* I stood as still as I could, afraid to move. Xavier was sniffling, trying to mute his cries.

"Dominique," I said in a frightened whisper. "Why are you doing this?"

"That's not Dominique," Xavier said in a tone that matched mine. His words made chilled me.

"Who is it?" I asked, still in a whisper.

"I don't know," he cried.

The front door finally sprang open.

"What the hell?" Daddy asked when he saw all the chairs piled up against the screened door.

He heard him prying his way out the door. I didn't turn to look at him. I was afraid to move and afraid to let go of Xavier, who had finally calmed down. I didn't say anything. It was as if I was planted in this spot. Once Daddy reached us, Xavier quickly made his way into his arms.

"What's the matter?" Grandma was asking him, and then she took one look at me and begins to pray.

"He's shaking," Daddy observed, "Why the hell is he shaking Angelique?"

I still did not move and I could not speak. The presence was still here, as if it was waiting on me to move -- daring me to move.

"Angelique," Daddy called out loudly.

"Take Xavier inside, William," Mama instructed.

"Now, William," She repeated when he did not move.

He glowered at her.

"What the hell is happening?" His voice was very demanding.

My mother turned and gave him a look that could make a man's blood boil. When grandma put her hand on his shoulder, he finally relented and went inside mumbling to himself. Grandma looked from me to my mother and stepped inside the house without saying a word to either of us.

Mama came and stood beside me. Then I heard her saying something swiftly in French, but she was saying it under her breath making it hard for me to make out exactly what it was. It was as If It was a chant of some sort. She just kept saying it over and over. *Praying?*

Whatever it was made the thickness around me collapse. Breathing came easier. I couldn't tell if this entity was still here or not, I only know that I didn't feel as though I was suffocating now. She grabbed my arm, turning me to face her. Now, I was the one trembling. She gently moved strands of wet hair from my face.

"Mama, something was here, standing right beside me," my voice cracked. "I swear it. Xavier saw her. I'm not making this up."

"I know baby," she said looking over my shoulder with squinted eyes.

My eyes widened with fear. In that moment, I knew that she was seeing something.

"Can you see her too? Is she still here?" I asked quickly.

She nodded her head slowly.

"Yes it's still here," she answered quietly.

I could tell she was trying to focus on something behind me.

"I haven't seen a spirit in a very long time, but I think I see it, and I definitely hear it," she said as a look of profound confusion came upon her face. "A woman, and she's crying."

"Is it Dominique, Mama?" I asked already knowing the answer to this unnecessary question.

Xavier kept telling me that this was not Dominique, but who else could it be. She shook her head slowly and brought her hand up to her chest.

"Lord, I hope not. This soul is tortured something awful.

CHAPTER 4

Mama grabbed me by the arm, and slowly began to lead me to the front door. Once I stepped inside the door, I turned around, trying to see if I could see anything. There was nothing there. It appeared as though me and Mama where the only ones present, but I know better. Something else is here; I could feel it; smell it.

Once we were inside, Mama spun around and just stood there staring out the door. Grandma appeared out of nowhere, She was about to ask me something when suddenly Mama inhaled deeply, taking me and grandma by surprise. We both turned to look at her. She looked as though she was holding her breath, her eyes were wide.

"Delphine?" Grandmother warily asked, "What do you see?"

Her hand was clasping that cross at her neck, she always did this when something weighed heavy on her mind or as she would put it, something troubled her spirit.

"I . . . can see . . . her."

There was a tremble in her tone.

"She is just . . . standing there with . . . her back to me. But one thang I know for sure, that's not my baby," Mama said softly.

She looked as though she was daydreaming.

"Do you know who it is?" Grandma asked quickly.

I began to walk towards my mother, but grandma held her hand out, halting my steps. She shook her head at me swiftly.

"Delphine?"

"I can't . . . see her face. She is covered . . . in dirt, from head to toe. It looks like she wearing man's clothes and . . . and she's doesn't have any shoes on," Mama said.

She paused a moment, tilting her head, "There is something familiar about her. I don't know what it is, but there's something," Mama said. "She is keeping her back to me. She don't want me to see her face."

Her voice was so full of emotion.

"I can feel her pain Mere, she carried a heavy load in life."

She walked closer to the door, bringing her hand up to her throat, "There is something terribly wrong here, but I don't know what it is. Why is she here? Why are you here?"

She screamed through the door. Suddenly, there was a loud crack. It was as if someone was trying to come through the front door with a sledge hammer. Mama cried out loudly as she began backing up from the door, almost knocking me and grandma over. I steadied her.

"Do you see her?" She screamed loudly, pointing at the screen door.

"No Mama, I don't see anyone," I answered.

The only thing I could see were the knocked over chairs near the front door.

"She's standing right there," she yelled as she continued to point. She began rambling off so fast in that Cajun language of hers that I couldn't make out what she was saying. I had never heard her speak that fast.

Crack! Crack, came the sound again.

"Her face . . . her face," Mama kept yelling over and over again and then she quickly covered her mouth.

She quickly dropped to her knees and started rambling again in French, hands locked in prayer as she rocked on her knees. Grandma quickly shut the door, and dropped down to her knee as well. She began mimicking whatever it was that Mama was saying. They both were speaking so fast. I couldn't catch a word of what they were saying. All of the words seem to just run together. Daddy came running from the back room, Xavier close to his side.

"What the hell?" He asked loudly.

He eyed the two women on the floor and was taken aback. He turned to me.

"Look, somebody need to tell me what the hell is going on up 'round here," he demanded fiercely. "Angelique?"

I just shook my head at him, "I don't know, Daddy."

I wanted to know the same thing he did. What in the hell is happening. And what in the hell had been unleashed into our midst? And who or what unleashed it? The prayer on the floor finally stopped. All remained quiet for a few moments.

Daddy stepped past the two hugging ladies on the floor and went straight for the front door. He swung the screen door wide open with harsh intent. I automatically glanced at Mama. I was waiting for her expression to change; letting me know if the spirit was still here or not. Her calm demeanor told me that it was gone. She stood up quickly, moving past Daddy and stepped out onto the porch with Daddy closely behind her. I walked outside as well, hoping to get an explanation for it all, now that things seem to be calm.

Daddy began to pick up the scattered chairs, placing them back in their rightful positions as Mama began to survey the surroundings. I knew she was hoping to see that which caused her so much fright only minutes before.

"Delphine?" Daddy began, "What's happening baby?"

Incomprehension was written all across his face. She didn't face him.

"I' m sorry, but you wouldn't understand," she said with such remorse as she continued to search for something that was now long gone.

"I understand more than ya given me credit for," he stated. "I know all about this here gift of yours, so try me, don't shut me out because ya thank I can't handle it."

She finally turned to look at him and began to explain what happened.

"There was the spirit of a woman out here," she started.

"What do you mean here?" Daddy asked, "You mean out here?"

He pointed downward at the porch. He began looking around as if he too would be able to see it. He looked at Mama and frowned. He was even more confused now than before. *Poor Daddy.*

"Yes William, here," Mama said. "When we were trying to get out of the door earlier, I knew something was wrong. And when you finally got the door open, my suspicions were confirmed."

She looked at him then, "Did you see how those chairs were stacked against the door?"

"I did," he answered sitting down.

Mama took a seat too. I was too wired to sit down. I just wanted an explanation.

"I knew the kids didn't do it that. And then I saw it, standing right there," she pointed to the spot where the spirit had stood, "right in front of Angelique."

She turned to look at Daddy again. I think she was trying to see what his reaction would be before she continued, but he remained silent, so she went on.

"It's shaped just like a person and it looked like a shimmer of sorts. You know how when you boiling water and if you look at the steam, I mean really look at it, everything behind the vapor appears to be a little distorted."

She stood up again and walked to the edge of the porch.

"When I was younger back in Louisiana, I use to see those shimmers all the time. No matter where I was; at school, at the store or just right in the street, I would always see them. But no else 'round me could. Sometimes they would walk right up to me, but they never spoke a word to me. It was as if they was surprised that I could see them. I think some folks thought I was a little touched in the head, but I knew what I was seeing."

She returned to her chair.

"When we came out here, I saw it standing in front of her," She glanced up at me, acknowledging me for the first time since I'd been standing here. "Then the form was starting to take shape and become a little clearer and I sensed that this was actually the spirit of a woman. I could hear it, her, crying. I could sense her sadness. So I began saying the first prayer that came to mind, The Hail Mary. I was raised Catholic and that prayer got me through many rough nights and there was many."

She glances out into the rain before speaking again.

"Something was different about this spirit though," she said with sureness.

"What was different about it?" I asked curiously.

A frown of confusion stretched across her face.

"When I saw the dead before, I saw them as they were before they died. Like when I saw my Daddy. He looked so good and healthy, as did my friends. But not this time, it was way different. After we came inside, and I turned to look at it again to see if I could still her shimmer. She started to become solid. And then she turned around and moved so fast. She was standing right in front of the door before I knew it. The screen door was the only thang keeping our faces from touching. She was pounding on the door."

She began rocking again and she had that look in her eye that I never wanted to see again. It was that look she had a few months ago when she was lost to us. Daddy put his arms around her.

"It's ok baby, I'm right here."

He looked up at me and I knew then that he saw the look too.

"Let's go back inside Mama," I said, not wanting her to lose herself again. "We can finish talking later."

But she just started talking again, not hearing a word I was saying.

"She looked to be pure evil. And I can tell she must have met a terrible end . . . a horrible death. Her skin looked gray and weathered. Flesh was missing from her hands, her feet and even her face, but I couldn't make out her face clearly. Her hair was long and stringy looking; full of dirt and it was all about her face, making it so hard to see her face good. She was just filthy. I could tell she was wearing man's clothes, overalls and a long checkered looking shirt."

She frowned, "I'm trying to figure out why is she so familiar to me."

My grandmother came out onto the porch with Xavier close to her side, "I think that's enough excitement for a day, now y'all come on back inside."

I notice the look that she gave my mama and I knew she was thinking the same thing I was. No one wanted to see her in that depressed state of mind again.

Mama looked across the street, looking as though she had just noticed all the cars lined on the streets.

"I'm going to go over and check on her later," she said. "I just don't have the strength right now. I don't want to be reminded of what I will be faced with in a few days."

We all knew she was referring to Dominique, who will be laying to rest soon.

She stood to her feet, "You ok baby?" She asked Xavier.

He nodded. She took both of his hands into hers.

"When you ready, I want you to talk to me about everything that happened out here today, what you saw, what you heard, but only when you ready to talk to me about it, Ok?"

She grabbed her only son into a warm hug, "There is nothing to be afraid of."

I watched as she tried to convince a frightened child not to be afraid of ghosts, but from where I stood, she wasn't doing a very good job of being convincing. If there wasn't anything to fear, then why was she so afraid? Why were we all so afraid?

CHAPTER 5

My grandmother took Xavier to the back to prepare him for bed, while the rest of us just sat in the sitting room, not really sure what to say to each other. Everyone scared to speak, scared to move. I noticed how each of us would take a peak from one corner of the room to the next, anticipating some ghastly figure to appear at any second. I turn my attention to Mama and the way she stared off into nothing, with a deep frown etched in her face led me to believe that she's thinking deep on something. She turns suddenly and catches me staring at her. My concern for her must have shown with great clarity on my face.

She extended her arms out to me, "Don't look at me like that, baby."

I went over to her, allow her to wrap me up in her arms.

"I'm ok; I'm just trying to figure all of this out, that's all."

"So am I," Daddy said, finally speaking. "I don't know what to say or what to ask. Do we need to move?"

He brought both of his hands up and rubbed his face briskly, then placed them on top of his head, "What does she want?"

"I don't know," Mama answered. "I don't know why she is here or what it is that she wants, but she is definitely here for something. And I don't think moving will help us all that much."

At that moment, I remembered that Xavier kept saying "*I don't know.*" She had to have been asking him something or telling him to do something.

"Mama," I began, "Xavier kept saying he didn't know how or he didn't know. She was definitely talking to him. Maybe he can tell us what she wants."

She stood up quickly.

"Oh my Lord," she said. "She has been around here for a long time. I remember about a month ago, Xavier kept saying that a woman kept scratching at his window and I told him that maybe he was dreaming and he told me that she was real and that she was always waking him up."

Daddy looked at her with wide eyes.

"Are you telling me we living in one of them spooked houses? Oh, we getting the hell up out'a here," he said loudly.

If this matter wasn't a serious one, I would have laughed. But I knew that this was no laughing matter. Something was going on around us. This woman wanted something and if she has been around this house all this time, this family must have whatever it is that she wants.

"No, the house isn't haunted," Mama said, "I guess you can say, in a sense, we are. This gift allows us to connect with lost souls, whether we want to or not, but each of us connect with them in a different way."

She walked to the front door again.

"It don't matter where we are. We can move way cross the country and it still won't matter, because they will find us or we will find them. Spirits are drawn to people like us. That's the way it's always been and that's how it will always be," she said as she sat down on the sofa once again.

The rest of the evening was full of hushed conversations between Mama and Grandma. I noticed how they would go out back whenever they wanted to discuss something that they didn't want the rest of us to hear. Xavier stayed very close to Daddy until it was bedtime. I took him to his room to tuck him in. He was afraid at first to go to bed, but I promised him I wouldn't leave his side until he fell asleep. I wasn't tired just yet and I wanted to find out what all the hushed conversations were about.

"Are you scared, too?" He asked me as I was readying him for bed.

I pulled the covers up around him.

"Didn't you hear what Mama said?" I asked lying down beside him. "There ain't nothing to be afraid of."

He looked at me as though he could see right through my lie.

"But I am scared," he said.

"I know you are, but don't be. You know Daddy won't let anything happen to any of us. You see how big and strong he is."

I was trying my best to make him feel at ease. I know I shouldn't be bringing this up to him now, but curiosity got the best of me like it always did. I have to ask him the question that had been plaguing me all evening.

"Xavier, Does the lady talk to you?" I asked cautiously.

"Sometimes, but not all the time," he answered.

"What does she say to you?"

"She said *'make it stop'* and sometimes she say *'when are you gonna make it better?'* She say that the most," he yawned.

"How long have you been seeing her?" I asked, not prepared for his answer.

"I always see her. I seen her all the time when I was a kid."

I smiled faintly at him. He spoke as though turning 8 years old made him an adult.

I rubbed his cheek, "Why didn't you tell us about her?"

I can't see someone his age not saying a word to anyone about something like this. Surely he had to afraid.

"I thought everybody saw her," he replied naively.

"She never frightened you before?"

I remembered Mama's description of her. The way she described her, I don't see how he wouldn't be afraid.

He shook his head, "No. I saw her at Belinda's funeral too. She was standing by that big tree."

This explained what had his attention.

"Where else have you seen her?"

"I see her in the backyard and I see her sitting behinds Phillips house all the time. But she is always right there," he said pointing at the only window in the room. "Sometimes she is out there walking around."

He moved a little closer to me. I wrapped my arms around him. I want him to feel safe in my arms, feel protected. I didn't want him to know that I was just as scared as he is. I stayed with him as promised until he fell asleep. I got up from the bed with ease, not wanting to wake him.

I walked over to the window and gazed outside, before quickly closing the curtains. There were raised voices coming from the front of the house. I looked back at Xavier to see if he had awakened due to all the shouting. My father was angry about something. Leaving the door open and the light on, just in case Xavier woke up, I made my way to the front to see what all the screaming was about.

"What the hell does that mean?" Daddy was saying.

He was standing in the middle of the sitting room, while Mama was sitting on the sofa and grandmother was standing near the kitchen.

"We living up in here with some damn ghosts that I can't see. How in the hell am I supposed to protect my family against something that I can't see?" He yelled.

"We have way more power over such things than we give ourselves credit for," a voice resounded.

Startled, we all turned around to see who had spoken from the front door. Someone was standing on the other side of the screen. It was dark now and we couldn't see who it was. The woman opened the door and stepped inside uninvited. My father was about to say something, but Mama stood up and grabbed his arm. I heard my grandmother gasp in surprise.

"I feel confident in saying that your spirit meant you no harm," said a woman who looked so regal, with her long gray and black hair braided to her scalp in three thick braids that almost reached her waist.

There was something colorful entwined in each braid, but I couldn't tell what it was from where I was standing. She wore long a colorful dress that swept the floor when she walked. The necklace on her neck looked so heavy with all of its different charms. On each of her fingers were rings with stones of different colors. She appeared to be about the same age as my grandmother. In spite of the many fine lines that were etched in her smooth chocolate complexion that came along with old age. She was beautiful.

"Aunt Celestine, *"Tu m'as manqué*," Mama said, running into the embrace of the old woman.

Celestine, this is my grandmother's older sister. The pictures I've seen of her didn't do her any justice. I only heard talk of my great aunt, and only seen pictures of her until today. And those pictures didn't compare to the woman standing before me. She is 11 years older than my grandmother and don't even look it. I knew that there was some sort of bad blood between the two women, but the

71

cause of it I never knew. My grandmother has one other sibling, a brother named Jericho, who is the oldest of the bunch. Him and my grandmother wrote each other quite often. I can tell by the way she spoke of him that she is very fond of him. Aunt Celestine began stroking Mama's hair.

"*Tu m'as manqué mon amour,*" she said pulling away from Mama so she could get a better look at her. "It's been way too long. You have grown into a beautiful woman, but then again, I knew that you would."

She had the same thick Cajun accent as grandmother, but hers was much thicker.

"My heart goes out to you for all that you have suffered through." She pulled Mama into another embrace, "Your strength has always been one of your most dominate qualities, even as a little girl."

"Thank you," I heard Mama whisper.

She turned to face my father, "And I take it you are the husband?" She said as she extended a hand to him.

"Yes ma'am, William," he said, "Nice to meet ya."

Before anything else could be said, Xavier came from out of nowhere extending his hand, mimicking Daddy, "I'm Xavier."

"You supposed to be a sleeping Xavier," Mama said looking down at him.

"Hello, young one," Aunt Celestine said as she took his hand in one of hers and raised his chin with the other.

"There is a lot of Jericho in him," she said to Mama.

She stared at Xavier a long moment. I saw her glance at my grandmother very quickly; it was so quick I don't think anyone else noticed it but me. She looked at Xavier again and smiled down at him.

"You have a beautiful light in you ya know. I can see it shining very brightly in your eyes little one."

I saw Daddy look at Mama and then at grandma. I knew he was probably thinking, *not another one.*

"I think that's called being sleepy," Daddy said, "Tell Aunt Celestine goodnight son, its bedtime."

"Goodnight," he said as Daddy led him to the back.

"Are you gonna stay with me until I go to sleep?" I heard him ask Daddy as they walked down the hall.

I heard the door close, I hope that meant Daddy was going to stay with him a while. I knew how frightened Xavier was right now.

"And you must be Angelique?" I heard her ask.

"Yes ma'am," I confirmed and extended my hand, but she opened her arms to me and I went into them.

There was a familiar smell about her, sweet, like the incense that grandma burned all the time. There was nothing fragile about this woman. There was vigor in her embrace.

"You are such a lovely thing," she said pulling away to look at me the way she did Mama earlier.

She ran her hand through my reddening mane of hair, smirking at my grandmother as she did so. I noticed then that her eyes were two different colors; one looked to be light brown and the other dark as coal. She looked at me and frowned.

"There is fire inside of you child. But," she paused, "why are you so afraid to feed the flame?"

"Celest," Grandmother called out with such ferocity. "Now is not the time."

"Isabelle," Aunt Celestine said as she stepped around me to stand in front of Grandma.

They began to converse in French. Grandma looked at me and motioned for Aunt Celestine to stop talking.

"They can understand what we are saying ya know," she said, letting her know that their conversation wasn't private.

"Really now?" She questioned then turned to look at me.

I can tell that she was quite impressed.

"You teach all the children?" She asked.

"Everyone except me," Daddy confessed making his way back to join us.

I knew Xavier couldn't have fallen asleep that fast.

"It's never too late to learn," Aunt Celestine told him, "they could be plotting against you right in your face and you don't even know It."

This caused a few chuckles.

She turned back to my grandmother, "Is there somewhere we can talk in private, Isabelle?"

My grandmother motioned toward the back of the house, indicating the back porch.

"We can talk on the porch out back, and I am called Odalia round here," she said sharply.

"Well, if I recollect correctly, our Mama did name you Isabelle too, did she not?" Aunt Celestine returned with a tone just as sharp.

Grandma just rolled her eyes and shook her head as she led her sister out the back door. *Boy would I love to be a part of that conversation.*

"Your Aunt is a little strange," Daddy whispered as he eyed the back door.

Mama turned to him with a smirk on her face, "Consider yourself privileged. That 'strange' woman you just met is one of the most powerful Hoodoo Priestesses in all of Louisiana."

CHAPTER 6

It was starting to appear as though Grandma and Aunt Celestine would never come back inside. Daddy, Mama and me were sitting at the kitchen table hoping they would soon come in and make us apart of the conversation.

"A hoodoo priestess?" Daddy asked Mama suddenly. "Are you fa' real?"

"Yeah, I'm fa' real. Just ask her yourself whenever she comes back in. I'm sure she'll tell ya," Mama said with a straight face.

"So she puts spells on folk and stuff like that?"

His curiosity was definitely peaked. Mama snickered.

"It's not all about spells and potions. It goes so much deeper than that," she informed him.

"Does she believe in God?" Daddy asked.

"One of the biggest believers," Mama answered, "That's one thing I admired about her when I was growing up. Despite what many believed about her, she believes in God."

Daddy frowned, "So, how does all that work? How can she believe in God, but play round with voodoo?"

"Don't confuse hoodoo with voodoo. They are the same in some ways, but different in just as many. Voodoo is considered a religion and hoodoo, well, hoodoo is not."

"So what is Hoodoo?" Daddy asked, confused.

Mama just smiled at him, "Ask Aunt Celestine."

She said motioning her head toward the back door.

"I don't want to know that bad," he said causing Mama to chuckle. "I hope she can help us figure out what's going on around here or else we got to go."

He leaned over to give Mama a kiss on her cheek. He was tired of waiting and decided to go on to bed, but not before telling Mama to hurry up and come to bed too. He wasn't too keen on going to sleep alone with ghosts lurking around.

I was tired as well, but I wanted to stay up and hopefully learn more about Aunt Celestine. A Hoodoo Priestess, in this family, Wow. I heard a lot of talk about the Priestess of New Orleans from Grandma, but she never said anything about her sister being one. I heard they could do some very fascinating things; some things that you could only imagine.

Mama made some tea for me and coffee for herself. I see she wanted to wait up as well. I wondered if she knew more than she was letting on.

"Why do you think she is here?" I asked abruptly, referring to Aunt Celestine.

She took a sip of her coffee, "Yo guess is just as good as mine, but I know she didn't come for nothing. But isn't it strange though, how she came just after what happened outside. It's almost as if she knew we needed answers. And I'm willing to bet my life that she will give them to us."

"Do you really think she can?" I asked skeptically.

This all seemed so unreal to me. And I don't even know why, because after everything that has happened, I should never doubt anything. She shook her head.

"I don't think she can, I know she can."

She traced her fingertip around the edge of her cup.

"I've seen her do some things that you wouldn't believe. Her and Jericho was like a team. And when I tell you they can make some things happen, things the average person can only dream about. She even knew that Genevieve was going to die."

I sat back in my chair with a look of shock on my face.

"Did she? How?"

This conversation was getting more interesting by the second.

"She went with me to see Jericho a week or two before the accident and Aunt Celestine was there. She pulled me off to the side right before me and Genevieve left and I will never, as long as I live, forget the words she spoke to me. She said, 'Tell your friend to continue to stay right with God, her essence is aiming for the stars and it's no fault of her own, but that of another.' I was so confused by what she was saying. At that time I didn't know what that meant, and I didn't bother to ask. I thought it was Celestine just being Celestine, but it wasn't. Genevieve died because of my father's carelessness. I've seen the fakes and I learned to spot the real. She is real as real can get. Now, if only they would stop all the fussing and fighting we can get to the bottom of some thangs," she said eyeing the back door.

That brought another question to mind.

"They don't like each other too much do they? That much I can tell. Do you know why?"

I figured I might as well ask all the questions I could think of while Mama was in the mood to answer them.

Shaking her head, Mama replied, "That's one I can't figure out either. To be honest, Aunt Celestine didn't come around our place much when I was growing up. The only time I would really see her is when I visited with Uncle Jericho, which was a lot. She was always really nice to me and treated me as if I was her own. I loved being around her, because she was so fascinating to me and to my friends. Even though they were afraid of her, curiosity always got the better of them."

She took another sip, "But it wasn't Mere who was the distant one; it was Celestine. I remember Mere always trying to go out of her way to please her. It was like she was trying to get approval. It was almost as if she hated Mere for whatever reason. After a while though, Mere stopped trying and she started treating Aunt Celestine the same way she treated her."

"Did you ever ask Gran why they didn't get along?" I inquired curiously.

Surely there was some driving force that caused the drift.

"Yeah, plenty of times. She would either ignore me or she would say I needed to ask Aunt Celestine that question," she shrugged. "But one thang I do know is that they both get along with Uncle Jericho well enough."

She smiled, "Ole Uncle Jericho was so much fun to be around. He was the one who kinda took care of everyone after my grandfather died. Most were afraid of Aunt Celestine. Everyone always went to Uncle Jericho whenever there was a problem or they needed some advice about anything. He was and still is a great listener."

"Do you ever talk to him?" I asked.

"Sometimes, but not as much as Mere. They talk at least once a week and write each other every other day it seems like."

I knew that to be true. I would check the mail sometimes and there would be letter's from Jericho LeBlanc. I've heard a lot about him, how generous and kind he was and still is. I have never met him before and I hope he would pop up soon too. It's sad that I have several family members in Louisiana and I've never seen or met any of them.

"Well," Mama said standing, "It doesn't look like their come'n in anytime soon."

"We could just lift the window up and eavesdrop," I suggested, eyeing the small kitchen window.

"Oh you mean how you and Dominique use to do?" She asked sarcastically with one eyebrow raised. "Y'all wasn't as slick as you thought."

"We kinda figured that out when y'all would stop talking all of a sudden," I smiled as I remembered how mischievous we used to be.

But the smile didn't remain for long, as the thought of Dominique lingered in my mind. There was so much we didn't know about our family, things she never got the privilege to know, and she never will. I still couldn't believe she was gone.

"What's wrong baby?" Mama asked, obviously noticing the look of sadness on my face.

I stared into my cup, "We will be burying Dominique soon. I still can't believe it."

She came and pulled a chair close to mine and sat down. She wrapped her arm around me, pulling me close to her. I rested my head on her shoulder.

"I can't believe she is really gone Mama," I said as the tears filled my eyes yet again, and raced across the bridge of my nose.

"Me either," she whispered. "She will always be with us."

"I already miss her so much," I cried. "I don't think I will ever get over this."

Mama didn't say anything else. She just wrapped her other arm around me and pulled me even closer. Her body was trembling slightly, letting me know that she was crying as well. *Will we ever get over this?*

"Let me go check on these old women cause they been out there for quite a while now," she said releasing me and wiping away fresh tears.

I know she didn't want me to see her upset. I don't know why it was so hard for her to show her emotions around any of us. She opened the back door and stepped out onto the porch, closing the door behind her.

A few moments passed and not one of the women had made their way back inside. Now, I was becoming irritated. I wanted to know what was going on too. I stood up and headed to the door, but Mama came inside before I could reach it. She looked as though something was bothering her.

"What's going on out there?" I whispered, not wanting to be heard.

"They are talking about something they obviously don't want me to know about, 'cause they stopped talking about it when I came out. Whatever it is must me mighty important, because they aren't done talking," she said, bending down to take off her shoes. "I'm too tired to make them tell me what they are talk'n bout. Not saying that I could make them if I tried."

She gave me a quick kiss on the cheek, "I'm going to bed and you should do the same. It's gonna be a rough couple of days for all of us. We need to try to get as much rest as we can. I love you."

"Love you too Mama. Good night," I said. I didn't have any intentions on going to bed, at least not yet.

"Good night. Wipe the table down before you lay down," she called as she head down the hall.

"Ok," I said, deep in thought. I quickly clean the table off, knowing exactly what I wanted to do next.

After I was done in the kitchen, I slipped quietly out the front door. I took off my shoes after making my way down the front steps. I walked softly along the side of the house. I had to know what they were discussing and why they were taking four hours to discuss it. I sat down on the ground quietly, when I got close enough to hear them. I stole a peek around the side of the house. They both were sitting with their backs to me. I had to listen closely, because it appeared as though they were going back in forth in both English and French.

"And what does that mean?" Grandma was asking.

"How do you not see that this is all your fault?" Aunt Celestine asked.

"Because it's not and you got some nerve coming here trying to start all kinds of confusion and devilment.

You can take that hoodoo voodoo or whatever it is that you are conjuring up these days, and head straight back to Louisiana," Grandma snapped.

"It's your fault because you have hindered them for so long," Aunt Celestine said motioning towards the house. "You have kept them from growing."

"That's no fault of mine," Grandma said angrily, "These are Delphine's children."

"And you are Delphine's mother and that alone gains you respect. She should have enough of that to take your words to heart."

"Don't you think I have tried," Grandma was saying, but was interrupted by Aunt Celestine.

"If you had tried harder I wouldn't be sitting here now would I," Aunt Celestine pointed out.

What did she mean by that?

Aunt Celestine continued, "I can see that you still don't like to own up to your wrong doings. You haven't changed in your ways at all. You never listen."

"That's a lie," I heard my Grandmother say. "Oh, I listen, but it is you that choose not to hear me."

She spoke with so much contempt. I don't think I have ever heard this tone from her before.

Aunt Celestine erupted with laughter, "Poor little Isabelle. Little weak Isabelle, always so spoiled and I see you still throw a fit when you are being chastised."

"I was never spoiled, nor was I ever weak," Grandma said in her own defense.

"Daddy's little girl, his little angel," Aunt Celestine tone was full of scorn.

"Oh so that's where all the hatred for me comes from? My relationship with Pere or is it something else?" Grandmother asked folding her arms across her breasts, acting as if she was truly surprised.

"Hate? I don't hate you Isabelle. I envy you," she got to her feet quickly, turning in my direction.

I jumped back quickly and waited for my name to be called, but it was not.

"You're too old to still be naïve," Aunt Celestine said.

"Naïve? What are you talking about?" Grandma hissed.

"Yes, naïve. The older you got the more you should have realized our father's true nature. You worshipped the ground that man walked on," the older sister spat.

"His true nature was one of sincere kindness and loyalty. He deserved the respect he was shown. And yes, I worshipped him. He was a great man who did good things for so many people," Grandma declared.

Another roar of laughter came from Celestine. I peeked around the side of the house once more. She had taken her seat again.

"Great things you say, humph," her words were bitter. "Let me tell you why I envy you my dear. You pretty much got to live your entire childhood in the light. You got to see all the 'good things' he did. Do you really think that's all he did? Cure ailments? No, he was as dark as dark can get when the time called for him to be."

What did she mean by that? I thought. I couldn't see my grandfather being a dark man. Everything I heard about him never led me to think otherwise.

"Stop talking all this foolishness and you know it's not wise to speak ill of the dead," Grandma warned.

"I'm not speaking ill of the dead. I'm just speaking ill truths performed by the dead," Aunt Celestine spat.

"So what you're trying to say is," Grandma began.

"What I'm saying is there were many nights that you lay sound asleep and Jericho and I weren't allowed to sleep because we had to help Pere. There were always ingredients that needed to be gathered. Some of them could only be gathered at the darkest hour to be potent and from some of the worst places in Louisiana. Places no child should ever have to go. We did things that no child should have to do. Do you know how many snakes I have slit from belly to head? All the tongues I have cutout from the mouths of animals, cats especially -- enough to last one thousand lifetimes."

My mouth flew open. This piece of information shocked me. I had only heard good things about my great grandfather Martin. I couldn't see him being into the things that Aunt Celestine is accusing him of. *How could my grandmother not know any of this?*

Grandma was still sitting with her back to me. The light from the kitchen window illuminated the porch slightly, allowing me to see my Grandmother's reaction to the news she had just heard. She was shaking her head from side to side quickly, her reaction one of disbelief.

"I won't believe any of this. I can't believe you just let filthy, satanic lies spill from your mouth so freely. You have always been jealous of me," Grandma was beyond angry now. "And you hated me ever since Eugene chose me over you?"

"Chose you?" Aunt Celestine threw her head back and roared with laughter once again.

"Is that what you've believed all this time?" She asked grandma.

"Eugene chased me for years. And when he saw that I couldn't commit to him the way that he wanted, he turned his eyes to you. I knew that he liked you and I allowed him to go to you. I encouraged it. I knew he knew about Pere, but I didn't want him to know about the things that I was made to do. I loved Eugene and I didn't want him to know about that side of my life. So, yes, I pushed him in your direction, and that was obviously a mistake. You turned him into a drunken fool."

What did I just hear? My grandfather was with Aunt Celestine before he was with my grandmother. I can see how that would cause several problems. Having to give up the man you loved to your sister would make any woman become bitter.

"That's a lie, just like all the other lies you're standing here tell'n. You and Eugene were friends. That's what he told me. And Pere wouldn't have allowed us to be married if that was not true. You're just a mean, evil old woman," Grandma was up in Aunt Celestine's face now.

But Aunt Celestine didn't back down.

"Pere knew the truth and he told me I had made a wise decision. He was never really fond of Eugene. He thought he was a better fit for you. He saw both of you as being weak," Aunt Celestine countered.

Her tone was one of sureness. Grandma took one quick step forward and slapped her sister.

"I hate the very ground you walk on Celestine," grandma spat. "You come all this way to try to hurt me, hurt my family! Telling all these sick lies about Eugene and Pere," Grandma paused, taking her seat again.

The older woman just stood there as if that hit to the face meant nothing.

"You can hate me all you want Isabelle, but I will never speak those words to you, because despite what you believe, I love you. I want to help this family not harm it. And if you don't believe my words, ask Jericho," Aunt Celestine advised slyly.

I could almost hear what sounded like satisfaction in her words. It was as if she enjoyed watching my Grandma hurt.

"There is no need to ask him, because he would have told me way before now," Grandma said.

"No he wouldn't. Thank Pere for that as well. He didn't want you to know the truth and we were given strict instructions not to tell you anything. He didn't want us to tell you anything about Eugene and nothing about his other activities and this is why. Our mother, rest her soul, wanted a child that wasn't tainted by our father's practices, one that he didn't mold in his own image. You were his gift to our mother. But ironically enough, you are quite gifted yourself, but in a different way from me and Jericho. Your gift comes from a good place: Ours, not so good. And not because they weren't meant to be, but because they weren't groomed to be. So, like I said, ask Jericho. There is nothing the old man can do to us now for telling you the truth."

Grandmother stood up again, "If Pere was so bad, why are you choosing to live the same life that he did?"

Aunt Celestine turned to look at her.

"Let me tell you something, I learned to stop being afraid of the dark before you were even thought of being conceived. I was introduced to this world at the age of 5 and this way of life is all that I know. It is buried right here," she said pointing at her chest.

"We didn't get to grow up the way most kids did, like you did. Other than schooling we had no free time, there was no playing with friends for us. It was all about learning the ways of our father, knowing which root could heal and which could kill. And getting the worse beating ever, if I chose incorrectly. Those are my childhood memories. But one thing that your precious father didn't bother to tell us was that this way came with a price and a hefty price it is. So you just keep right on praising him and I will keep right on wishing that he is in that cold dark grave of his sinking deeper and deeper into the murk. You have no idea how much that man took from us. I hated him."

I think I have heard enough for tonight. This was too much information for me to absorb for one night. I slowly and as quietly as I could, stood up from my crouched position. I didn't realize how long I had been sitting, because when I stood up, my legs almost gave way. I stumbled backwards and almost yelled out when I bumped into someone standing behind me. Phillip placed his hand over my mouth to keep me from screaming. He had scared me so, that my heart felt like it was about to jump clean out of my chest.

"What'chu doing?" He whispered, removing his hand from my mouth. "Why you?"

"Shush," I said and quickly turned him around and headed for the front of the house.

"Why are you sneaking round on the side of my house?" I asked fiercely.

I didn't want to explain what I was doing on the side of the house with a boy, if we were caught.

"You tell me," he returned folding his arms, as if he had just caught me doing something I didn't have no business doing.

Well, in a sense, I guess he did.

"I was eavesdropping on my grandmother and her sister," I confessed. "And you almost got me caught."

I slapped him hard on the arm.

"Ouch," he squeaked, rubbing the spot I had just hit. "And, what did you hear?"

"What did you hear is the real question," I said, "How long were you standing there?"

"Not long at all," he answered.

Not long could mean anything from five minutes to thirty minutes.

"Hear anything good?" He teased bumping my shoulder.

"I don't know about that, but I do think I heard a little too much," I answered taking a seat on the front steps.

He looked at me with a puzzling look on his face.

"Never mind all that," I said changing the subject. "What are you doing out here?"

"I s-saw you when you came out the house. And you looked like you was up to no good," he explained as he sat beside me. "I s-sat outside and waited, but when you didn't come back. I g-got a little worried."

"So you decided to come to my rescue?" I said batting my eyelashes, causing him to laugh.

I turned to look back at the close door, knowing I shouldn't be out here, "I have to get on back inside, before my Granny comes inside and find me outside, or worse, Mama waking up finding me outside."

He rose up from the step and smiled down at me, "We sho don't need those troubles."

"No we don't," I said in agreement, standing on my feet. "You want to hang out tomorrow?"

I don't know where this came from, but the words were out of my mouth now and couldn't be taken back. He looked just as shocked as I was.

"S-sure," he stammered, "I'd like that."

He bent down and gave me a light kiss on the lips and headed home. I stood there watching him for a few moments before sneaking back inside. I made my way to the kitchen and walked over to the window and peeped out. The two ladies were still at it, and with great reason. My grandmother is just now, after all these years, learning that her father was not the man she thought he was, and to find out that she was her husband's second choice, his first being her sister, had to be like a kick to the stomach. I just wonder how many more skeletons are hidden in the closet.

CHAPTER 7

I checked in on Xavier before getting ready for bed. Today had been so terrifying for him. I opened the door quietly and a cold gust of air came out. It was freezing. I looked around the room to see if I could figure out the cause, the window was closed. The nights were cooler now, but not that cool to cause this type of chill. I looked down at him. I thought he would have a hard time going to sleep, but he appeared to be in a deep slumber with his covers pulled up over his head. I knew he was still afraid from everything that had transpired earlier. To have a gift such as his at such a young age had to be frightening. I glanced over at the window again, remembering our conversation from earlier, a chill ran along my spine. I rubbed my arms briskly and stepped back into the hallway, leaving the door slightly ajar.

I walked down to me and Dominique's room, which seemed so strange to me now. I hadn't slept in this room for a few days now. I glanced at Dominique's side of the room when I flipped on the light; still the way it was the night she left; nothing out of place. I took a seat on her bed and allowed my hands to run across the soft lavender covers. Lavender, her favorite color, was in abundance on this side of the room. I brought one of her pillows up to my face, hoping her scent was still there. My heart sank when I realized it was fading and that the time would come when I would try to find her scent and find it completely gone.

I placed the pillow back in its proper place and walked over to the closet to begin undressing. The first thing I noticed when I opened the closet door was all of Dominique's things. Everything on her side was neat like always, sorted by color. I remembered there was a time that I would always tease her about her obsession with neatness. But I quickly learned to stop teasing her, when I realized it took her absolutely no time at all to get herself dressed for the day. I would be looking everywhere for my things; under the bed, on the side of the bed, the closet floor, but not her. She always kept everything in order. I can't count how many times she would fuss at me.

"Maybe if you would straighten your junk up, you would be able to find what you need," she once said to me with that scornful look of hers when we were both getting clothes out of the closet for the day.

I was digging and digging for something, but she just went straight to what she wanted.

"I know exactly where everything is. You have your way of staying organized and I have mine, now just mind yo own business," I told her while still in search for my garment.

Sometimes I think she thought I was the messiest person on the face of the earth. I would give anything to see her again, to have her scold me the way she use to do. I quickly pulled out one of my night shirts to sleep in and closed the closet door. Slipping into the shirt quickly, I started for the door and nearly tripped on Dominique ribbon box. *Had this been here before?* I don't remember moving it from its place at the foot of her bed. After placing the few ribbons that had fallen out back inside, I slid the box back in its place, but I noticed something sticking from out the side of it.

I picked the box up again and dug inside to see what the object was. Mixed in with the ribbons was a neatly folded piece of paper. I sat on the bed and unfolded it. Belinda's handwriting was the first thing I recognized, my hands began to tremble. The last time I saw her immediately came to mind. I had come into the room and saw her sitting on the edge of Dominique's bed. She had snuck in through the window. Something heavy was on her mind that night; the night she took her life. She must have left this here then. I took a deep breath and began to read:

Angelique,

I know you probably wondering why I'm writing a letter instead of just talking to you. I know you may not understand, but I can't face you right now and to be honest, I can't really face myself either and I guess I'm doing this to break the ice a little. These past few weeks have been really hard for me. A lot has been going on. Things I have no idea how to handle.

I found out that my Daddy ain't my Daddy. I overheard him and Mama talking a few days ago and I heard her tell him that he knew from the start that I wasn't his and that he chose to take on the role as my Daddy and that he needed to send money like he promised. And from what I could gather, they are the only two that knew the truth, and now I know and so do you. It broke my heart to find out that the man I called Daddy my entire life ain't even my Daddy, but that's only a small thing compared to what I need to tell you.

I overheard something else and it's big, real big, but there is something I need to do first before we talk. I'm placing this letter in a place I know you would surely look. I noticed that you always wearing Dominique's ribbons nowadays, so I know you will find this. I know how much you miss her. I miss her too. When all this is over, maybe everybody can start putting their lives back together again. All I need is a little time.

Your best friend in the entire world,

Belinda

P.S. We can't trust nobody round here, and I mean NOBODY!

I didn't realize I was crying until I saw a tear hit the paper. She needed me and I didn't realize it. Why didn't she just come to me the way friends are supposed to do? I didn't know what to make of this. Confusion settled deep in my mind. This proved one thing without a doubt, deception wasn't just attached to my household.

Mrs. Kirkland didn't seem like the type of person that would do something that would intentionally cause someone pain. She must have a good reason for not telling Belinda the truth, and was only looking out for her daughter's best interest. We all have our reasons for doing something that doesn't always make sense to others, but makes perfect logical sense to us. I know that Amos left when Belinda was still pretty young, but her parents never divorced, which I thought was pretty odd. If Amos wasn't Belinda's father, then who was? And what did she need to talk to me about that was way more significant than finding out about her true parentage?

That night began to play over and over again in my head. The way Belinda looked, the way she sounded, she was not herself. She wanted to talk to me, but she couldn't, but why. I knew without doubt that Claire was what she wanted to talk about. I'm still so angry with her for not telling me what she knew. How long had she known this information about Claire? Mr. Monroe had a business to run so they had to return home soon enough. They're probably just trying to put together a story for Claire. She must have played a vital part in whatever happened to Dominique.

Belinda wrote "Claire knows," but what exactly did Claire know. I could feel the anger building again. That icy feeling of betrayal was consuming me. I looked at the note again. Belinda was right about one thing, I was always going through Dominique's ribbon box, but I haven't touched it since our altercation, not until tonight. The soft knock on the door interrupted my thoughts.

"Come in," I said, quickly folding the letter and stuffing it underneath the mattress.

I don't know why, but I didn't want anyone to see this. Mama stuck her head inside.

"I saw the light on. Are you sleeping in here tonight?" She asked.

I looked around the room. Surprising myself, I answered.

"I think so," she smiled at me and walked into the room and sat beside me on Dominique's bed.

She rubbed her hands across the spread just as I had done earlier.

"We are going to have to get back to normal one of these days," she said, "so tonight will be a good starting point as any."

I turned to look at her.

"I don't think we will ever get back to being normal, I think we will just learn to be better at accepting things for what they are, because we weren't given a choice. To me, that's a big difference Mama," I said looking her straight in her eyes.

She needed to understand that things would never be normal. Dominique is gone, and so was Belinda. Me and normal could never be used in the same sentence, ever.

"I can see how you feel that way. But, like I told you before, time is a wonderful healer." She rubbed her hands across my cheek, "Get some sleep. I want you to come with me tomorrow to pick out something nice for your sister to wear, ok?"

Her voice cracked. I see that she is trying to control her emotions. I took her hands in mine.

"You don't have to try to keep it together for me. I'm hurting just like you." For once, I pulled my mother into my arms to comfort her for a change, "You can't keep all this inside Mama. Let it go."

She squeezed me tightly as she sobbed heavily. All these pinned up tears she was holding back had to be released. I held onto to her until she was done crying. She stepped back and wiped her eyes with the back of her hands.

"Thank you baby," she said and quickly left the room. I just stood staring at the door long after she had left, realizing that what I said earlier was definitely the truth. Nothing would ever be normal, not for any of us.

After I got into bed, I stared into the darkness for a long time. So much was running through my mind. I thought about Belinda's letter and quickly got out of bed to retrieve it. I turned on the lamp and read it over and over again before putting it back inside the ribbon box. So many questions are dancing around in my head. And the only people who could possibly put all this into perspective are sitting out on the back porch having bouts of sibling rivalry.

I glanced around the room, shuddering as I thought about my encounter with the spirit from earlier. I quickly opened up the bedroom door, hoping she was gone for the night and didn't feel the need to appear again anytime soon. There are so many questions that needed to be answered. And the main one is why are we being haunted. What does this spirit want with us? I yawned, climbing back into bed, putting the many questions out of my head and greeted sleep with contentment.

I didn't recognize where I was immediately, but then it came to me. I was sitting on the back steps of Belinda's house which faced the woods. I looked around and realized I was alone. I heard someone singing. I turned to see someone coming from the woods. Belinda. She was smiling at me as she sang. I tried to get up from my place on the steps, but I couldn't move. It was as if I was glued to that spot. Belinda came and sat down beside me, she took both of my hands in her.

"Be still, Angelique," she giggled. "You are always searching for something. When all you have to do is sit still and you will see that all you have been searching for will find it's way to you."

She looked so happy, so peaceful, this was the Belinda I knew and loved. I bring her hands up to my lips and kissed them.

"Why did you have to leave me too?" I asked her.

She squeezed my hands tightly, so tight that they were starting to bleed. It was as if she had a million knives attached to her hands that were penetrating mine.

"BELINDA," I screamed, "you're hurting me, let go."

She was crying, not tears, but something dark. Is it blood?

"I didn't want to leave you, but they said I had to," she said as she continued to squeeze blood from my hands.

I looked down and saw both of our hands covered in blood. She let go abruptly and she was gone, just disappeared into thin air. Then, all of a sudden, she appeared on my left, so close to my ear that I could feel her lips there.

"Now everyone has blood on their hands," *she whispered swiftly.*

"Angelique, wake up."

It was Grandma.

"Wake up," I could hear her say, but I could also hear someone whispering, "Look in the box."

I opened my eyes and sat up. Aunt Celestine was standing at the foot of my bed and my grandmother was on the side of me, helping me sit up.

"One of those dreams again?" She asked. "You haven't had one in quite a while now have you?"

"The last one was the night before Belinda died," I answered

"You didn't tell me about that one," Grandma eyed me with her narrow slits.

"No, I didn't. It was not on my mind after everything that happened afterwards," I said looking down at my hands, remembering my dream.

I looked up at Aunt Celestine. She was staring at me so intensely. She didn't even blink, just started right at me as if she could see my darkest fears. I quickly looked down. Her unnatural eyes made me nervous.

"Why do you stare down at your hands like that?" Aunt Celestine asked. "What did you dream tonight girl?"

I took a deep breath and told them about my dream. When I was done, my grandmother turned to look at her sister, as if she was waiting for her thoughts on the matter.

"The longer you wait, the harder it will be. You are wasting precious time and I didn't come all this way to lose a battle, and you know I don't take kindly to losing. You know some things are better handled in numbers. If you don't know anything else Isabelle, you should know that. You better decide quick or I will just have to get Jericho down here to get the job done. I have enough blood on my own hands without adding anymore. And dancing with a hank only makes this situation worse," she stated snidely and stormed out of the room.

Her manners weren't the best as far as I could see. Grandma kept her eyes on the spot were Aunt Celestine had just stood.

"Go back to sleep child," she said, heading for the door.

"Gran," I called, "what did she mean by that?"

"By what?" She asked.

"Dancing with a hank?" I asked interestingly.

"A hank is just a fancy term for ghost or spirit," she answered reluctantly.

"So does Aunt Celestine know why we are being haunted?" I asked.

I knew now that they talked about everything that happened today. Judging the exchange that just took place between the two, apparently Aunt Celestine knows why the spirit is here and how to get rid of her.

"I have to speak with Delphine first, you are her child. All decisions about this matter are hers to make."

She didn't even give me a chance to reply, before switching the light off and closing the door behind her. I lay back down and stared into the darkness once more. I sat up again when something that I didn't think about before popped into my head, something that didn't make a bit of sense to me.

Why would Belinda take her own life the same night she left a letter saying she needed to talk to me? I hopped out of bed and grabbed the ribbon box again. *Look in the box.* I turned it upside down, allowing all the ribbons and the letter to fall onto the floor. I started digging through the fabric, unsure of what I was looking for, until something silver caught my eyes. A necklace. I place it in the palm of my hand and continued digging until I found *them*. My hands began to shake as I held the crescent shaped earrings in one hand and the necklace in the other.

CHAPTER 8

I woke just a little before dawn after a restless night. My mind kept going back to the jewelry that I know had to have come from Belinda. I guess she wanted me to have it, because Dominique had a set just like it that she was wearing the night she went missing. I arose and walked over to the only window in the room and looked out into the darkest. I looked at the woods, which were directly behind the house. I thought about Willow's Creek. I hadn't been back there for a while. It was my place of solitude and peace. A visit there was long overdue.

I chose something from Dominique's side of the closet to put on. Wearing her things made me feel closer to her. After I was done with my bath, I quickly dressed and stared at myself in the mirror for what seemed like a long while. My eyes were all swollen; my hair looked so uncared for. Revolted by my appearance, I brushed my teeth and quickly took down my two braids and brushed my hair until it actually looked decent. It appeared to be even redder than before.

On my way to the kitchen, I noticed that Aunt Celestine was asleep on the sofa. She definitely didn't look like the type that should be sleeping on anybody's sofa. With the air of authority that she carried around, I'm surprised she didn't demand that someone give up their bed for her. I'm sure that an entirely different argument would have ensued if she had tried that with Grandma. Those two really seemed to have it out for each other and after last night, I'm sure things won't be getting any better anytime soon.

Trying to remain as quiet as I could, I began getting together everything I needed to make myself some tea, but I guess I wasn't quiet enough.

"Make me a cup too if you don't mind," Aunt Celestine said as she came into the kitchen tying her robe.

She took a seat at the table. Her long braid was tucked underneath a colorful head wrap. I was amazed at the way she looked after a night's rest. Most of us looked pretty bad first thing in the morning, but not her. She was still beautiful. It was still hard to believe that she is older than my grandmother. I guess father time has his picks and chooses.

"Ok, I don't mind," I stated, grabbing another cub from the cabinet. "I'm sorry for waking you. I tried to not make too much noise."

She waved her hand at me, "You didn't wake me child. I don't sleep for too long these days anyways. Have you ever heard the saying 'every shut eye ain't sleep?'"

I shook my head, "I can't say that I have."

"Well," she began, "never assume that just because one's eyes are closed that they are asleep. They may just be faking sleep so they can hear what ain't meant to be heard."

She looked around the kitchen as if she was noticing it for the first time, "This is a cozy little place. It's nice."

"Thank you," I said.

I didn't want to tell her how I really couldn't stand this house anymore. The place that I once loved so much was now a constant reminder of the things that I've lost. There were so many good memories here, but the magnitude of the bad ones has almost completely diminished the good.

"I take it you didn't sleep too well since you are up before the rooster's crow," she assumed as I placed the steaming cup in front of her.

"Not too well. I couldn't really get comfortable after waking up from that awful dream," I replied.

"Hopefully, tonight will be a little better for you," she said. "So, you are almost done with school I'm told."

"Yes, this year is my last."

I sat in the chair across from her.

"When will you be returning?" She asked.

That's something I had been thinking about for a while now and I think I have made my decision. School started a week ago, so I really haven't missed much. I would return this week.

"Tomorrow," I told her, "I will be returning tomorrow. It's gonna be different going back there without my sister and Belinda, but I'll make it, I guess."

She looked at me and smiled.

"You will be ok child. I'm glad to see that you are very well spoken. That's almost unheard of among you young folk nowadays. I guess that white school you go to have a lot to do with that."

I sort of took offense to that. So did she think I wouldn't be well spoken? I wonder what she was expecting when she met us. A house full of dumb relatives from Mississippi; well she was sadly mistaken. Just like her, I am well educated.

"Thank you. Mama makes sure we read a lot."

Yeah, I can read and write too, I even know my colors, I thought to myself rather than telling that to her like I wanted to.

Mrs. Vermont, the lady Mama work for, was always sending us tons of books to read. Whenever she saw us, she would ask what book had we read and she would ask us questions about it to be sure we weren't lying. The variety of books allowed us to learn many different things and our imagination allowed us to travel to many places. We loved when Mama would bring a new box of books home allowing us to go on another adventure.

"That's good. My father was the same way. He didn't want any of us to not be educated. He wanted us to sort of stand out from the rest I guess you can say. He made sure we did just that."

She took a sip of her tea, staring at me with those strange eyes of hers, over the brim of the cup. I quickly thought back on the conversation that I heard last night and I knew she meant that in every sense. They definitely stood out. I think now is the perfect time to get her to tell me a little more about herself, about her beliefs.

"Tell me about your sister," she said suddenly, taking me completely by surprise.

"Uh, well, what would you like to know?" I wanted her to be more specific.

There was so much to tell about Dominique.

"Anything that you would like to share will be ok," she answered.

113

"Well, we looked exactly the same, but no one really got us confused. She was so different than me. She was better than me in so many ways," I said rubbing my arm absentmindedly.

"She was a caring person who loved people, always wanting to help those who needed it without asking for anything in return. But she didn't mind setting anyone straight either, especially me," I said with a smile, looking up at Aunt Celestine, who was looking at me with interest.

I was quiet a moment, trying to hold back tears.

"She was brilliant and smart. Everyone liked her," I paused wiping at the tears the came pouring out against my will. "She had the heart of a giant and no one understands why someone felt the need to take her from us. She was too trusting and that's why she is not with us today, because of that trust."

I looked at Aunt Celestine again, not caring about the tears that were spilling down my cheeks, "She was the good one, not me. I know I shouldn't say this, but I think that it would be more likely that someone would want to harm me before they would her."

"Why do you say that child?" Aunt Celestine asked.

I thought a moment before answering.

"I don't get along with people the way that she did. I'd rather be to myself, because I don't trust people like

114

that, it's a feeling I get sometimes. And I'm not always right about some of them, but I have to say I'm right at least ninety percent of the time," I truthfully answered.

She reached across the table with her hand opened to me. I placed my hands in hers.

"Just because your ways weren't like hers, doesn't make you a bad person," she said. "It makes you a different person. You both are individuals and you have to live your life that way, always. That's how a lot of us lose ourselves. We are too busy trying to be someone else. We fail to understand that if only we would just be ourselves, life might not be so complicated. So don't change for anyone, be who you are and then you will certainly be who you are meant to be."

Squeezing my hands gently, she looked at me and narrowed her eyes. Then she glanced back sneakily over her shoulders, making sure no one else had arisen to listen in on whatever she was about to tell me.

"You are unique, as is your mother, as was your sister, and your brother," she said shaking her head, "Your brother has something in him that I see in my brother Jericho. A light that shines brighter than any sun and in that light is pure greatness. I see your brother doing great things in his lifetime. He will help many people, as will you. But you have to nurture what you have. Learn to interpret your dreams, because your dreams aren't just any ole dreams, they are prophetic and you must learn how to understand them. And unfortunately that is not something that can be taught. You must learn that in your own way and it will take time."

I looked at her. I had so many questions, but I didn't know where to begin, "I just found out about our family history a few months ago. And even though I have seen many things over the past few months. It's still kinda hard to believe."

"I know and what a shame that is," she said frowning, "and that truly makes me angry, because I know that if you would have known long before now, you would have known the signs and a lot of tragedies could have been prevented."

"Even with Dominique?" I asked her without thinking as a fresh set of tears sprang to my eyes.

But before she could answer, we heard a door in the back open, and heard someone coming down the hall.

She pat my hands lightly and pulled back, "We will finish this later."

"Ok," I silently mouthed.

"You are up early," Grandma said looking at me.

"I couldn't really get back to sleep after my dream," I said.

"You are a growing child and you still must try to rest," she said pulling out some pans, obviously about to cook breakfast.

"You're talking as though the girl has been up for ten nights straight. We all have a few restless nights," Aunt Celestine said in my defense.

"Yeah, I'm sure you have more than most," Grandma shot at Aunt Celestine as she put on her apron.

"You have no idea," Aunt Celestine said maliciously as she got up from the table and headed down the hall.

Grandma just shook her head.

"That woman," she murmured to herself. "Hope she didn't put all sorts of nonsense in your head."

"No," I said, "she didn't."

"Good, cause she can surely do it."

I went to the stove to warm up my now cold tea. As I stood there watching Grandma as she prepared breakfast, I asked her a question that I hadn't had the courage to ask Aunt Celestine.

"Gran, Aunt Celestine's eyes, was she born like that?"

After I asked the question, I realized that I didn't recall seeing her eyes like that in any of her photos. Grandma kept on mixing her biscuit batter.

Not bothering to look at me, she said, "No she wasn't."

I waited for her to finish, but that was it, nothing more. I'm not satisfied with her answer.

"Well, how?"

"No she wasn't born that way, she did that to herself," she seemed to be irritated by my questions.

She did that to herself. How? How could someone do such a thing to themselves? Is something like that even possible? I wanted to ask more questions, but the look on her face told me to shut up. She was always so cryptic with her answers. Why couldn't she just answer a question straight out. I was really getting tired of not being told anything. I'm seventeen and still being treated as though I was seven.

Aunt Celestine made her way back into the kitchen. He head wrap now gone. She walked over to the stove and stood in between me and Grandma. She wrinkled up her nose at Grandma.

"Why do you do the biscuits that a way?"

Grandma turned to stare at her with her hands on her hips.

"Will you get away from this stove and let me cook how I cook? There ain't been any complaints till now," she told Aunt Celestine in such a way that told her, "You are getting on my nerves."

"That's because they don't know no better," Aunt Celestine returned with a raised brow. "Move over because I don't want bricks for breakfast. That's too much flour, and why?"

I walked out of the kitchen shaking my head as I chuckled, leaving the two ladies to quarrel in their native tongue about whose biscuits are better.

CHAPTER 9

I left the house before everyone else woke up. Grandma and Aunt Celestine seemed to be ok with one another for the moment. They were preparing breakfast together when I left the house. Hopefully that was a sign of some sort of reconciliation, even if for a little while. Grandma told me not to be gone too long. She didn't want my parents to be worried about me. They wanted me in their sight at all times these days and understandably so.

I really need some alone time and I know Xavier would not allow me to have any, especially if he knew I was going to Willow's Creek. The path I took had been taken by me and Dominique so many times, I'm sure I can get there with my eyes closed. The creek finally loomed ahead of me. It was still as beautiful as it was the first time we seen it. I stood at its edge, looking into the water as the suns gleam was finally starting to shine through the trees.

Like everywhere else around here, Willow's Creek was so full of memories, but it only held those that I would always cherish and look back on whenever I wanted to see Dominique's smile again. I took a seat on my usual stump and just took in the surrounding. It was so peaceful here, and that's what I liked about this place the most. The sound of nature was the only thing that could be heard, the water in the creek flowing over the rocks, the musical sound of the chirping birds, and other sounds that I couldn't place, but didn't mind hearing. This is the one thing in my life that never seemed to change.

I could sit out here all day, but today wouldn't be the day. We were going into Jackson to buy something nice to bury Dominique in. As much as I liked shopping, this was not a shopping trip that I was looking forward to. Having to find a dress to lay my sister to rest in was not something I wanted to be a part of. If I could avoid the funeral all together, I think that I would. It almost feels as if I'm the one being buried, and well, in a sense I am.

Belinda had made dealing with Dominique's disappearance a little easier for me. She was both of our best friends. She knew just as much about Dominique as I did. But now, not only do I have to deal with the death of my sister; I also have to deal with the death of my best friend. I walked to the edge of the creek once more and I closed my eyes. I prayed to God to help me deal with all the loss and to keep my family surrounded by his grace and mercy so that we may try as best we could to move forward in this world full of hate.

By the time I made it back, the house was in full swing. Everyone was up doing whatever is was they needed to do. Noises could be heard coming from all directions. I heard someone in the bathroom, Mama and Aunt Celestine talking about the pattern for a new dress. On the way to my room, I could hear Xavier in his room talking to himself letting me know that he was acting out some imaginary role with those toys of his like always.

I opened the door to his room only to discover that he was sitting on his bed alone, not a toy insight. Walking all the way into the room, I looked around expecting to see Daddy, but no one was inside, he was definitely alone. I glance at the window to see if someone had been standing there, but the curtains were still closed tight.

'Who are you talking to?" I asked taking a seat beside him on the bed.

"My friend," he answered looking up at me. "I'm hungry."

He quickly hopped off the bed and I know he is going for kitchen.

"Wait," I said grabbing his arm, "Who is your friend?"

I wondered if the lady had returned, but how could he be so calm about it. He was so frightened yesterday.

"You don't know him. He said he just moved here from out of town and he's the same age I am."

Him? That took me by surprise. There was assurance in his words. He spoke as if someone was really just in here.

"He just moved here? What's his name?" I asked him.

"Jacob," he answered without pause, "Jacob B. and guess what?" He asked with excitement, eyes wide. Before I could reply, he said to me in a loud whisper, "He's white, I ain't neva had no white friends."

I know Xavier has a vivid imagination, but this here was a little too vivid, even for him.

"Come on eat," we heard Grandma yell.

Xavier dashed out the door quickly without saying another word about his new friend, this Jacob B. I quickly made up his bed, something that had become a habit of mine over the past couple of days. On my way out of the room, his curtains flew upward as if the wind had blown them. I walked over to the window and pushed the curtains aside. The window was still shut tight and locked.

So where did the gust of wind come from? I left the curtains open and stood back, folding my arms across my breast. My thoughts suddenly went to this Jacob B. I quickly shook off the thought. *Maybe there are a couple of cracks along the seal.* We definitely couldn't deal with two different spirits.

I quickly headed for the door, not wanting to meet this spirit for myself, hoping that my imagination was getting the better of me and Xavier's was as well. Just as I was about to close the door, it closed on it's on, almost knocking me off balance. I turned around and stared at the closed door. That was definitely not my imagination. I slowly opened it again and peeped inside of the room cautiously.

"You ok, Angelique?" Aunt Celestine said, catching me completely by surprise almost causing me to lose all of my bodily fluids. With a pounding heart, I quickly closed the door. What I intended to say was, "Yeah, I'm ok," but that's not what rolled off of my tongue.

"No," I said turning to look at her.

She was dressed in one of those colorful dresses of hers. This one hugged her figure perfectly. To be as old as she was she still had the figure of a young woman.

"I'm not ok. I think something strange is going on around here again, very strange and I think some of the adults around here know more about it than they are letting on. I'm smart enough to know when something ain't natural, and whatever this here is ain't natural," I said a little too unkindly.

She walked a little closer to me and tilted her head slightly. "You," she had begun to say, but she abruptly stopped talking.

There was a strange look in her eyes. She stared at the closed door of Xavier's room and reached for the knob.

"You go on to eat a little something now," she instructed without even turning to look at me, but I didn't budge.

"I know something is in there," I whispered.

That's when she turned to acknowledge me. She just looked at me and smiled as she opened the door and stepped inside of Xavier's room. She stood in the middle of the room for a moment before walking over to the window. She swung the curtains open with force. She stepped back from the window with a slight smile on her face.

"Innocence is abundant in this room," she declared. "It's not's what's inside that we need to be worried about. What's on the outside of these walls is what causes me grave concern. Whenever the light has entered, the dark will surely follow."

Her and my grandmother are truly sister's. I thought no one could confuse me like Grandma, but I don't think she has anything on Aunt Celestine. That eerie feeling was beginning to come over me.

"So there is something in here?"

She turned to me, "Yes," she stated without hesitation. "But it's something good that's on the inside. Innocence, nothing harmful," she said, indicating the room.

Jacob B, I thought. An innocent child?

"Xavier was talking to someone earlier and when I asked him who he was talking to, he said a little white boy named Jacob B."

Aunt Celestine smiled broadly at this, "That child has no idea what he can do."

"Neither do I," I said. "And I want to know what it is that I can do. I am not a little child anymore. I'm practically an adult and the decision to know certain things shouldn't be left up to everyone else. The decision should me mine."

It was time for everyone to stop treating me like a kid. I was forced to face some harsh realities. Any remnants of the child inside of me died a long time ago.

"You're right," Mama said stepping inside of the room.

She looked at Aunt Celestine with tears in her eyes. I didn't know she was listening, but I'm glad she heard me.

She stepped in front of me, "Angelique, I've tried so hard to keep you and your sister in the dark about who we are and the background we came from, but I can't do that any longer. I can't keep certain things from you now even if I tried, not with everything that's goin on."

She looked at Aunt Celestine again, "She is not a child anymore, she is right."

"Yes she is. I've been telling you and that stubborn mother of yours that," Aunt Celestine gloated. "Now, what do you want to do about it?" She asked Mama.

"I want you to teach her all there is to know," Mama said.

I looked at her elated that she had come to that conclusion.

"But I have a few conditions," Mama said.

Aunt Celestine looked at her and tilted her head, something that she did often.

"And what are these conditions that you speak of Delphine? I don't think that there should be any conditions of any kind regarding these things. The more she knows, the better she will be," Aunt Celestine stated.

"I need for you to go slow with her. I don't want her to be frightened by anything you say or do, because you have a knack for doing just that if my memory is still intact," she raised her brow at her aunt. "Teach her only what she needs to be taught. There is no need for her to know about anything outside of that."

I knew Mama was referring to the Hoodoo/Voodoo practices. I'm sure I will be finding out soon enough whether Mama wanted me to or not. Aunt Celestine was about to protest, but Mama raised her hand, silencing her.

"But, I especially don't want her to get her hopes up about certain things either. So you be sure not do or say anything that will do that. She is my child, and if you can't respect any of these things that I ask you not to do, then there is no need for us to continue with this discussion." Mama looked at her Aunt and tilted her head, "So, do we agree?"

Aunt Celestine receded, but I can tell that it was with hesitation, "Agreed."

She looked at Mama and then at me, "There is much to teach you. Are you sure you're ready to know these things?"

I remembered when my grandmother asked me almost that exact same question and at the end of our conversation, I found that I wasn't truly ready to hear some of the things that I heard, but this time is different. I am ready to know all there is to know about my family, about me.

"Yes, I am ready," I said with enthusiasm, maybe a little too much enthusiasm.

She looked at me with those weird eyes of hers, "We will see."

She didn't appear to have a single ounce of confidence in my ability to learn. Well, I will definitely prove her wrong. Not only will I learn and retain the knowledge that will be instilled in me, but I will master it, all of it.

"Now you go on and get something to eat. I want to go ahead and head to the stores to find something nice for your sister," Mama said to me.

I knew she's only rushing me out of the room so she can talk with Aunt Celestine in private.

"Ok," I said, "and thank you so much Mama."

I had finally made her see things my way for once. That was a huge victory for me, because before now, I may as well been talking to a brick wall. I know this was a hard decision for Mama, but I'm so grateful that she put her fears aside and have a little faith in me and in Aunt Celestine ability to teach me.

"You're welcome baby. I hope I don't have to end up regretting this."

She shot a knowing look at Aunt Celestine. I left the room knowing that they were about to discuss the things I am forbidden to learn.

CHAPTER 10

After eating breakfast, I freshened up a little, touching up my hair and putting on some lip gloss. That's the least I could do to myself presentable to the public. I could hear Daddy's voice coming through the walls. By some of the things he was saying, I could tell he didn't want us going to Jackson today, and he did have a valid reason not wanting us to go.

"Is there any place here you can find a decent enough dress?" Daddy asked.

He was really concerned about us going downtown. There is supposed to be a protest taking place there today to boycott several of the businesses there that still didn't take kindly to colored folks being able to come inside their establishment. If we were coming in there to buy something for the whites we worked for was more acceptable than coming inside to buy something for ourselves and our money was just as green as everybody else's. There were a couple of store owners that didn't mind us coming inside, but only a couple.

Just the other day, a black woman was accused of trying to stealing from one of the stores, which she denied. The way it was told, she even had more than enough money to pay for the items she was accused of trying to take. The store owner's wouldn't let her leave the store after they had called the police on her. Once they arrived they treated the woman badly causing her to spit at one of the officers. They say the two officers beat her real good, right there on the sidewalk. This made a lot of folks angry.

"I understand your concern, but the stores there are better. If it will make you feel better just come with us," Mama was saying coming out of the room.

"Angelique," she called once she was in the hallway.

I made my way out of the bathroom.

"You ready?" She asked as she rambled around in her purse.

I heard Daddy jiggling the keys behind me.

"You look'n for these?" He asked. "You are the most stubborn woman I have ever met in my life."

Mama extended her hand, waiting for the keys to be dropped into the.

"Come on," he said heading for the door. "I'm going with y'all."

Mama just smiled as we headed for the door, knowing that Daddy was weak for her and always won him over. On our way to Jackson, I realized that the last time I was downtown I saw David there with his parents. I wouldn't dare admit this to anyone else, but I think about him often. His face still materializes in my dreams sometimes, that handsome face with those haunting eyes.

I still regret not listening to what he had to say to me that day on my way home from the center. I'm still bothered by the fact that something had him so disturbed that he took his own life that very same day, and like Belinda, he took many unanswered questions to the grave with him.

My thoughts were interrupted as we finally made our approach into the Downtown area of Jackson. There was absolute pandemonium in the streets.

"See what I mean?" Daddy said to Mama.

There had to be at least 200 colored people in the streets. Majority of them had their picket signs raised high as they sang:

We shall not, we shall not be moved
We shall not, we shall not be moved
We're fighting for our freedom,
We shall not be moved

We shall not, we shall not be moved

We shall not, we shall not be moved
We're fighting for our children,
We shall not be moved

Every police in the city seem to be here. They were all armed with shields and batons. The men obviously thought they could disburse this crowd, I hope they realize that when there's a bunch of black folks banned together and are fighting for a good cause it will take more than baton clutching policemen to disband them. There were two fire trucks making their way up the street as well.

"Thangs bout to get real ugly round here," Daddy declared. "We gonna have to come back another day. I don't want Angelique around this. At times like these the police don't care who gets hurt."

Daddy tried to turn around, but just that fast he was blocked by other cars filled with angry protesters who were now making their way to join the rest of crowd.

"Damn it," he said hitting the stirring wheel hard.

"It's alright," Mama was saying, taking off her hat staring out at the massive crowd.

"Don't you remember how many of these we have taken part in?" She said motioning at the crowd. "We fought so hard to have the little bit of rights we do have and they wanna take that away from us too. We use to live for the fight."

"Things are different now. I support what they doing but we have a family to protect from the backlash of all this," Daddy explained.

"And it's the same family we had back then," Mama pointed out. "The same struggles that existed then exist now, and our family is already suffering the backlash, can't you see that. Our kids suffer it every day, in these stores, on the damn sidewalk, and especially in that precious little white school that we fought so hard to get the girls in. They suffer there the most because they're too light to be fully black and too dark to be fully white. As long as we show our colored faces in this white society there will always be backlash."

She turned around and looked at me, then back at Daddy.

"Our lives begin to end the day we become silent about the things that matter," she said in Daddy's direction. "I'm sure you remember who spoke those words."

Mama reached across my lap and opened the door, "Get out the truck, Angelique."

I snapped around quickly and stared at her. She wanted me to stand in the streets while this war was brewing? I climbed out of the truck slowly. The panic was apparent on my face.

"Don't be afraid," she said.

She lifted my chin, "You are almost an adult and you're a very intelligent girl. So I know that you know the struggle for us is real around here. The world we live in baby is ugly as ugly can get. And if things like this here ain't done, the struggle will be just as hard for your children, and your children's children. Today you will see how some fights are fought. They think we so dumb and stupid, but they fail to see that we realize there is strength in numbers, so we ain't as dumb as they think."

She grabbed my hand in hers as we headed for the crowd. I was basically being dragged down the street. It was as if everything was moving in slow motion. My heart is pounding so fast. I took a quick glance behind me, in search of my father. He's directly behind me. Noticing how frightened I am, he grabbed my free hand and held onto it tightly. There is so much noise, the singing. I could hear people yelling obscenities at some of the officers. One man even had a bull horn, so his voice could carry above the crowd.

"Y'all trying to scare us into submission, but no sir, that slave mentality doesn't exist around here. You got the wrong generation for that. That old age of subjugation has faded away," he said as the crowd roared in agreement.

"Things have transformed in that regard. Where respect is due, respect is given, and it's a sad day when we see the little children out here replicating their father's, their mother's actions in this generational journey of hatred. SHAME ON YOU MOTHERS! SHAME ON YOU FATHERS," he shouted, "For raising little monsters who will grow into gigantic beast."

Then someone yelled, "But that's okay too, because the bigger they are, the harder they will fall."

I looked out into the crowd and saw children of all ages. My parents never let us take part in any of the protest before, but now, here I am. We finally came to a stopping point near one of the hardware stores. The signed on the door read closed, but I could plainly see three white men inside. I am certain that several of the businesses closed due do the protest. I stuck close to Daddy. Mama had let go of my hand and made her way into the crown. I could hear her voice blending in with the other's as they began singing:

It's been a loo-oo-ng,
a long time coming
but I kn-oo-w,

a change gone come.
Oh, yes it is.

    I could tell just by looking at some of the faces here that this was a serious matter to them, as if the injustice had been done to them personally. Mama is right. The struggle was and still is real for us. When someone is harmed and mistreated because of the color of their skin, it was taken to heart by the entire black community. The evidence of that was shown by the crowds in the street.

    Tears were flowing down my face as I realized that one person's battle is not theirs to fight alone. It's personal for me, personal for everyone who's was raising their voices in unison. Not only is there strength in numbers, but true power resides there as well. We must all fight and continue to fight until we are treated as equals; respected as human beings and we don't have to accept nothing less than that.

    Pulling my hand away from Daddy's, I walked into the crowd with him close behind me. I joined Mama, grabbing her hand I lifted my voice as high as everyone else's. I could hear the officers telling everyone to go home. People in the crowd were yelling at them to go home and saying a few more things I dare not repeat. Suddenly there was a loud crash. Some of the store windows were being broken out by some of the demonstrators.

Suddenly the crowd started shifting. People were running towards us, so the only thing we can do is turn around to keep from trampled. Daddy grabbed my arm, as I held on tightly to Mama's had. He fought through the crowd to get us out of the street and onto the sidewalk. He found a place for us to stand as mayhem continued to manifest in the streets.

Men, women and children were being hosed down in the streets like they were nothing. Fights seem to be breaking out everywhere between the officers and the protesters. A girl, no older than me was fighting as well, and she was holding her own until the officer hit her with his baton across her head. I screamed as she fell limp to the ground. The officer just stepped right over her and went on to the next person in the crowd. Daddy grabbed me and put my face in his chest.

"Don't look," he said into my hair.

I placed my hands over my ears to shut out the screaming and the sirens.

"Daddy, I wanna go home," I said through my tears. "Please, Daddy just take me home."

I was so afraid. This is something I only heard about, but to witness it first hand was devastating. Mama wrapped her arms around my waist as Daddy held us both close to him.

"I'm trying baby, as soon as I see it's safe for us to move, I will take you home."

The moment I raised my head from Daddy's chest, I regretted doing so. There are so many people lying in the streets. I don't know whether it's from received from the batons or the force of the water hoses. There were several being arrested and loaded into the back of the police vehicles. I saw the girl again, the one who was hit earlier by the officer. She is sitting up against the wall on the other side of the street. Two women are with her, one fanning her, and the other was talking to her, I guess trying to make sure she is ok. She seems to be a little disoriented, but still responsive.

As soon as it was safe enough, Daddy ushered us across the street. I could still hear the crowd screaming above the sirens after we climbed into the truck. It took us a long time to get out of the madness, but we finally did. No one said much on the ride home. We all are in deep thought about what had just happened. Mama kept kissing me and asking was I ok as if she didn't remember me saying I was for the hundredth time.

I'm still in disbelief at how men could just injure one another without just cause. To inflict the type of pain I saw delivered today, you have to be a heartless individual. I am more determined than ever to be a part of cause. I want to stand up and fight for equal rights just like everyone else was doing today. My thoughts went back to that injured girl again. She will forever be etched in my mind as a reminder to me that the price that we have to pay for demanding equality is one that you not only have to be willing pay, but most importantly, strong enough to pay it.

CHAPTER 11

Sleep did not come easy. I'm not sure if it's because I was still afraid of the spirit that was lurking about, what happened downtown, or the fact that I would be returning to school in the morning. It definitely could be a mixture of all three. It's gonna be strange walking those hallways without my sister or Belinda. They were the only ones I really talked to at school. The other's only talked to me because of Dominique. She was the one who had all the friends.

Once we returned from Jackson, Mama had gone and spent the rest of the day with Mrs. Kirkland. She said that she wasn't doing good at all. Belinda was her only child, so I can only imagine how she must be feeling. I only knew how she must be feeling surrounded by all of Belinda's things, that was something I can relate to. Being surrounded by my sister's things was still a constant reminder of what we've lost. Mama also said that Mrs. Kirkland was thinking about moving, because she couldn't stand walking by her bathroom knowing that's where her daughter took her own life. I didn't blame her.

I got out of bed and headed to the kitchen for a glass of warm milk. I really needed to get some kind of rest before morning. I remember my grandmother said it worked wonders when you couldn't sleep. I could see that the light is on so I knew I wouldn't be the only one up at this late hour.

"I see I'm not the only one who can't sleep," Aunt Celestine said as I entered the kitchen.

There was a steaming cup of coffee in front of her.

"That coffee is gonna keep you up all night," I said grabbing a cup from the cabinet.

"Humph. It's thangs much stronger than coffee that keeps me awake at night," she proclaimed, taking a sip of her hot brew.

I poured some milk in a small pot and placed it on the stove. I walked around the table and took the seat beside her.

"And what's that? What keeps you awake at night?" I asked.

I don't think she ever sleeps. She is always up at night, but I noticed she did nap a little during the day, but only a little. She looked at me for a moment before answering.

"I have been doing what I do for as long as I can remember. I have done a lot of good but I have done just as much bad. I can control my thoughts when I am awake, but when I am sleep, my mind is no longer mine to control. Some of those bad things find their way into my head, and into my dreams. So I find myself having to do battle in my dreams more than when I'm awake."

She took a sip from her cup. I wasn't expecting her to be so candid, but I can tell that something is heavy on her mind.

"Do you get any sleep at all?"

She looked at me and nodded.

"Sometimes," she smiled at me slightly.

"So why do you do the bad things if they bother you so?" I asked curiously, wondering why anyone would want to continue to do something that caused them distress.

"But I didn't say the bad things bothered me. I am the one who bothers the bad things," she smirked as she took another sip of her coffee.

She pulled a pack of cigarettes from the pocket of her robe. She lit one and turned her chair around to face me.

"I want you to understand something that no one else seems to get," she said. "This way of life was chosen for me from early on. It's who I am; it's all I know. But I had to find out on my own that there is a cost for doing some things. Oh, and how I've learned that a million times over."

She took a long pull on her cigarette.

"I remember Grandma saying something about choosing to take certain gifts to a darker level taints the soul. Is that what you mean when you say there is a cost?" I asked as I quickly went to the stove and removed the pot of milk.

I filled my cup quickly and returned to the table.

"Yes, that's exactly what I mean," she said.

She took the head wrap from her head and let down her braids.

"You see here, on these pieces of cloth I have braided in my hair. Attached on each piece is hair," she said pointing at one of her braids.

So, that's what that is.

"This is the hair of my children, Magdalene and Henri, and of their children, Lisette, Ines and Simon, and the hair of my husband, Victor, as well. It's for their protection. I try my best to keep them protected from certain things even when I'm not around."

"Do you believe in God?" I heard myself ask.

I remember Mama saying she did, but I wanted to hear it from Aunt Celestine. I noticed when we got back from Jackson earlier today. She was sitting on the ground out in the backyard with her eyes closed and arms outstretched on either sides with her palms raised. Grandma said she was in prayer, but it didn't look like any praying I'd ever seen. She was out there for a long time.

"Yes I do," she looked at me quizzically. "I pray to God every day and I go to Him as humbly as I can. I just worship him in a different way than most do. God is all around us. A part of him is in every breathing thing. I don't have to be behind the four walls of the church to worship him. Do you think that makes me any less spiritual than you?"

I didn't want her to misunderstand what I was trying to imply, "No. I don't think that it does. I think in a way you have to be even more spiritual than me, in some ways at least. I don't know a lot about what you practice, but I know enough to know that to do what you do, you have to believe in something, something spiritual, something not of the natural. But I guess what I'm trying to say is, how can you believe in God, but do some of the things you do?"

She said, "You just don't know how many times I've been asked that question and my answer is always this. Even the demons believe in God. The question that you should ask me is, Do I trust in him and his word, do I worship him, do I love Him and the answer to all of those are yes, with all my heart. Do I believe in the devil just as much, yes I do. He is a deceiver, a master of manipulation and what you saw today when you were out with your parents is some of his handy work. There was nothing Godlike about what happened there. It was all Satan. He is mighty, but God is Almighty. I believe that fully, but I am who I am. I am full of light and dark energy and they both know it. You know how I know this?"

She asked, leaning close to me as if she were about to tell me something so forbidden. I was so drawn into this conversation that I was afraid if I said one word she would stop talking.

"How do you know?" I whispered looking straight at her.

I wanted her to know she had my full attention and I wanted her to continue.

"Look at my eyes. They weren't always like this you know," she said leaning back. "I'm the only one who inherited my mother eyes, the prettiest shade of brown."

"How did they become this way?" I asked looking into her mismatched eyes.

I had asked my grandmother this very same question, but in her typical fashion, she just danced around it without answering it.

She pointed to her light brown eye, "For a long time in my life, I chose only to dance in the light because that's truly where my heart dwelled. I wanted to do only good things with what I knew. I wanted to make people happy and I did that for a very long time. When your mother was only a little younger than you are now, she reminded me so much of myself -- of that young girl I had once been, so happy and full of the light's energy."

Then she pointed to the eye black as night and frowned, "Then your grandfather began to make me play in the dark more and more and I found myself liking it, loving it really. In the darkness is a power so seductive that it consumes your every thought, but wherever lies seduction that is that powerful, you better believe that danger dwells there as well."

Aunt Celestine rubbed at her temple as if she could feel a headache coming on, "Jericho tried to pull me back. He knew I was in way too deep, and he tried to teach me how to keep the black at bay, but I wouldn't listen. He was skilled at not allowing himself to get consumed by what he did. He is so much stronger than I am, always has been. I ventured deeper and deeper into the abyss. To watch my enemies suffer, to watch my friends enemies suffer and knowing that I was the cause of that suffering brought me such satisfaction. Like I said, it's so seductive there in the dark, but the consequences are not so seductive. The darker the deed, the darker the eye became. And if you look closely, it's starting to stretch out into the white part. Strange isn't it? How such things work? The eyes are windows to the soul may sound like a cliché, but believe me when I tell you that it is the truth. So you see there is a battle for this old darkened soul of mine and I'm fighting very hard for redemption and He knows that," she stated looking upward, "But so does he," she looked at the floor now.

"I do want to dance in the light once again, while I still have a chance to do so," she said and pointed to her brown eyes one again before she took my hands in hers. "One good thing about all of this is that you never knew your grandfather, and you can choose to always partake of the light and leave the dark to those who have already succumbed to it. There are a lot of things that's going on in the world today that would make anyone want to do some terrible things to one another, but you are a strong girl. So choose to do good things always and you will prevail over all that is bad."

She patted my hands and stood up, "Don't stay up too late child you do have school in the morning."

"When will you begin teaching me some of the things I need to know?" I asked quickly before she headed out of the kitchen.

I couldn't wait to have my mind full of other things besides death and cruelty. She turned around and smiled at me.

"We just got done with Lesson Number One – 'knowing the consequences of what you choose to do with your knowledge.' I hope you're good at making the right decisions," she said as she rubbed her temple again.

"Do you have a headache? I'm sure Mama got something you can take. I can go grab something for you," I offered, standing up, but she quickly motioned for me to sit back down.

"I'm ok. There is no remedy for what ails me," she said.

She walked out of the kitchen, leaving me staring at the place she just stood. We all have our own personal demons to battle, but some of our demons are way bigger than other's and Aunt Celestine had some giants. I always wished my grandfather had lived long enough for us to meet him, but now I'm starting to think that it's a good thing we didn't. If he could inflict this much pain to one of his children by the things he taught, I could only imagine what he would have done to any of his grandchildren.

I finished off my milk and headed back to bed. I thought about something Aunt Celestine had just said about me making the right choices. I know I am far from perfect at making the right decisions, because I've made a lot of wrong ones. I never think before acting; I just act and never think. This is something that Dominique was always on me about. I would never choose to take my gift to a dark place no matter how tempted I may be. At least not on purpose, but it frightened me to know that I could if I wanted to, because there are quite a few people I would love to oblige with a hex or two, Claire Monroe would be the first and the last name on my list.

There is something that I wanted to know, something that no one else seemed to care enough about or either I was just left out of the loop as always. I climbed out of bed once more, and made my way to the front. Aunt Celestine was laying on the sofa. Mama had told her that one of the sofa's let out into a bed, but she said she preferred the sofa. She had her eyes closed, but I knew she wasn't asleep.

"It's not nice to spy on your sleeping guest," Aunt Celestine said turning on the light.

I smiled at her as I took a seat in Daddy's favorite chair, "Well it's a good thang you weren't asleep."

"Why are you still up child?"

There is something that I wanted to know, something that no one else seemed to care enough about or either I was just left out of the loop as always.

"I want to ask you something," I said to her, hoping that she would be open with me.

She waited a moment then replied when I didn't say anything, "Then ask, I can do a lot of things, but I can't read minds."

"Oh, sorry," I said hurriedly. "I'm not sure if you know or not, but there was a something here on yesterday. A ghost or something."

"Yes, I know. I could feel the energy the moment my taxi turned onto your street," she answered.

"Do you know what she wants?" I asked, really hoping she knows what this spirit wanted.

"I have an idea, but I was told not say anything to you about it just yet," she whispered.

This revelation made me so angry. I'm sure the conversation she had with Mama earlier had a lot to do with everything I didn't need to know.

"Why am I not surprised by that?" I said with irritation.

"They only want to protect you child, but the sooner you know about you, the sooner all of this will be over."

"Does she want to hurt us?" *It wouldn't be safe for us to stay here if she wants to harm us.*

"Hurt you?" She said in a surprised matter, "No, I don't think so."

I was confused, "I remember you saying something about once the light is in, the dark can enter also. The little boy is the light, and the woman is the dark."

She nodded her head, "Yes, I did say that, but I'm starting to feel that the dark is not among the dead, but among the living. This spirit, this woman, is not trying to harm any of you, she is trying to help you, but she isn't getting through to any of you besides the young one. His innocence allows him to see and hear things that some of us cannot, but he doesn't understand what's happening. But things have changed since your mother saw her, and you felt her and she knows it."

I could feel my hands trembling, I don't know why, but I am afraid. "Help us? Help us how, for what?"

"She will come again, because it is crucial that she does, so be prepared to face her, but you can't be afraid. Open your ears and your mind. Listen to her and she will answer your questions. I'm willing to bet my life that she has a story to tell that will make you question everything you think you know. Now, go to bed child. That's enough for tonight."

CHAPTER 12

I don't know why it was taking me so long to choose something to wear. It wasn't like I had tons to choose from. I bought several skirts, shorts and blouses with the money that we saved up. Half of that money I put up for Dominique, because I knew she would be coming home, or so I thought. Now here I am, returning to school alone.

Choosing a dark blue skirt with a matching top, I quickly dressed and went into the kitchen for a bite to eat, not that I had much of an appetite. Xavier was sitting at the table finishing off the last of his breakfast.

"Good morning," I said patting the top of his head.

"Morning," he replied with a mouthful of food. He didn't even bother looking up at me. He was sitting there stuffing his mouth with food not even bothering to swallow. Then I noticed it was already after seven; that would explain that.

"Aren't you gonna be late for school?" I asked as I grabbed a piece of toast.

He shook his head.

"Nope, leaving now," he said getting up from the table.

"Come here," I called out to him as he was heading for the front door. "You have food all over your face."

I grabbed a towel and cleaned him up.

"And don't you think you will need these?" I asked, handing him the books that he forgot on the table.

"Oh," he said grabbing them from me. "Bye."

"Bye," I said and watched him almost knock Daddy over as he headed out the door.

Our neighbor, Mr. Morrison, was kind enough to take Xavier to school in the mornings since he had to take own boys who attended the same school. It saved Daddy an extra trip in the mornings. I could have ridden the bus this morning, but Daddy insisted on taking me. I must admit that I am a little relieved. That gave me a little more time to get myself together before having to be faced with all the stares I'm sure I would be getting.

I notice that the back door is slightly opened and I see Mama and Aunt Celestine sitting with their heads together. I could tell that they have a deep conversation going on by the furrow in Mama's brow. Aunt Celestine had that effect on you. She had a way of holding your attention when she spoke, making you want to hear more. It was almost hypnotic. I am willing to bet they are talking about me. When will everyone stop acting so secretive and keep me in the loop of thing? They are starting to drive me crazy.

Some of the things Aunt Celestine said to me last night were still fresh on my mind this morning. I really didn't need to be thinking about any of that right now if I want to make it through the day. My heart is still racing at the thought of me returning to school today, but I know I need to go ahead and get it over with. I couldn't dodge that place forever, no matter how bad I want to.

"Are you ready to go?" Daddy asked grabbing his lunch from off the table.

"Not really, but I may as well be," I stated, heading to the back to grab my satchel and take a final glance in the mirror behind my bedroom door.

I ran my hand across my hair, which I chose to wear down instead of wearing my usual braid. The red tint was becoming more and more apparent in the spiral array. I ran my fingertips underneath my hides, hoping that this would rub out the puffiness there. I wish I could have gotten more sleep last night. Every sound I heard caused me to wake up. I was scared to even open my eyes for fear of what may have been standing in front of me. The door open slowly, Mama peeped around the door to find me standing behind it.

"One last look," she said noticing that I was giving myself another look over on last time. I give her a simple nod. "You look beautiful."

She stepped inside of the room. "If you find it a little too hard to be back at school, you be sure to let me know. Like me and your Dad said before, you can take all the time you need."

"I think I will be ok." *I hope I will be ok.* "Daddy is waiting on me," I said.

I quickly grabbed my satchel from the bed and giving Mama a quick kiss on the cheek. I headed for the door hoping that this day would be over just as quick as it had started. As we pulled off, I notice Phillip coming from the back of his house with a wheel barrel. He was always doing something out in the yard. I hate that he wouldn't be returning to school. He didn't think there was a need to even though he had low marks from last year. He said that he could learn more on his own that what he learned in some classroom.

Once we arrived at the school, Daddy got out of the truck too and walked with me. This was something he never did before, but on the other hand, there was never a reason for him to do so. I always had Dominique and Belinda by my side. I never had to enter this building alone, not until now. I'm truly grateful that he is with me now. It was too bad that he could stay with me all day. Once we walked inside, several of the other kid's eyes went straight to me. *And so it begins.*

We walked into the office to get my schedule. Mrs. Dillon, the office secretary, told me that all students were to report to the auditorium before going to class, because the principal, Mr. Hollander, is just reporting back to work today due to illness and he wanted to address all the students.

Once we got back into the hallway, Daddy turned to me, "Do you want me to walk you there?"

I shook my head, "No, I'll be ok."

He put his arm around my shoulders, "What if I wanted to?"

I looked up at him and beamed, "Then I'll let you."

"All students report to the auditorium," a male voice was instructing the many teenagers piled in the hallway.

I looked around trying to find the owner of the voice. It was coming from someone I didn't recognize, but the strangest sensation surged through me when I heard him, as if his voice was drawing me in; almost like it was entrancing. This had to be a new addition to the staff. He looked a little too young to be a teacher. I finally got close enough to get a better look at him.

A word hasn't been invented yet to describe his looks, because handsome wouldn't do him any justice. The perfectly tan skin was a nice touch to his athletic frame. His eyes were the same color as his hair, dark brown. He was definitely something to look at. I noticed how some of the other girls were starting at him. I'm pretty sure they're thinking the same thing I am; *I hope I'm in his class, whatever it may be.*

"Let's keep it moving young people! You all can discuss what happened over the weekend later. Keep it moving, no lingering," he instructed.

Daddy walked me to the door of the auditorium. He pulled me close to him and hugged me. I didn't want him to leave me. Maybe it was a bad idea for me to come back. I quickly put that thought out of my head. *I know I can do this.*

"Try to have a good day today. I really think that being back here will do you good." Daddy said staring at me so intently that I was beginning to wonder if my face reflected the panic that I feel on the inside. I smiled at him and watched as he turned to walk away from me, keeping my eyes on him until I could no longer see him. I walked into the auditorium, taking the first seat that I came to in the back of the room. I didn't want to bring any more attention to myself than I had to.

The auditorium began to fill up quickly as more and more students piled in. I reached in my bag to get a pencil and a sheet of paper. I knew they were about to tell us all the rules and such like always.

"Hey, Angelique," a soft voice said.

I turned to see Cynthia Gaines taking a seat beside me. She was one of Dominique's closest friends. Whenever Dominique wasn't with me at school, she was with Cynthia. I had talked to her a few times over the summer, but all she wanted to do was talk about Dominique and that was something that was really hard for me to do and still is. Cynthia's parents also fought along with the many others for the acceptance of their colored children into this once all white establishment.

"How are you?" She asked as she dropped her satchel on the empty chair beside her. Her page boy haircut was sleek and shiny as always. "Glad to see you made it back."

"Thank you. I've been better," I replied, trying my best to give her a warm smile.

"It's so good to see you," her smile was one of warm welcoming. "For a moment, with your hair down like that, I thought you were Dominique."

I turned and looked at her. Then I realized that I had never worn my hair down at school before. She saw that I was taken aback by her comment.

"I'm sorry," she said quickly. "I guess I needed to keep that to myself."

"No, it's ok."

This was all I could manage to say before the Principal took the stage to give the usual speech. Looking straight ahead, I gave him my full attention, or at least I acted as though he had my full attention. I noticed that there were a few more colored kids this year. I smiled at this, maybe a change will come sooner than any of us expected.

Mr. Hollander gave the same boring speech: no fighting, being courteous to your teacher's and fellow students; rule breakers will be handled accordingly and so on and so on. I'm sure he already knew we know the do's and the don'ts, but there was always a few that thought the rules didn't apply to them; those like David. He was one that used to get away with any and everything just because of his father.

It's going to be different not seeing him with his friends harassing everyone they came in contact with in the halls. Dominique and I always stood our ground when they tried to mess with us, even Belinda stood firm and actually bullied a few of the bullies herself, but of course we would be punished for standing up for ourselves, while the others didn't even get a slap on the wrist. That was much of a surprise to any of us.

I looked down at the sheet of paper on my lap as if it held the secrets to mending a broken heart. I am attempting to clear my mind of the days of old while trying to fight back tears. This is my last year of high school and here I am about to complete it without my sister. I have never felt so alone in my entire life. The tears that I was trying to hold back finally broke free.

I reach inside my bag in search of a tissue. Cynthia handed me a tissue from her pocketbook before I could find my own. I wiped at my eyes quickly and when I was done she took my hand in hers.

"Angelique, you will be ok. It's just gonna take a little while, but you will be ok. I can only imagine how hard this gotta be, but I'm here for you and I know Dominique would want me to be. You are not alone in this."

I smiled on the inside because I knew that this was God's doing. He wanted me to know that know that all is still well and that no matter how I felt or what I was going through at any moment on any day, I would never be alone. *Thank you God.* I turned to Cynthia.

"Thank you," I said quietly.

She gave my hand a gentle squeeze and we turned our attention back to our principal. Cynthia never let go of my hand. She held on to it firmly and that alone steadied my troubled spirit.

CHAPTER 13

In a lovely twist of fate, Cynthia was in several of my classes and I must admit that I was thankful. That would make things a little easier. Throughout the day, several students as well as some of the teachers offered their condolences for my loss. I know they all mean well, but every time someone came up to me with their little scripted line, I just want to scream.

As I make my way out of my first period English class, I see David's best friend (Matthew Reed) in the hall. There is something a little different about his demeanor. The other boys around him were their usual loud and arrogant selves, but not Matt. He walked past me and that's when I saw it -- that look in his eyes that mirrored my own. It was a longing for something that we would never have again in this life. For him that was David. I know he missed his friend and there isn't anything he can do to bring him back. I can relate to that, because that something that I longed for was Dominique and yes, Belinda too. So yes, I understood his pain all too well, and I think my pain is a lot worse than his, but then again, pain is pain.

I somehow managed to get through the day without any major hitches. I'm glad I decided to come on back. With all the work that's being handed out, I have more than enough to concentrate on. Cynthia was waiting for me near the entrance of the cafeteria once I finally made my way there.

"Hey," she said when I approached. "I thought maybe you'd like to eat lunch together."

"Yeah, I'd like that," I replied with honesty.

I really was glad that she decided to wait for me. That eliminated me having to awkwardly look around for a place to sit. The moment we sat down is the moment I almost immediately regretted sitting with her. I never realized before now that Cynthia talked way too much for me. I mean from the time we sat down she starts rambling on and on about her vacation and all the new things she bought. I wanted to say who cares, but that wouldn't have been nice of me. She is the only one who seemed to want to hang out with me. I could be a little more appreciative.

After lunch, the rest of the day just seems to fly by. I get to my last class of the day, which just happened to be my favorite subject, Math. *Dominique hated math.* I suddenly think. I smiled as I remembered the way she would always frown the entire time during a math assignment. For her to hate the subject so much, she always managed to get all A's though and even tutored. I use to tell her that she must of didn't hate it that bad if she got A's all the time.

She would say, "Just because I don't like it, don't mean I want to fail it. You can be good at something and not enjoy it one bit."

I made my way to the back of the class without looking around to see if I knew anyone I could possibly want to sit by. I'm sure there was no one. Once I got to my seat, I glanced around the room only to notice that I am the only black in the room. And by the look on some of their faces, they were just as shocked as me. I guess that's the reason why they were staring at me the way that they are, or could it be because I have the look of a girl who has ghost running around her house.

Can a person have that look? The look of someone that's being haunted? I seriously doubt it. I glance around the room. I recognized just about everyone in this class. Some of them are pretty nice and some aren't so nice. I immediately go into defense mode, waiting for that one bold one to make his stupidity known, because there was always one.

"Hello everyone, welcome back," a familiar soft voice said as she made her way to the large desk at the front of the class.

What a delight it is to have my favorite teacher enter the room, dressed in a long brown dress with her auburn hair pulled back in her signature bun that's always so neat. Ms. Clincy was the best teacher in this entire school and probably one of the most hated by some of her peers because of the genuine kindness and concern she showed to her black students. She really did care about us and our education.

"I hope everyone had a pleasant weekend and is now ready to get back to learning about the wonderful subject of mathematics," she said cheerfully.

There were a lot of groan coming from around the room.

"Hush now," she commanded. "I know no one in this room ever wants to get cheated out of anything in life, so I think a big part of making sure that don't happen is to know something about numbers. Now, raise your hand when your name is called so I can see who all is here today."

She took out a thin booklet and began calling out the names listed. When she got to my name, she looked in my direction and gave me a warm smile.

"It's a pleasure to have you in my class once again, Angelique."

"Thank you," I replied softly. *Why did she put me on the spot like that? She didn't say that to anyone else.*

I hear Sally Carlton say in a loud whisper, "Well we know who the teacher's pet will be."

She looks back at me. I act as though I don't hear or see her. Like I said, there's always one. Ms. Clincy continued calling out the names until she was done.

"Now," she began, "I know we didn't do a lot last week. I wanted everyone to get all settled in and get use to your classes and all, but this is a new week and it's time for us to dive into some real work. I am proud to admit that I have some of the smartest kids in this school right here in this class and I know this because I handpicked each and every one of you based on your scores from last year. As I look around this room, I know that each of you can handle a little more advance teachings and I know everyone is definitely up for the challenge."

She went on to tell us what she expected from us, as well as some of the assignments we would be completing during the year. And if anyone had any problems with what she wanted done, please see her after class. She came across as being mean, but I know that she's one of the nicest people ever. But I also know that she's not too fond of some of these snobby kids and she doesn't care who knows it.

I look up from my notebook to see Matt looking back at me and his girlfriend from last year, Marla Grove, looking over at him then back at me. I looked away and smiled to myself. Not even one day? I couldn't make it just one day without being tangled up in some foolishness?

Ms. Clincy didn't give us much work to do. She just had us work on a worksheet filled with multiplication and division problems. I hope this isn't what she considers advanced work. This is something that we did in the 5th Grade. Oh well, I guess I shouldn't complain since I'm sure I will be getting an easy A. At the end of class, Ms. Clincy asked me to stay behind for a moment.

"I just wanted to check up on you Angelique," she said kindly. "I know you have a lot going on in your young life and I just won't you to know that you can always come to me if you need to talk or anything, even if it's just to blow off a little steam. Call on me anytime, day or night, you hear?"

"Yes ma'am," I replied appreciatively. "That's very kind of you."

She smiled at me and placed her hand on my shoulder, "I know it may not seem like it now, but trust me when I say that things will get better, it will."

"I can't wait for that day to come." I said.

"Do try to enjoy the rest of this beautiful day," she smiled at me once more.

"I will definitely try," I said, giving her a smile of my own.

Once I stepped outside the door and rounded the corner, I almost ran into Matt.

"Excuse me," I said with an acidic tone, which he didn't have any problems detecting.

"No, excuse me," he replied as I stepped around him.

I give him a look that let him know that I didn't fall for this fake demeanor of courtesy for one second.

"Hey, can I talk to you for a second?" He asked quickly, seeing that I was trying to get away from him.

"About?" I ask, not hiding my suspicion.

"Look," he began, "I just won't to say that I am very sorry for your loss."

I study his face a moment, searching for something to let me know that he isn't being sincere. *I have never been this close to him before.* He actually could be a very attractive man one day if he ever decided to grow up. I can see the freckles sprinkled across the bridge of his nose. His eyes were the palest of blue. His hair was the same shade of blond as those little white baby dolls. It has a look of fakeness to it. I actually resisted the urge to touch it.

"Thanks," I finally said, "I guess I should say the same to you since you and David were the best of friends."

"Yeah, we were," he said looking down at the floor. "I hope that this year will be different from all the rest. I guess what I mean to say is that I hope we can find a way to somehow manage to be friendly."

He walked away before I could utter a reply. One of his friends caught up to him and says something, but not before glancing back at me. I'm sure I know what that conversation will be about. As I make my way to the exit door, I see that good looking teacher again. Cynthia gave me all the information on him at lunch today. Mr. Fuller is his name. He teaches History to the lower grades. His family just moved here from somewhere up North, Maine I think she said.

"Study those chapters now," he said to a group of students walking past. "You never know when I'm going to be quizzing you."

He made his way down the hall. There is something very intriguing about him and it's not just his good looks. It's something else.

"How was your day?" Cynthia asked, catching me off guard. I hope she didn't notice me ogling at Mr. Fuller.

"Ok, it was actually not that bad. I just got to get caught up on everything," I answered.

"Which is no problem at all for you since you are probably the smartest person here after all," she bumped me teasingly. "I was gonna see if you wanted a ride home instead of riding in that hot bus, but I see your Daddy is already here."

I turn around to see Daddy standing outside of his truck. He waved at me when he saw me looking in his direction, I wave back. It was not time for him to get off work, but I'm glad he is here.

"See ya later," Cynthia said, giving me a hug.

"See ya," I said, hugging her back.

She did after all make this day more tolerable.

"Hey Daddy," I greeted as I make my approach. "I wasn't expecting you to pick me."

"I know, I left a little early so me and ya mama could handle some business." He explains as we both climb into the truck.

"So was today ok for you?" He asked.

"It was. Nothing to complain about really. Just have to get use to certain things I guess," I said.

"Like I told you earlier, it will take some time and being back at school will be good for you."

I nodded in agreement. Being back in school would give me something else to focus on besides sitting at home letting my thoughts consume me. But if I be honest with myself, I know that it really doesn't matter what I do at any given moment of the day, I will never forget everything that's going on right now, my heart won't allow me to.

CHAPTER 14

As soon as I walk through the door, Xavier starts to tell me about his day at school. He tells me all about his new friends, following me into my room. This is the longest conversation that he has ever had with me. I remember how he would do this to Dominique and she would actually sit there and just listen to him, showing no signs of aggravation. I'm trying to follow her example. I'm tired, but I try not to let him see this. So, I listen to him and I even ask a question whenever he takes a breath.

He seems to enjoy when I ask him a question. It gives him just that much more to talk about. After he leaves out, Mama comes in and asks for a recap of my day. Even though her voice sounded exciting, cheerful even, her face told a different story.

"You ok, Mama?" I ask, not bothering to tell her how my day was.

There is plenty of time for that. She nods.

"It's just been a very long day."

Her eyes began to glaze over with tears. We both take a seat on the bed. Now that I am this close to her, I can see that she's already been crying. Her eyes were puffy and her face red, as if she spent the entire day in tears.

I take both her hands in mine, "What's wrong Mama?"

I asked, but I already knew what was wrong. I know the answer before she could even part her lips to tell me. She said nothing at first, but then fresh tears start to run down her cheeks.

"We went over to the church today to talk to the Reverend about the funeral arrangements for Dominique." She put her face into her hands and starts to moan. "Lord, why am I burying my child? I shouldn't have to bury my children. This is not how it should be."

I wrap my arms around her. This is all I can do for her at the moment. There are no words in existence that will dry her tears, and I know this first hand. She wiped at the tears sliding down her face.

"I went to check on Martha today and I could barely keep it together. She was trying her best to console me while I'm trying to console her. It was a big mess. We've been friends for years on top of years. We've been through a lot together. We've witnessed so much turmoil and injustice. So in a strange way I guess it's only fitting that we're suffering the loss of a child together, too. Life is such a strange, horrible thing sometimes. I'm really starting to believe that Satan has a big part to play in certain ironic happenings."

She gave me a kiss on the forehead before standing.

"I know you need to wind down a little bit."

I got the feeling that she just wanted to get out of the room so that she could be alone, which I didn't think she needed to do.

"No, you can stay if you want to," I tell her as I grab her hand and give it a gentle squeeze.

She touched my hand, "I know, but I have a few things to take care of, but we can talk later on."

She brings her hand up to her mouth for a quick kiss and she leaves the room, leaving me to stare at the closed door long after she had left. I stay sitting on the bed a while longer, not feeling a need to be in a rush to do anything besides what I'm doing at the moment, which is nothing. It's so quiet in this room now and I wish I could change that.

There was once a time that I wanted it to be this hushed. There was even a time when I didn't want to hear Dominique's stories about what happened in school or after school; or hear the gossip about what someone said about someone else or all the plans she made for us without getting my consent to do anything she decided we should do. I hated when Xavier would come in and Dominique would horse play around with him for what seemed like days. This room was never quiet, this house was never quiet. I wanted silence for so long and now I have it, satirical isn't it. Now it dwells within these walls, making this house its own, not minding the occupants who lived here that never made it go away. There is a tap on the door.

"Come in."

Daddy stepped inside.

"There is something I forgot to let you know. I think the Monroe's will be back in town real soon. I heard some talk at work."

I stood up quickly, "Do you have idea when? Are we going to see them?"

"I don't know when and we aren't going to see them. As much as I want to, we can't do that without getting in no trouble. The detectives said they will be talking to them," he told me.

"And when will that be? They shouldn't have been allowed to go anywhere after what happened with Belinda. They probably just needed time to rehearse the lie that I'm sure they're going to tell. If that would have been one of us, we would have been dragged into jail the same day, or worse," I said to him. "The Monroe's act as if they run

177

Mississippi and can just go around doing what they want without having to worry about consequences. I guess if everyone treated them as such, why wouldn't they act like they world belonged to them?"

"I know you're angry, we all are, but let's just focus on what matter's right now. When they get back, we can get to the bottom of what's going on. And if Claire had anything to do with what happened, she will have to answer for it. If any of them had anything to do with this, they will pay," he says and gives me a quick kiss on my forehead and heads for the door. "Don't worry. We will not lay down on this, so just try to keep it together for your Mama while we figure all of this out."

I nod at him, angry that he did not join me in my rant. After he leaves, I walked over to the window and see Aunt Celestine sitting on the ground in the back yard, in the position that I've seen her in before. Her eyes were closed and her arms were stretched out on either side of her, palms raised towards the sky as if she were waiting for something to fall into them. Her lips were moving rapidly. I knew that she was praying. Suddenly, she stopped moving her lips and brings her arms down quickly. She frowns. She jumps up quickly from her spot on the ground and heads towards the front of the house.

Out of curiosity, I rushed out of my room and head outside. Just as I make it out the front door, I see her standing beside the porch; just standing there staring at something across the street; her eyes constricted. I look in the same direction that has her attention. The only thing that I can see that could have her attention is Belinda's mother, who was standing there gazing out of her screened door. I turned back to look at Aunt Celestine to see if this was indeed the object of her concentration, and indeed it is. Mrs. Kirkland retreats inside, closing the door.

"You ok?" I say, but she doesn't answer me.

She just keeps right on staring. Making my way down the stops, I call out to her again.

"Aunt Celestine?" I said a little louder.

I stood in front of her. This seemed to bring her out of whatever trance she was locked in.

"You ok?" I asked her.

"Who all lives in that house over there?" She asked me pointing at Belinda's house.

"No one besides Mrs. Kirkland, Martha, my friend Belinda's mother," I answered suspiciously.

She looked at me, "Belinda? She's the young girl who just recently passed on?"

"Yes," I answered, now confused by the questions. "Why?"

179

There has to be a reason why she is asking me all of these questions. She wiggles a finger in the direction of Belinda's house.

"Something ain't right about that woman. I can smell her stench from here."

I turn and look at the closed door of the Kirkland's household. My heart is racing and I don't know why.

"Her stench? What do you mean by that?"

"Yes, her stench. She smells of dead things. Those with hearts as dark as the tar usually do," Aunt Celestine said.

She turns and walks towards the back of our house, leaving me standing there with my mouth wide open. There are a million and one questions running through my mind. I've known Mrs. Kirkland as long as I've known Belinda. Mama has been friends with her just as long. She's always kind to everyone. I don't think there is a mean bone in that woman's body.

What is Aunt Celestine sensing that all of us who have known her the longest are not? I turn around to see Mrs. Kirkland staring out of Belinda's window. She waves at me and I wave back. That's when I noticed my hand was shaking again. *She smells of dead things.*

CHAPTER 15

I walk around to the back of the house to find Aunt Celestine has gone back to her praying as if nothing has happened. I head for the back door, as much as I want to interrupt her to ask questions, I decide against it at the moment, but I'm definitely not letting this slide.

"She's a strange one isn't she?"

It was my grandmother. I hadn't noticed her sitting there on the back porch. She had a blanket about her legs, protecting herself against the cool air that seemed to come out of nowhere. I make my way to the empty rocker beside her.

"Yeah, a little bit," I remark as she puts a portion of the blanket across my legs. It was nice and warm.

"Seeing her makes me miss it," she said softly, as she pulled the blanket up around her arms.

"Miss what?" I ask.

"Miss home," she says with a slight smile. "She reminds me of everything that I left behind."

"So why don't you just go back? Even if it's just to visit," I propose.

She speaks of Louisiana often, but she has never said anything about wanting to go back. It was where she was born and raised. I know it had to be hard for her to leave it all behind. She had tons of friends and family still there. I understand the reason why she left, but all that was so long ago. Surely everyone had moved on with their lives by now. The past was the past.

"I've thought about it, but it's just hard. There are too many memories there. Not all of them bad, but not all good either. But I do miss it, just not sure it misses me," she said as she closes her eyes and begins to sway slowly in her rocker.

I lay back and do the same. Thinking it's Aunt Celestine, I open my eyes when I hear footsteps approaching, only to see Phillip standing making his way towards the porch. Hands stuffed deep in his pockets. Just as he reaches the steps, Aunt Celestine jumps quickly to her foot and looks in our direction. Grandma sees this too and narrows her eyes.

"Hey there Miss Odalia," Phillip says kindly.

"Phillip, how you doing today?" Grandma returns, rising up out of her chair, following me down the steps.

"Doing good, just try to s-s-stay warm," he says, taking notice of how the atmosphere had drastically changed. It wasn't this cool earlier.

"I know what you mean," Grandma declares with a smile and headed toward Aunt Celestine.

Phillip stuffs his hands into the pocked of his worn jeans as he watches my Grandma.

"So, what's up?" I ask him, causing his attention to drift to me, but only for a moment.

He turns once more, placing his focus back on the two women who are now conversing in the yard.

"Your Aunt's kinda s-s-scary," he said frowning.

I give him a playful shove causing him to smile. I place my hands on my hips.

"Scary? I didn't think there was anything that existed that could scare you," I tilt my head to the side and look at him.

He smiled at me, causing me to melt, something I did whenever he smiled.

"There are a few things," he said.

"And they are?" I ask playfully.

"If I tell you, then you might be scared too," his tone had changed slightly and the smile was gone.

He stared at me a moment.

"Let's take a walk."

He suddenly holds out both of his hands, I apprehensively place mine into them and he gives me a little tug causing me to walk forward.

I frown.

"And just where are we taking this walk to?" I ask nervously.

His change in mood was a little concerning. He suddenly smiles from ear to ear.

"Oh, just to your favorite place."

"Oh," I said teasingly, "and I wonder just where that is."

I know he's talking about the creek. He started walking galloping backwards, faster and faster causing me to do the same since he was still holding on to both of my hands. He laughed as he dropped one of them and we both ran off towards the opening that led to Willows Creek. Laughing, I turn around, about to tell Grandma that I would be right back. But when I turn around to call out to her, I see that both women are quickly heading towards the house. They both turn to look at Phillip and me as we dashed into the woods. Grandma hand was playing with the cross at her neck. Something was wrong.

"Phillip," I call out as we are running through the woods, dodging branches.

He just kept on running as if he didn't hear me.

"Phillip," I call out louder, pulling my hand from his. This got his attention.

"What's wrong?" He was puzzled by my actions.

I look back towards the house, "I think something is wrong. Gran and my Aunt were acting strange back there."

He steps closer to me taking my hand in his once again, "We won't be gone long, I just want to show you s- something."

He obviously saw the hesitation in my face, "I think they will come get you if any thang is wrong. Come on, we won't be long."

I glance back towards the house once again. I think he is right. Obviously they know where I am going and they will surely come get me if something is wrong.

"Okay," I give in, and we head towards the creek.

Once we reach the creek, I am surprised by what I see. In the spot where our favorite sitting stump used to be, now sits a white bench. I turn to Phillip and smile.

"What is this?" I ask.

I make my way over to the bench and take a sit. The wood is cool against the back of my thighs. *This is really nice.* I think back to a time when me and Dominique was talking about getting Daddy to make us something to sit on for when we came out here so we wouldn't have to sit on the stumps or the ground and ruin our clothes, which we often did to Mama's dismay.

"Did you make this?" Phillip slowly makes his way over to me and sits down beside me.

"Only if you like it," he said slowly.

"I do like it," I said earnestly. "I really can't believe you did this. Did you make this for me?"

This was definitely handcrafted. It didn't look like some of the ones you see in the fancy houses, but it was still very nice looking.

He nods, "I did. That little s-stump didn't look like it was too comfortable."

He took my hand in his and looked over at me, "I'm glad you like it. I wanted t-t-to make you s-smile, and I did."

I see the genuineness in his eyes and it warms my heart.

"Yes, you did. Thank you. This is so kind of you. I love it."

Smiling, I look down at the white wood and rub my free hand across the wood, intrigued by its smoothness. To get the wood to feel like this had to take precise sanding I would think. The painting was done perfectly also. It must have taken him days to put this together.

"That's what I been wanting," he said in a low voice.

I turn to him, and he notice that I don't understand his meaning.

"You s-s," he began.

I held up my hand, stopping him, giving his hand a gentle squeeze I say, "Slow down. I'm not going anywhere. You don't have to be in such a hurry to get your words out, and we have known each other for a while and there is no need to be nervous around me."

I smile at him, "It has been proven that if you talk slower and not think about your stammering, you will stammer less. So now, let's try shall we?"

He looked at me and smiled, talking more slowly this time, he whispered, "You're . . . a . . . nerd."

I shoved him slightly. He looked at me with one of those serious expressions he often displayed. He stood up, pulling me along with him. He put his hands around my waist.

"You smiling is what I been wanting to see."

Before I can say or do anything, he bends down to kiss me. Somehow this kiss is different from the others. The tenderness is so evident. The longing he displayed for me made my heart race. He pulls back. I can feel my arms trembling and so can Phillip.

"You cold?" He asks.

"No," I say softly.

I can't make myself utter another word. We just stare at each other, neither one of us saying anything. It was as if we were both asking, "Now what? What's next?" He gathers me in his arms once more, but he doesn't kiss me again. He just pulls me into a tight embrace. I rest my head against his chest. *Wow, Phillip and me, me and Phillip.* I smile, thankful that he couldn't see my face right now. It wouldn't be awkward trying to explain my thoughts to him. Never in a million years would I have ever imagined this day and I'm sure he would probably say the same.

"You want to go back now?"

He kissed the top of my head. I look up at him and shake my head.

"Not just yet, we still have a few hours of sunlight left, there's no hurry, unless you have something to do."

He looks thoughtful for a moment.

"Not right now."

Catching me off guard, he suddenly says, "Go out with me."

My reply comes out so quickly that I surprise myself, "Would love to."

The look on his face lets me know that he wasn't expecting me to say yes. Now it was my turn to catch him by surprise. He was always initiating, now it's my turn. I place my arms around his neck, rising up on my tip toes. I place a soft kiss on his lips. I pull back and look at him. He is definitely stunned.

When the red settled at his cheeks, I smile. Pleased with myself for making him blush. He wrapped his arms around my waist once again. He pulls me so close to him that I can feel the hardness of his chest. Now, it's my turn to blush. He moves the stray hairs from my face with the back of his hand as he leans in. I close my eyes, anticipation flowing through me, settling in that place that's sacred to me -- the place that awaits the one I will call my husband. His lips finally press against mine.

"Angelique!"

Phillip and I quickly pull apart, putting several feet in between us as Mama stands there all wide eyed. Why is it that every time Phillip and me have a private moment, she somehow manages to interrupt us.

"Didn't you hear me calling you?" She said to me, but her eyes didn't leave Phillip.

He drops his eyes quickly.

"It's time to come on home now, supper is almost ready," she continued.

I see that she notices the bench, but she didn't say anything about it. She just glanced at it, showing no interest. *Did she really just have to come out here and embarrass me like this?* I fold my arms and let out a small sigh to let her know that I was not pleased with this show of parental authority.

"Yes ma'am," I reply as I join her at the opening of the pathway.

Turning back to Phillip, giving him an apologetic smile, I say to him, "Thanks again for making the bench. I really do like it."

He flashed me a smile as he looks from me to Mama. I see flash of something in his eyes just then, something that overshadowed his smile. The soft features he displayed earlier were no longer there. His dark eyes appeared even darker as if that were even possible. Even though he didn't say or do anything, I knew without a doubt in my mind that he was furious, the sudden flare of his nostrils only verified what I already knew. Mama grabbed my hand without saying anything to him and pulls me quickly through the thicket of bushes, letting me know that she noticed the change in Phillip as well. The branches tore at our limbs as walked quickly up the path.

"Mama," I said, "slow down."

"No time to be slowing down. I got thangs to do and it will be getting dark soon," she answered angrily.

The sun was still shining so bright that it was blinding, it was definitely not getting dark anytime soon.

"And what the hell are you doing out here with that boy?" She asked as we made our way out of the foliage.

That boy. Why is she talking as if she hasn't known Phillip for most of his life and mine for that matter?

"I didn't raise no fast tail girls, and I don't won't you off in the woods alone with him, you understand? Boys that age only want one thang," she said pointing her finger at me.

"But Mama," I began, wanting to let her know that she was wrong and that we didn't do anything wrong and I am seventeen after all so she shouldn't be treating me like a little kid.

"I said do you understand me?" She interrupted me before I can get anymore word out in my defense.

Her voice is raised, her way of letting me know that I didn't have a say in this matter. "I'm not always right, but I am never wrong" was one of her favorite things to say and boy was she far from the truth.

"Yes ma'am," I mumble.

What I wanted to say was, "No I don't understand, so please explain it to me lady. Explain to me why you are trying to destroy your daughter's life with your stupid paranoia."

If I could say this without getting beaten within an inch of my life, I would scream these words right in that pretty face of hers.

"Now, let's go on inside so you can get out of those good clothes and get washed up before we eat."

Mama leads the way to the back door and just as she steps inside I turn back and look towards the woods. I didn't see Phillip emerge yet. I stand there a little longer hoping to see him emerge. Just as I was about to go on inside I finally spot him, but I had to squint my eyes a little just to be sure it was him. He is just standing there in the woods, hidden by the thick brushes of trees as if he didn't want to be seen. I know he sees me looking in his direction, but he didn't move. I stepped into the kitchen and closed the door behind me, locking the top lock as well as the bottom. I moved the curtain aside to peer out, but he is no longer standing among the trees. I jumped when I felt a cool hand being placed on my shoulder.

"Everything okay, child?" Grandma asked as she glanced out the opened curtain trying to see what I'm looking at.

"Yeah," I say and quickly close the curtain. "So what are we eating?" I ask hoping she won't ask any other question.

The slamming of the front door made us both turn around. Daddy came rushing into the kitchen looking all wide eyed. We didn't have to ask to know that something's wrong.

"Where's ya mama?" He asked then headed swiftly down the hallway before I could answer him.

I move past Grandma and follow my father. Before I made it to the doorway of my parent's bedroom, I heard Daddy speak the words I had been longing to hear for days now.

"The Monroes were spotted today. And from what I gather, I don't think they ever left town."

CHAPTER 16

"I don't thank it's a good idea for everyone to go running over to them folks house," Aunt Celestine was saying when she saw Daddy, Mama and me headed for the door. "Shouldn't you be waiting on the law to go out there?"

"I mean you no disrespect Celestine, but the law can go straight on ta hell for all I care! They have been lying to us day after day, covering up for those people," Daddy said with vigor. "They been taking precious time trying ta get to the bottom of all this. I thank we have a better chance of getting answers on our own. We're going over there."

Grandma walked up to me and places her hand on my arm, "Angelique, why don't you stay behind and keep us old folks company?"

"You the only old one standing in this room Odalia," Aunt Celestine mumbled loud enough for all to hear, causing Grandma to roll her eyes in annoyance.

If this wasn't a serious situation, I may have found that quite funny.

"I don't want to stay here," I said without hesitating. "I'm going too."

I wanted to stare them dead in the eyes while they told their lies. And I say "they" because I'm sure that little vacation was just a ruse so they could come up with some concoction of a story for Claire. Belinda's message kept playing over and over again in my head for days now, "Claire knows." But something else kept playing over in my head also. *How did Belinda know what Claire knew?* There are too many questions, zero answers and everyone who could tell us anything are not around to tell -- no one but Claire.

"You need to let grown folk handle grown folk business," she said sternly not taking her eyes from mine.

I could tell by the wrinkle in her brow that she was picking this moment to assert her position and make her authority over me known. I turn to look at my parents, because neither of them spoke one word in my defense. They had no idea how slick Claire was. She was so manipulative. But I know her and she wouldn't be able to pull the wool over my eyes.

Aunt Celestine got up from her place at the table and headed in my direction as she declared, "There are a few things I would like to discuss with you precieux, and now would be a good time. Actually, I think your Mama should stay as well."

Mama snapped around so quick, you would have thought Aunt Celestine had said something filthy. She stared at her aunt for a few seconds before speaking.

"Do you really expect me ta just sit here? My daughter is dead and somebody in that house knows what happened," Mama said, pointing as if the Monroe's house was right outside our own door. "And somebody in that house has got ta pay for it!"

"I don't think any of you are thinking too clear right now," Grandmother spoke this time. "We all love Dominique and want somebody to pay. Oh and they will, one way or the other."

When she spoke this, she exchanged a knowing glance with her sister, "If everybody go running up over there at one time, those folks will feel threatened and probably won't talk to any of you. Now, you know the law already taking their time trying to figure this thang out. Don't give them a reason to take even more time."

I saw the look of defeat cross Mama's face as Grandma walked over and place her hands on Daddy's shoulders, "William, I know you want to get answers and help this family move pass all this, but do it the right way son. Call the law and let them know the Monroes are back."

"I'm sure they already know," I mumbled more to myself than to anyone else.

At that moment, I heard the front door open and close. Xavier made his way into the kitchen covered in dirt as usual, but that wasn't what got my attention. It was the look on his face. He looked as though he was somewhere else and he acted passed through the kitchen and headed down the hall. It was as though he didn't even notice the small crowd gathered in the kitchen. No one seemed to notice this but me. I left the chattering adults to themselves and followed Xavier down the hall. Just as I entered his room he was climbing his filthy body into bed.

"Xavier," I said as I head over to his bed, pulling back the covers the he has just yanked over his head. "What are you doing? You're as filthy as a pig. Mama will spank you raw if she finds out you're in this clean bed."

"I don't care," he said roughly, pulling the covers back over his head.

"What's the matter?" I ask as I kneel down beside the bed.

I pull the covers back a little so I can see his face at least.

"What's the matter?" I ask again.

"Nothing," he answers once again with the same rough tone as before.

I didn't want to push him, but I knew he was lying to me. I knew that he and some of the kids could play a little too rough sometimes and the next thing you knew somebody was fighting. Xavier was pretty big for his age and the kids weren't too quick to pick on him, but I wanted to make sure.

"Did one of the boys do something to you? Cause you know I can go out there and fix that."

"No," he said in a low voice. "I just want to go to sleep."

Sleep? There was still a little light outside, and he usually took advantage of it until the last minute.

"Well, you know it's almost time to eat and I know you're hungry. So come on let's get you cleaned up before Mama comes in here and see you in this bed."

He was hesitant at first, but then he succumbed and let me help him out of bed. *I don't know what is wrong with him, but I will find out one way or the other.* After we finished eating, Daddy made a call to one of the detectives to let him know the Monroes were back, and he asked the detectives when someone would be going to speak with the Monroes. Of course, they wouldn't give him any information really. They only told him that they would be speaking with them this week, and that Daddy had to stay away from their residence or else he would find himself in some trouble. But they did say that they would let Daddy know when they called them in for questioning. Daddy was not too pleased with this piece of news, but it had to do for now.

Grandma suggested they go for ride to ease their minds. It didn't take much suggesting because they quickly agreed to it. They asked me if I wanted to come along, but I felt they needed the alone time as well. After they left, I went and took a seat on the front porch. Leaning my head up against the rail, I admired the beauty of the evening. The sky was now a brilliant orange in color signaling the beginning of the end of another day. The heat that was beating down on us earlier was no longer present. A cool breeze now took its place.

My thoughts went to Dominique and I could feel the heaviness consume my heart again. I close my eyes tightly, trying to prevent the tears from coming yet again. I tried to concentrate on the good memories of her, the type of person she was, how loved she was by many. Those are the things I try to focus on the most. But sometimes the awful things make their way in. What happened to her? Did she suffer much, or was her death a quick one?

I open my eyes just in time to see Mrs. Kirkland coming from the side of her house. I'm willing to bet she's putting that screen up again. I don't see why she just won't nail that thing up and safe herself the hassle. She noticed me and gave me a wave. I waved back. I remembered what Aunt Celestine had said about her, "She smells of dead things." I wandered what that meant. But, like my grandmother, I could never get a clear answer from Aunt Celestine either.

Mrs. Kirkland has always been so kind and she spoiled Belinda something serious. I couldn't imagine her being any other way, definitely not in a bad way. I stood up and made my way across the street. I haven't spoken with her in a while and this would be my first time going over to the house since that terrible day. Finding Belinda like that and then coming home with my best friend's blood still on me to hear that the body of your sister has finally been found after months of searching. I think the pain I felt that day will ever be matched. In fact, I know that it won't ever be.

When I stepped into the yard, Mrs. Kirkland turned around at the door.

"Hey there Angelique," she said.

I don't know what I was expecting to see when I saw her, but I wasn't expecting this. I guess some people bounce back quicker than others. She looked . . . good . . . very good. She looked nothing like Mama did after Dominique disappeared. There were no dark circles under her eyes from lack of sleep, she looked well rested. Her hair didn't look as though birds had nested in it for a week, but it was pulled into a neat ponytail. There wasn't a single hair out of place, nothing about her appearance was out of place. *Why is this concerning to me?*

"How are you?" I ask her.

She smells of dead things is echoing in my head. She folds her arms across her breast.

"Just trying to make it baby," she softly answers. "You wanna come in for a while? I just made some lemonade."

I smiled and nod my head. She holds the door open for me to pass through. I was hesitant for a moment, remembering the last time I had passed through the door and the horror that lay on the other side of it. I walk inside a quickly sit on the sofa the sat facing the door. That way I didn't have to stare down the hall. The scent of fried chicken swam up my nostrils.

"Are you hungry?" She asked me. "I just got down frying up a few pieces of chicken. I just got my appetite back and I have so much meat in there and if I don't start cooking it up it will just go bad."

She smiles as she takes a seat on the sofa across from me.

"No, I've just got done eating myself," I explained.

"Ok," she said staring at me, "It's so good to see you."

She ran her hand across the arm of the sofa, not taking her eyes off me.

"I've been meaning to come by sooner, but so much has been going on," I told her.

I thought that explanation would suffice. I just couldn't come out and say, "Well, you know our house is haunted, and we have a voodoo/hoodoo priestess visiting for a little while. And by the way, I have a letter from Belinda telling me how you lied to her about her father all her life. Oh and my little brother can see and talk to the dead." There was plenty going on across the street.

"Oh I understand. And I am so, so sorry for the loss of your sister. Dominique was always a lovely girl, so sweet and kind to everybody she came in contact with. I hope they find whoever is responsible for doing such a horrible thang to a child. Have the arrangements been made yet?" She asked.

Tears had formed out of nowhere.

"No, not yet. They haven't released her body to us just yet."

"I know that's something you want to put behind ya," she said. "Closure is the key to healing."

She came over and sat beside me.

"I thank you and your sister for being friends with Belinda. She loved the both of you as if y'all were her sisters," she paused a moment before speaking again. "Two lives gone and for what? Why?"

She exclaimed and started to cry. I wrapped my arm around her shoulder, trying to soothe her as best as I could. She turned and pulled me into an embrace and it felt good. Both of us were heartbroken over lost loved ones gone before they had a chance to truly live.

Through the opened curtain, I could see Xavier coming across the street. Someone must have sent him to come and get me. But he did the strangest thing. He stopped on the walkway and just stared up at the house.

"Angelique," Xavier screams.

I stood up from the sofa, "Mama must've sent him to come and get me. I will see you later."

"Please come and see me again sometimes. It's awfully quiet in the house now with Belinda gone and all. I could use the company," she said as she gave me a quick hug and walked with me outside.

As soon as Xavier sees me in the doorway he yells, "Grandma wants you," and then he bolts back across the street almost falling as he turns to look back at us.

"Is he okay?" Mrs. Kirkland asks quizzically.

"Yeah. Just Xavier being Xavier. Bye."

I quickly make my way across the street. I see Xavier heading for the back of the house and I follow. I find him sitting in me and Dominique's favorite spot in the backyard, underneath the willow tree. I take a seat beside him and wrap my arms about his shoulders.

"You know you can always talk to me about anything right? I can be a pretty good listener sometimes."

I really wanted him to open up to me more. I wanted him to talk to me and not keep whatever it is that's bothering him locked up inside. I know something is wrong and I want him to talk to me about it.

"What's wrong?" I gently say to him.

That's something that I haven't always been to my little brother, gentle. That's another reason why he favored Dominique more than me. I can still hear Dominique's criticism in my head.

"Do you have a heart that pumps blood Angie? Or were you born with one that pumps mud?"

I would never have a comeback for most of her snide remarks. I would usually just stick my tongue out at her like a big kid and walk off or just ignore her altogether. I realize now that I was not always nice to Xavier. I guess it's his job as the younger sibling to annoy the older ones or one in my case. I was nothing compared to Dominique. She was always the better of the two of us. I'm certain Xavier wouldn't have any problem at all talking to her.

Xavier remained quiet. He kept his head down, resting upon his knees, which he held tightly to his chest.

"Please tell me what's wrong," I pleaded.

I was really starting to worry about him.

"Are you seeing that lady again?"

I hope the answer to this is no. After a few seconds, he finally lifted his head and turned to look at me. There was fright in his brown eyes.

"Yes, she never left."

I hugged him then, wishing there was someone I could make this better for him. He is too young to have to deal with something like this. How can I protect him from something I don't understand? I only sensed her before and I was scared out of my mind, but to see her and hear her had to be horrifying on a whole new level. His next statement was shocking to me.

"She don't really scare me no more, because Jacob said I don't have to be scared of her and that she isn't a bad person. He said he can tell when ghost are bad," he explained to me with a shaky voice.

Jacob B is the little boy he has been talking to in his room. I turned and looked back out our house wondering how many spirits lurked in our house and why did they choose to make themselves known now.

"Jacob told you that?"

He nods and then wipes at the tears coming down his face.

"Angie, is something wrong with me?"

I pulled him closer to me, "No, there is anything wrong with you. Nothing, you're perfect."

I tried to draw him even closer to me. He is blessed with a curse that's been handed down through the generations; taking away innocence, snatching childhoods with ease, leaving only the craving for normality. But I already knew what Xavier is only finding out. Normal does not exist in this family. It never will. I felt him shudder in my embrace.

"Xavier, why are you so afraid if Jacob told you not to be afraid?" I asked, noticing the trembling had not subsided.

He pulled back enough to peer into my face.

"Is Belinda really in the ground now?" He asked wide eyed and confused.

"Yes, that's why we went to her funeral, to say our final goodbyes to her," I said wiping tears from his face.

A look of puzzlement spread across his face, "Why is she standing at her Mama's front door then?"

I froze at his question. This caught me totally off guard. It even frightened me a little. That explained why he didn't come into the yard.

"You saw Belinda?" I said nervously.

He only nodded.

"Did she say anything to you? What was she doing?" I asked then noticed that my hands were shaking.

"No, she didn't say anything. I don't even think she saw me, cuz she didn't turn around to look at me. She was just standing on the front porch looking in the door," Xavier said.

"Angelique," Aunt Celestine called from the back porch. "Come. Let me talk to you for a minute."

"Okay," I called back.

"We will finish talking about this later, okay," I stated to Xavier as I pulled him up from the ground.

"Okay?" I repeated.

"Ok," he whispered.

We made our way across the yard. I looked in the direction of Belinda's house, wondering what was really going on around here. I was beginning to get scared now.

I can't help but to look around for Phillip, I know he isn't far away, he's never far away. I can almost feel his eyes on me now. He was acting so strange earlier. Something's out of place with him. I stepped onto the porch with Xavier in tow. Aunt Celestine stepped aside to let us pass, but she suddenly blocked our way. She kneeled down in front of Xavier and she just looked at him without saying a word. I could feel his hand tighten around mine.

"There is no reason to fear the dead little one. They can bring you no harm," she spoke softly to him. "Go on inside now."

Xavier dropped my hand quickly and ran inside the house, no doubt scared of this strange eyed woman who knew what he had seen without him having to tell her.

I must have given her a curious look, because she looked at me and smiled before saying, "Yes, I know. Sometimes when one has just had an encounter such as the one he has obviously had, the aura around them tends to change. I watch your little brother closely and I know that the light of the sun always follows him. But just now, it's like all the dreary days of winter decided to linger above him today. It's the same look that was surrounding this house when I first arrived."

She exclaimed, "So tell me, what did he see?"

"He said he saw Belinda standing there looking inside the door of her house," I told her.

This would have sounded so crazy to the average person, but she just looked at me knowingly.

"Isabelle and I finally agree on something. We both think it's about time we talked about some things, some serious things. Now is the perfect time since you're parents aren't home."

After I stepped inside, she closed the door and locked it. It is strange how we use to always leave the doors opened until it was bedtime, but now, no door is ever left open and unsecured. It was as if there was something or someone we wanted to keep out. Grandma gave Aunt Celestine a knowing look before speaking.

"You better make this as quick as possible. I don't know when they will be back. But if they find us up to no good when they get back, we all gone be in for it," Grandma said.

She then turned to me, "I was against all of this at first, and ya Mama still is, but if what she is saying is true, then I need you to listen to her and you listen well, and then just maybe things will be as they should be."

She took Xavier's hand and led him out of the kitchen, and as always leaving me confused. Aunt Celestine disappeared down the hall. When she came back, she had something wrapped up in a tan colored cloth.

"Come," she said leading me to the back door, "we don't have much time, and I hope you are as strong as I think you are."

210

CHAPTER 17

Once outside, we made our way to the part of the back yard where Aunt Celestine always sat to pray or do whatever it was that she did when she sat out here.

"Sit," she said to me.

I did as she asked and sat down on the cool grass.

"Has Isabelle ever told you anything about your ancestors; where they came from?" She asked as she laid the cloth on the ground.

It was filled with candles, incents and other things I never seen before, some of them very frightening to look at.

"No, she doesn't talk about our family history much," I replied, watching her as she laid the weird looking trinkets about.

"Well let me tell you a little about your heritage," Aunt Celestine said as she began spreading the candles around us. "We are descendants of Maximilien Nazaire St. Amante, a slave from Saint Domingue, Hispaniola."

"Haiti?" I asked.

"Yes, now Haiti," she looked surprised that I knew that. "He took part in the Revolution, fought alongside

Toussaint Louverture, a former slave himself, leader in the revolution. Maximilien's father was one of the Frenchmen who liked to have their way with the African slaves. The island was full of Mulattos and what they called 'gens de couleur libres' or Free People of Color. After some time, many of them settled in Louisiana, and all of what they knew traveled across the waters with them. They passed it down throughout the generations. So what you see me doing now is nothing new, it's something ancient that's just as powerful now as it was back then."

She put a pile of sticks in the middle of the circle she made around us. She sprinkled a dark powder on the wood, she struck a match and through it into a pile. The blue flames blazed, but I have never seen flames as blue as these. She began to put this white substance all over her face adding a little black in certain places.

She placed a weird looking necklace around her neck. She placed an identical one around mine. I raised the necklace closer to my face to see what was dangling from it. I was revolted to see what looked like some sort of animal paw and teeth, the necklace itself looked as though it was made from snake or some sort of reptile skin. My neck went stiff once I realized I was wearing dead animals around my necks like this was really ok to do.

"Everything is not what it seems around this place. So I need you to put everything you think you know out of your mind, because it will keep you from seeing the truth and if you cannot see the truth, all of this will be for nothing. I want you to relax and open your mind, allow reality to flow in. And don't be afraid of what you hear, but most importantly, don't be afraid of what you see."

Don't be afraid of what I see? Those words alone frightened me. *What would I be seeing?* She dipped her thumb in a small bowl that had a red liquid in it. She started at my forehead, spreading the liquid straight down to the top of my lip. She sat down beside me and began to say something that I couldn't understand. She began to rock from side to side as she repeated her chants over and over again. I looked at her, not knowing what to do. Her eyes were closed, her hands reaching toward the blue flames in front of us that now crackled loudly as the flames seem to grow. Fear was taking over me. I could feel my heart pick up speed.

"Aunt Celestine," I began.

But before I could get any more words out, she turned toward me and her eyes were white as snow, which caused me to shrink back. She raised her opened palm towards me and with a strong breath, blew into my face. Something flew into my eyes and mouth, causing me to fall backwards. It felt as though gasoline has been thrown into my face and I had been set on fire. It seemed as though my entire body was in flames. I open my mouth to scream, but no sound would come. I couldn't open my eyes. Now, I was truly without a doubt afraid. I feel Aunt Celestine's hand on me.

"Be still child," she said, "The burn will pass. I need for you to calm down and take three deep breaths, calm down."

Her voice was gentle, relaxing. It was hard to calm down when you are in pain like this, but I did as instructed and took deep slow breaths. Just as she said, the pain subsided. Only numbness remained.

"Now," she said as she pulled me into sitting position once again, lifting my bowed head up, "slowly open your eyes and tell me what you see."

Again, I did as I was instructed and slowly opened my eyes. All I see is red around me. The sky looked red as blood, but the atmosphere around me was a lighter shade of red. I look all around me, not understanding any of this. It looked like I was still in my backyard, but something was different about it. I look to Aunt Celestine but she is not there.

I call out to her in a shaky voice, "Aunt Celestine?"

"I'm here," I could hear her, but I couldn't see her.

"Where are you? I can't see you," I say and stand to my feet quickly.

"I'm right here," she said.

I could feel her touching my arm, but I still don't see her. I look down at my arm. The hand she placed there was invisible to me.

"Look around and tell me what you see."

I began to look all around me, "I can't see very clearly. Everything looks so red."

"Do the best you can," I hear her say.

I took in the red surroundings.

"It looks like our backyard. I can see our house, but there is no back porch, and I can see the neighbor's houses, too."

I look all around me, turning in a circle, looking for something, not sure what exactly.

"You are seeing things as they were," I hear Aunt Celestine say.

"What is it that I am supposed to be seeing?" I ask.

She quickly replied, "I'm not sure, but you will know it when you see it. Just look carefully. Something has to be different."

Well, thank you, that helps a lot, I think to myself. *This is what I get for wanting to know more about my abilities and more about our family history. I should have*

215

just left well enough alone, but no, I allowed curiosity to
get the best of me.

I turn to walk towards the back of my house when, suddenly the small patch of grass if front of me (a patch of grass that I knew was not in our yard) started to move as if a breeze passed through it. But, there was no breeze and nothing else was moving, only this lone patch of grass -- followed by that sweet smell of flowers that I longed to smell again.

"Do you smell that?" I asked, but there was no response.

"Aunt Celestine," I called out.

She didn't answer back like before. I walked around the patch of grass, only looking back at it once as I headed toward the house again. Suddenly, I hear crying behind me. I turn around swiftly, seeing nothing, but hearing plenty.

"Why?" I heard a soft voice say, "Why did they do this to me?"

The scent of flowers seems to grow stronger, overwhelmingly stronger. I began taking slow steps forward.

"Aunt Celestine," I said in a loud whisper.

I was on the verge of tears now.

"Aunt Celestine, do you hear that?"

Why isn't she answering me? The earth seemed to move, causing me to sway a little. Fear like I have never felt before took over me. *Where is Aunt Celestine? Did she leave me out here alone?*

"AUNT CELESTINE," I scream out.

That small patch of grass suddenly stopped moving, but the soft crying continued. Just then, I realized that the crying seemed to be coming from the grass. I kneeled down beside it and stretched my hand out towards it, wanting to see if I could actually feel it. Then, without warning, the soft crying turned into a rage filled scream, "*WHY DID THEY DO THIS TO ME?*"

The sudden scream caused me to retreat backwards, not taking my eyes from the ground. Something was coming out of the grass! A hand! A hand was clawing its way up from the earth, and then the other appeared. I could not stand up. I tried my best to stand, but I couldn't.

"*WHY DID THEY DO THIS TO ME?*" The woman screamed again.

Now I could see her head coming up from the ground. She was digging her way out of her grave with all her might. I tried to find my voice but I could not. I kept moving backwards, unable to make a sound. The woman

217

looked up quickly, her eyes fixed on me as she continued to pull herself up.

"WHY DID THEY DO THIS TO ME?" She kept screaming at me.

She was now completely out of the grave slowing dragging herself toward me. She stood up quickly and moved towards me in a slow twitchy motion. Her hair was matted on her head and hung in strings around her face. There was flesh missing from her face, neck, feet and her hands. Her dark shirt and overalls where filled will holes. My back hit something hard. I turned around to see that my back was now up against my house. I could go no further. I looked at the woman again coming towards me.

"WHY?" She screamed.

She looked at me as though I had the answer that she sought. I opened my mouth and let out a scream. I felt hands on my arms, hands that I could not see.

"Don't be afraid."

It was Aunt Celestine's voice. It was her touch that I felt.

"Now I need you to see things as they were meant to be. See things as they are," she said.

I felt something being blown into my eyes once again. Things suddenly began to change all around me. The red seemed to be lifting from my eyes. Daylight seemed to be taking over as the sun began to feel warm against my skin. This is strange, because the sun just set not too long ago. So, this couldn't be my reality. The woman had stopped moving towards me. She was only a few feet away from me now, but she didn't move.

"What the hell is goin on out here?" I heard someone say from far away, followed by a swift "shhh" from someone else.

I realized it was Mama's voice that I was hearing. I couldn't see her, but I knew it was her. I allowed the voices to fade away. My focus was on the woman in front of me. The woman whose appearance was changing right before my eyes. The grotesque person I saw only minutes before was slowly changing into someone else.

That matted hair was now beautiful and chestnut in color. It flowed around her oval face, the decayed flesh now a smooth golden brown. The tattered clothing, no longer tattered. She was beautiful in appearance, but there was sadness in her brown eyes. Eyes that were filled with tears. She walked a little closer to me. It was as if she was moving in slow motion, but I was not afraid anymore. I didn't sense that she wanted to cause me any harm.

She stood directly in front of me and then kneeled do so that she could look me in the eyes. Her hair lifting slightly in a breeze meant only for her. She smiled at me

219

through as tears slid down her cheeks. It was a smile I knew all too well, a smile that was filled with unhappiness. She was saying something to me. Her lips were moving, but no sounds were coming from them.

I was trying to say something to her, but no sounds would come. She stooped up and walked away, placing a straw hat, that appeared from nowhere, on her head as she took slow, long strides across the yard. That sweet smell trailed behind her. I kept my eyes on her as she walked towards the Thomas's backyard. She stopped at a flower bed that I knew was no longer there, but it was full of vibrant colors now. She sat down beside it and allowed her hand to dance over the beautiful arrangements. She was smiling as if this brought her the greatest joy.

The sun began to quickly disappear and her along with it. I was back in my own reality now. I knew this because Aunt Celestine, Mama and Grandma where all kneeling down beside me, but I didn't turn to acknowledge them right away, I kept my eyes on the overgrown place that use to be a beautiful flower garden.

"Angelique," Mama called, turning my face to face her.

She wiped at the tears that was flowing down my face, "Are you ok baby?"

She turned on the two older women beside her and said fiercely, "What the hell were y'all thinking. I told you no?"

"It was as if I could feel the pain she felt," I said, talking to no one in particular.

"Who baby? Whose pain?" Mama asked, her attention back to me.

I turned to focus on Phillip's backyard again, knowing that the woman was long gone.

"I don't know who she was, but she was so sad."

"Was it someone who seemed familiar?" Aunt Celestine asked.

I shook my head. I had never seen this woman before.

"Can you describe her?" Was her next question.

I thought a moment before speaking.

"She came up from the ground," I said, pointing at the ground where she came up from. "She kept saying, 'Why did they do this to me?' At first she was scary to look at. She looked as if she was . . . decayed, I guess you can say. Flesh was missing from her and her clothes were all torn up. But then, she began to change before my eyes. She was . . . pretty and she was so sad."

"Tell us what she looked like child," my Grandmother speaking this time.

"She was about my complexion, brown shoulder length hair, brown eyes. She was barefoot. She wore overalls and a dark shirt."

At that moment, Mama and grandma looked at each other.

"She had a straw hat on her head, and she walked over to that old flower bed and sat down," I said pointing to that place.

"Could it be her?" Mama was asking Grandma with a look of shock or horror.

I couldn't determine which at the moment.

"It sure sounds like it, but I thought she had run off," Grandma replied as she looked into Phillip's backyard.

"Do you all want to tell me who you're talking about?" Aunt Celestine asked.

She was clearly annoyed by their exchange, "Why you acting like nobody else is here."

It was Mama who answered as she pulled me to my feet, "The woman she described sounds a whole lot like, Pearline Thomas, right down to those overalls and straw hat she wore whenever she tended her garden."

She brought both hands up to her face and turned to look at Grandma, "Pearl always smelled like flowers. Whenever you did get close enough to her, that's all you would smell, fresh flowers."

Mama shook her head rapidly, "Oh my Lord, that's who I saw that day on the front porch. It was her. It was Pearl."

"Pearl Thomas?" I asked, "Phillip's mama? I thought you said she'd run off?"

"Let's get inside, quickly," Aunt Celestine demanded as she looked around as if she felt someone watching us. "Hurry."

We were obviously moving a little too slow for her. I swayed a little as I stood, dizzy for some reason. Mama grabbed my arm to steady me. Daddy was coming out as we were heading in. He saw the look on each of our faces and panic sat in.

"What's wrong?" He asked.

His voice was filled with alarm, and who could blame him with everybody rushing inside as if we were being chased by a back of wild animals.

"I need you to do something for me," Aunt Celestine said to Daddy, not bothering to answer his question. "And I need it done real fast."

Daddy looked at her for moment as if he were afraid of what she was about to ask. He looked at all of the women in the room before replying.

"What do you need me to do?" He spoke rapidly.

He looked at Mama as if she was the one making the request.

"I need to see her body, your baby's, Dominique," Aunt Celestine said in a whisper, looking at each of us. "And I need to see it soon. Something ain't right around here. I know you feel it. Something's wrong and we need to find out what that is, and soon.

"The longer we wait, the darker it will get 'round here. I need you to find a way for me to see that girl's body. And you need to see it as well," she said to Mama.

The look Daddy gave her was priceless. Everyone was looking at her now as if she was a person that had gone completely insane.

"See her body?" He looked at Mama, "Is she for real?"

"Why do we need to see her body?" Mama asked her. "Why would you want to put me through that?"

"I think you need to just do was she says," Grandma said, finally speaking.

"MERE," Mama said loudly.

She was also a little shocked by this request.

"Why do you need to see her body?" Mama asked again, turning her attention once again to her aunt.

"I think you know why I am asking this of you?"

Aunt Celestine sat down at the table and grabbed her little purse that was filled with cigarettes.

"No, we don't," Mama replied.

Aunt Celestine lit her cigarette and took a long pull. She chuckled a little as if she knew something the rest of us did not.

"But you are going to tell us," Mama stated.

Aunt Celestine continued to smoke on her cigarette a while longer before finally answering.

"From the moment I pulled in front of this house, I sensed death all around me, like four walls squeezing in on me. But I've walked around this house, every corner of it and I have lain in that child's bed and touched her thangs. And I feel something, something weightless, light. Nothing heavy like death."

"What does that mean?" I asked, looking around the room to see if everyone else was just as confused as me.

"William, you were the one who saw the body. Are you 100% sure that the girl laying on the table in that morgue belongs to you? You said that you couldn't really make sure, only that the clothing and other little valuables led you to believe so," Aunt Celestine said.

Daddy just stared at her. I don't think he knew exactly what to say to her.

"Yeah, that's what I said," he finally responded.

"Are you sure it was her, without a doubt?" Aunt Celestine asked.

"I don't know," he whispered, "Her body is in really bad shape."

He turned to look at Mama, "I don't know."

"What?" Mama said as tears filled her eyes.

She looked from Daddy to Aunt Celestine, "What are trying to say?"

Mama voice was loud again. Anger and confusion had taken the place of the curiosity. Aunt Celestine now showed irritation. Her voice was just as loud as Mama's was now.

"What I'm trying to say is that you gave birth to that child. You know every inch of her body -- from the crown of her head to the sole of feet, regardless of what shape it's in. You are her mother and you are not like most mothers, you're special. I want you to be the one to say if that's Dominique's body on that table, because I don't think that it is."

"What the hell you trying do?" Daddy yelled in Celestine's direction.

Mama was in tears now. I haven't seen her cry like this in a while.

"Are you trying to drive this family crazy with all this foolish talk you talk'n? We have suffered enough," my father snapped.

He was so angry. But, Aunt Celestine was a tough old woman. And, she wasn't backing down. She looked at him the entire time she slowly rose up out of her chair.

"This suffering will be nothing compared to the suffering you will go through if you don't heed my words," she said. "Don't you want to know for certain that your child is truly dead? What wouldn't you do to see have her back if it was a chance she could be still alive somewhere?"

"I would give anything," Daddy yelled.

Then, he stopped talking altogether for a moment. You could see by the look on his face that he's trying to keep his emotions under control.

"I would give anything to have her back," he said in a much calmer tone.

"Then stop treating me like the enemy and let's do what need to be done," Celestine replied. "That girl you are about to bury, I truly don't think she's yours?"

Only silence followed the exchange. I sat down on the floor, not bothering to sit down in one of the many empty chairs. I was trying to process all that had just been said. My heart was racing so fast. We are supposed to bury Dominique in a few days and now it's possible that the girl we are about to bury is not my sister. Could that even be so?

Could Dominique really be alive somewhere? Who would be so cruel to keep her away from us this long? The thought of her being hurt came across my mind and I quickly had to bring myself back to reality. As much as I wanted to believe that she could still be alive, I was afraid to have that hope. I didn't want to be destroyed all over again. So, no. I will not allow myself to hope. That way, my heart will not be crushed all over again when it's realized that she is truly gone.

"I think I know how we can see the body," Mama suddenly said as she wiped at the tears.

CHAPTER 18

"Mason Wiggins works down at the morgue. He keeps up the yard, keeps the place clean and such thangs like that. They even trust him enough to leave him there alone," Mama said.

"They will be releasing the body to us in the next day or two. Can't we just wait til then?" Daddy asked.

I don't think he wanted get involved in all the sneaking around. I can't say I blamed him.

"Time isn't on our side. Do you think he can get us in there?" Aunt Celestine asked.

Mama shook her head, "I don't think it should be a problem. We just need to talk to him and see when we can come down there."

"I need y'all to talk to him as soon as you can," Aunt Celestine instructed with urgency.

I knew who Mason was. I use to attend school with his kids. Him and his wife was among the parents who didn't want their children to attend one of the desegregated schools. They felt as though it was too much trouble and just a waste of time, because his kids were doing just fine at the school they were at.

"Let tha blacks fool wit tha blacks and let them whites fool wit tha whites. That's how it is and how it'll always be. Ain't got no time to be stirr'n up trouble, cause that's 'xactly what's gone happen if everybody try'n ta get they kids over there wit them white kids," I remember him saying that as clear as day.

I don't think he will be too quick to want to help us do anything if it involves doing something to defy white people, but then again, he did help in the search of Dominique. He was always willing to help, so maybe he will be this time too.

The opening of one of the doors down the hall startled me. We could hear the sound of bare feet against the wood floor as Xavier walked down the hall. He was probably woke up by all the yelling. I looked back over my shoulder, expecting to see him at any minute, but instead I heard another door being pushed open, a door I knew to be mine by the distinctive squeak. Mama started to get up, but I motioned for her to sit back down. I needed a break from all this, even if it's just for a few minutes.

As I walked into my room, I see that Xavier had made himself comfortable in my bed. He had the covers pulled up over his head. I didn't have the heart to make him go get back in his own bed, and honestly I didn't want to be alone, not after everything that had happened tonight. I will admit that I was afraid now, afraid because all the stories you hear about things that go bump in the night are not stories at all.

I removed my shoes and got into bed beside him. He peeked up at me from under the covers.

"So I guess you wanted to sleep with me tonight huh?"

"It's too cold in my room," he drowsily answered.

"Too cold?" I asked.

He just nodded and turned his back to me, pulling the covers back over his head. I guess this was his way of telling me that the conversation was over. *Too cold?* It was still pretty warm outside and even warmer in here. The cool weather was on it's way, but hadn't quite made it just yet.

Out of curiosity, I got out of bed and made my way down the hall. I could hear murmurs coming from the kitchen, letting me know that they were still trying to figure out how they are going to handle the situation. I head for Xavier's room. Once I get there, I stand in front of the closed door. Just as I reach out for the handle, it opens slightly. I could feel the cool breeze coming from inside the dark room. I place my hand on the door and slowly began to push it open.

Just as I did so, I notice someone or something standing at the foot of the bed. At the same time I noticed them, they noticed me. And without warning it came running towards the open door, gliding would be more like it. I screamed and turn to run, but collided with Mama instead. We both fell onto the floor. I got to my feet as quick as I can, pulling Mama up with me.

"MAMA RUN," I screamed, trying to push her backwards as she had a tight grip on my arm.

I turn to look back at the opened door, but it was no longer opened. It was closed. I see the other's running down the hall trying to figure out what was going on.

"Something's going on in there! SOMEBODY'S IN THERE," I yelled.

I finally broke away from Mama and tried to get as far away from that door as I could.

"In where?" Daddy said quickly.

"In Xavier's room," I said quickly with a quiver in my tone.

I don't know what's in there, but I didn't want to see it again. I have never been so terrified in my life. Daddy tried to open the door, but it wouldn't budge. He tried bumping up against it with his shoulder, but that didn't work either.

"If somebody's in there, you gonna be a hurt son of a bitch when I get my hands on you," Daddy screamed at the closed door.

"William," Mama said in a quiet voice, "move away from the door."

She exchanged a knowing glance with her aunt.

"You can sense it, too," Aunt Celestine said as she walked up behind Daddy.

"Move aside, William," she commanded.

"No, if someone is in there," Daddy begun, but he was cut off.

"I'm afraid you want be able to handle what's in there the proper way," Aunt Celestine said before she gently moved Daddy to the side and held her palm up to the door.

Mama came and stood beside her. Aunt Celestine reached for the door knob, giving it a slow turn, opening it with ease. Daddy looked surprised, because 10 seconds ago it wouldn't open no matter what he did. The cold air pouring out of the room seemed unreal. There is no way it should be that cold when it was pretty warm outside. Each one of us could feel it.

"Where is that air coming from?" Daddy asked Mama as he folded his arms across his chest.

Aunt Celestine pushed the door open even wider. The room was dark, not even the light of the moon poured into the opened curtain. She started to walk inside the room, but she stopped and placed a hand over her chest. She started to hyperventilate as if she couldn't breathe, but she still ventured further into the room. Mama grabbed her and pulled her back out into the hall and quickly shut the door again. Aunt Celestine leaned her back up against the wall.

"That poor boy," she said.

"Who?" Grandma whispered, clutching her necklace.

"Xavier," she answered, "That room is full of the lost and, for some reason, they are drawn to him."

"We are getting the hell away from here," Daddy said, "and soon!"

"William, I told you before that wouldn't do any good," Mama tells him.

"And she's right," Aunt Celestine said. "They will follow him no matter where he goes. It's as if he's a magnet for them, they are attracted to him. I knew there was something about him that reminded me of Jericho, but Jericho has nothing on that little one."

"Why him?" Mama asked.

"Children are more vulnerable, more sensitive to these sorts of things. The older they get, the less sensitive they become. That's the case for most, but I don't think that's the case with your boy. It's different with him. I hope he can handle what's in store for him."

"What's in store for him?" I looked to Mama for a response. "What does that mean, Mama?"

She didn't get a chance to answer, because a strange look crossed Grandma's face.

"Mere, what's wrong?" She asked.

"Something's off with all of this," Grandma said. "Why now? We have been in this house for years and nothing like this has happened. Something is setting all this in motion."

"Yes, you are right," Aunt Celestine agreed.

She turned back to the door, opened it slowly.

"You going back in there?" I asked.

I was starting to realize that this old woman was not normal at all. Nothing frightened her, nothing at all. Grandma looked at me as if I was the crazy one.

"It isn't the dead that you should fear child," she said. "There are plenty living folk walking around that you should reserve that fear for."

Aunt Celestine made her way back into the room with Mama trailing close behind her, but the rest of us remained at the door.

"Y'all gonna go right on back in there?" Daddy said, shaking his head.

He walked past us and headed into my room where Xavier was sleeping. Aunt Celestine looked all around her as if she was searching for something she lost. She made her way over to the window, she peered out of it. Mama was just standing in the middle of the room when she quickly turned around as if someone had touched her. "Do your hear that?' She said in a loud whisper.

"What do you hear?" Grandma asked

"Whispers," she said looking around the room "and they are getting louder. You can't hear them?"

Aunt Celestine got close to her. "What are they saying to you?"

"I don't know," she said, "I can't make out what they are saying..."

"Try," Aunt Celestine demanded. "Close your eyes and listen."

Mama did as she was told and closed her eyes, listening intently. She opened her eyes and looked first at Aunt Celestine, then to Grandma and me standing in the doorway.

236

"What?" Aunt Celestine said impatiently.

"Lies," I can hear one voice say clearer than the others. And it keeps saying, "So many lies."

"I think y'all mess'n with thangs that shouldn't be messed with," Daddy whispered.

I was in total agreement with hlm. It was as though we opened a door that shouldn't have stayed welded shut.

CHAPTER 19

Xavier was moved from my room, which was now as cold as his, and brought to the front with the rest of us. Everyone slept in the living room that night. Daddy felt like too much was going on for anyone to be left alone. I think he was the most afraid to be alone, and wanted as many people around him as possible, but I am thankful that he suggested it, because I was afraid too.

Things were going from bad to worse without hesitation. I didn't know what to make of any of this now. Daddy's idea of getting out of this house didn't seem like such a bad idea. It wouldn't do any good though since Xavier seemed to be the focus of whatever is going on. And if Dominique is alive somewhere, this would be the first place she would come to if she saw a chance for escape. I found myself starting to feel hope again and I quickly put the idea that my sister could be still alive out of my head. I had learned the hard way how it felt to put so much hope in something only to find that hope turn to nothing more than dust.

My thought went to Phillips mom, Pearl, and the events that happened earlier. Something awful had happened to her. I don't think she ran off at all. I remember Grandma saying that when someone meets a tragic end, their spirit will sometimes remain bound to the place where the tragedy happened. That could explain the reason why Xavier seen Belinda standing at her front door, but what about Pearl? Everyone said she had run off. Could she be dead and did she die somewhere around here? What really happened to her and why?

"Why did they do this to me?" She kept saying this over and over.

They? Who was she referring to? I had many questions and no one knew the answer to any of them.

"Are you okay, baby?" Mama whispered softly, trying not to wake up those who may have fallen asleep.

But I could tell by all the stirring that everyone was wide awake, except Xavier, who could sleep through anything.

"I don't know Mama," I began, "so much is happening right now. It doesn't seem real; none of this seems real. Just the thought of Dominique being alive makes me feel so good, but I know better than to hope for that. What if that girl in the more really is her? Then we will have to start the mourning process all over again. I'd rather not have my heart ripped apart for a third time. I don't think I can bear it Mama."

"I feel the same way, but we gotta find out," she said, then turned to look at Aunt Celestine. "And when I think about all the people that she's helped, I don't think she's ever let anyone down."

"I hope the letting down don't start with us," I said.

Mama turned my head to face her, "I love you. I know I haven't said that in a while, but I want you to know that I love you more than anything, and even if we are let down, we still have each other, and our love for Dominique will remain unchanged. We will carry her with us always."

I wiped at her tears that were sliding down her face, "I miss her so much. And even though I don't know what part Belinda may have played in all this, I miss her too."

I suddenly remembered her letter. The only person I shared it with was Aunt Celestine.

"Mama, I want you to read something."

I went to retrieve Belinda's letter from underneath my mattress. After reading it, Mama just looked at the pages for a long moment. She shook her head slowly.

"I wonder what that child knew. Belinda never seemed troubled to me, but I do recall her acting a little strange and I just wrote it off to her being a teenager. Y'all do have those strange acting days," she said.

We both smiled at that knowing that it was definitely the truth.

"What are you two whispering about down there?" Daddy asked.

He was laying on the sofa, next to Xavier while me and Mama was on the floor.

"This."

She handed him Belinda's letter. He sat up and leaned towards the light so that he could read it.
He looked at Mama then at me.

"Did she ever say who her father is?" Daddy asked me.

"No," I answered. "She left this letter the same night she died."

"Seems to me she had a lot going on," he said as he handed the letter back to me.

"Yeah, it would appear so. We were friends for so long. I don't know why she just didn't talk to me. We talked about everything or at least I thought we did," I stated, remembering the many times we all were there for one another.

"Sometimes people like to keep thangs to themselves, work out their own problems. It's not always a good idea, but that's just how some folks are built, so don't blame yourself, baby," she pulled me into her arms.

"I'm sure Belinda knew you would be there for her if she needed you, but whatever she was going through, maybe she felt like it was her battle and hers alone."

I hope she knew that; knew that I was truly there if she need me. It's hard for me to think bad things about her. All my good memories of her overshadowed the bad ones.

"Things are so different now without Dominique and Belinda. I feel so alone most days. Don't you know I can go an entire day without uttering one word?"

"Now that's something," Daddy said sarcastically, "I've never seen that mouth of yours not mov'n."

I could hear the low chuckles coming from everyone including Grandma and Aunt Celestine, who had obviously been listening the entire time. I had to smile too. Mama use to tell me that my mouth ran like a motor, whatever that meant.

Mama tapped me on the head lightly and said, "Try to get some sleep. You got school in the morning. We can't let whatever this is interrupt our lives completely."

I did as I was told and closed my eyes, thinking that sleep wouldn't come, but I guess being surrounded by family made me feel at ease. The murmurs in the room didn't bother me. It was actually kind of soothing. I felt protected, as if nothing could touch us as long as we stuck together like this.

I was sitting on top of a roof, but it wasn't mine. I looked around me, looking for something familiar that would give me some sort of clue as to where I was. I stood up and noticed that I was surrounded by nothing but woods as far as the eye could see. Walking over to the edge, I begin to look for a way down.

"Angie," a voice said.

I turn around to see Dominique sitting on a bench in the middle of the roof that wasn't there before. A bench that looked exactly like the one Phillip had made.

"Dominique!"

I ran to her and threw my arms tightly around her.

"Sit with me a while, Angie," she said.

We took a seat on the bench.

"Where have you been Dominique?" I ask her.

"She's been with me."

I turn around to see Belinda standing next to the bench.

"Slide over," she said, "there is plenty of room for three."

She sat down.

"Where are we?" I asked.

Neither one of them bothered to answer me.

"Will you just look at that?" Dominique said.

"At what?" I ask.

"The sky," Belinda answered. "Have you ever seen wings so bright and beautiful?"

"Wings?" I gave her a look that let her know I was puzzled.

Dominique pointed, "The wings of dawn."

I looked out in the direction she was pointing to see the sun starting to rise and the clouds surrounding it were shaped liked wings; massive wings with brilliant colors that stretch clear across the sky. It was beautiful.

"Your dawn is coming soon, Angie." She put her arms around me, "Just hold on a little while longer."

"Your sisters love you," Belinda said, putting her arms around me as well.

"Why did you have to leave me all alone?" I ask.

Dominique giggles.

244

"What are you talking about? I didn't go anywhere," she said. "You see me every day. All you have to do is look out the window."

"You're so blind, Angelique," Belinda said with annoyance.

Her happy demeanor now gone. She was becoming enraged.

"Open up your eyes before it's too late," she warned, as she rushed towards me.

"Too late for what?" I asked.

"Too late for you to see!"

She grabbed my arm and pulled me to the edge of the house. I tried to pull away from her, but she was too strong. I turn to look at Dominique but she was gone.

"OPEN YOUR EYES NOW," Belinda screamed as she pushed me off the roof.

"Angelique, come on baby. Time to get up," Mama said, gently tugging at me, waking me from my dream.

I sat up and grabbed my arm. It was as though I could still feel Belinda's hand there.

"You okay," she asked.

"Yeah," I answered, "Just had the strangest dream."

"I would like to hear about it," Aunt Celestine said as she came from the kitchen.

Mama help up her hand, "Well, she will have to tell us all about it later. They have to get ready for school."

"Mama, are you going to see Mr. Wiggins today?"

I knew that they were going to talk to him and I really wanted to be there as well. Missing one day of school wouldn't hurt. I would be able to catch up on my school lesson with no problem.

"Yes," she answered, then gave me a knowing look. "And you're not. So go on and get ya'self ready for school. That's enough of all that."

She walked away quickly before I could even utter a word. I picked up Belinda's letter from the floor beside me and headed off to my room. I placed it in Dominique's ribbon box and walked over to the window. Gazing out, I thought off all the times me and Dominique stood at this window, talking about everything or nothing at all. My life was like a bad dream that I couldn't wake up from.

Catching a glimpse of Mr. Thomas in his backyard, I move away from the window. Seeing him caused me to think of his wife and the mystery surrounding her leaving. My thoughts then went to Phillip. Something about him was different and not in a good way. I was trying to keep my distance from him. But I knew, sooner or later, he would pop up. He always does.

CHAPTER 20

As soon I walked into school, Cynthia comes up behind me.

"Good Morning, Angelique."

She was always in such a cheerful mood.

"Hey Cynthia, Good Morning," I replied as nicely as I could. "How's it going?"

"Oh it's going pretty well, especially with it being our last year of school and all. Me and Dominique would always talk about," she stopped talking and turned to look at me with her mouth open wide, as if she had said something she knew she had no business saying. "I am so sorry."

"Don't be," I said grabbing her hand, "It does me good to hear people talk about her. She is missed by a lot of people."

"She really is," she replied. "Oh, and I thought you might like to have this."

She reached into her bag, "I found this last night."

It was a clamp of ribbons. Dominique use to take a big rubber band and tie several ribbons around it in such a way that the ribbons wouldn't come off. She wore them whenever she pulled her hair back into one ponytail. But this one was different. She would usually use one color, but this one had several.

"I remember when she made this one at my house," Cynthia said handing the colorful band to me.

"Cynthia, I would love nothing more than to have this, but she made it for you and I know this means a lot to you," I said.

"It does mean a lot to me. But when she made it, her intent was to give it to you. She said you were always bugging her to make you one with every color there was, but I liked it so much that she gave it to me and said she would make you another. I want you to have it Angelique, because she made it with you in mind," she said, then closed my hand around the hair piece. "She loved you so much Angie."

She gave me a quick hug and rushed off down the hall, not wanting me to see her cry. I clutched the ribbons tightly. Cynthia had no idea how much this meant to me.

"Thank you for thinking of me Dominique," I whispered.

"Let's get to class people."

It was Mr. Foster, looking as handsome as ever, telling us stragglers to get to class.

"You all have about five minutes."

I made my way down the hall, not realizing that Cynthia and I had spent so much time talking. Being late for class was something I tried hard to avoid. I already have enough problems in this school as it is.

"Angelique."

I turn around to see Mathew coming toward me.

"Hey," he said.

"Hey," I replied frowning at him.

This was just weird. He has never said too much to me and now all of a sudden he acts like talking to me is normal.

"We need to talk about something," he said, looking everywhere but at me.

"Talk?" I asked. "About what?"

His eyes widened. He looked at me as if he was seeing me for the first time ever.

"About David."

I took a step back, "What about him?"

I folded my arms across my breast and waited for him to reply. He suddenly started to act as if he no longer wanted to talk. He looked down at the floor.

"We can't talk here."

"Well, I guess we won't be talking then," I spat.

"Don't the both of you have a class to get to?" Principal Hollander called out as he was heading in our direction. "Matt, I don't want to see any late marks on you this year son."

"I'm just heading there now sir," Matt replied.

"Catch up with you later," he said to me in a low voice, making sure Principal Hollander couldn't hear him. He hurried down the hall before I could say anything.

"On your way now, Miss James," Principal Hollander said to me with a scowl.

"Yes sir."

I quickly got on my way. I already had enough attention on me and I didn't want anymore. The remainder of the day was pretty much a blur. I really couldn't concentrate on much of anything, not after talking with Matt. What could he possibly have to tell me about David Monroe? He was part of David's clique and was well aware of my feelings toward all of them.

They were mean arrogant bullies. Even if some of them didn't actually do the bullying, they allowed it to take place and even laughed at some of the cruel jokes that were played on certain students. I could hear Dominique talking to me now, telling me to calm down and ignore the ignorance being displayed.

"Angie," she would say, "you need to learn how to just tune folks out and not let them get you to the point where you ready to somebody in the eye."

I smiled at the thought of her. She always knew how to calm me down, even though I would get mad at her for not allowing me to deliver a good right hook to whoever rightfully deserved it.

I sat with Cynthia and a few of her friends at lunch in our little corner of the room. There were three tables on the left side where all the blacks sat, and the whites sat everywhere else. Sometimes a white student would come over to say something to one of the black ones, but there would always be a teacher that told him to leave "them" alone and get back to your seat. But, they were able to get up and talk amongst the other white students as often as they liked without anything being said. It was almost as if we were quarantined.

Cynthia was carrying on about something that happened at home the night before, but the girl talked 100 going North as my Daddy would say when somebody talked so fast and so much that nobody else was able to get a word in. I could barely keep up with what she was saying, so I found myself tuning her out. But I was starting to see why Dominique was so close to her, they had a lot in common. Dominique used to talk like that sometimes too, but I didn't mind telling her to slow down or just flat out tell her to shut up, which led her to say that was very rude of me, and then she would keep right on talking as if I hadn't said anything at all.

After school, I waited for Mama. Daddy had finally got her old Ford back to running and today was the first day she was actually driving it. I scanned the line of cars to see if I could spot her light blue one. A familiar face in the crowd stopped my search for Mama. I would remember that face for as long as I lived. It was the girl from the protest who was attacked by the police. She was standing alone apparently waiting for her ride as well. It was only about 17 blacks at this school and I thought I had seen them all. I was actually acquainted with most of them. She had to me new. Her body language told me that she was uncomfortable standing there alone. I made my way over to her. I am not sure why I did, but I felt as though I needed to say something to her.

"Hi," I said extending my hand to her, "I'm Angelique James."

She was a pretty girl, a brown smooth complexion. Hey shiny black hair was pulled back into a thick ponytail that fell past her shoulders in beautiful waves. Her face told me that she was surprised by my approach.

"Hello," she said in a soft voice, "my name is Raven, Raven Tucker."

She flashed a radiant smile.

"Are you new here?" I asked curiously.

"Yes, this is my first year here," she answered.

"Okay. I was just wondering because I don't remember seeing you before this week, but this is my first week back due to some family things."

I don't know why I am telling her these things. Strange as it may seem, it almost felt as if I had to.

"Yeah, trust me I know how those family thangs can go," she said, looking away. "There's my Mama. It was nice to meet you, Angelique."

"Nice to meet you too," I said as she made her way down the step and climbed into the waiting vehicle.

"Bye, Raven," Cynthia called as she came and stood beside me. "I'm so glad that you got to meet her. Maybe you all can help each other."

I turned and looked at her, "Help each other how?"

"Well, her older sister Robyn went missing." A strange expression came across her face, "You know, it's so weird, because I think she actually went missing not too long after Dominique did."

"Really?" *Why haven't I heard about that?*

"Yeah, they have pictures of her posted all over town," she said. "I better get going. See ya later."

"Okay, bye," I said more to myself than to her.

I was lost in my thoughts.

"Angelique," Cynthia called out, stopping on the steps. "Maybe we can do something together sometimes."

I smiled at her, "Yeah, I would like that."

Yes, I could definitely see why Dominique and her were friends. Sweet as sugar, the two of them.

"Good," she said.

I watched her as she vanished in the midst of all the others.

CHAPTER 21

After we made it home, I was sort of hesitant to go to my room -- a little unnerved about what may be lurking in there. But, I went in anyway and took in the surroundings. I didn't want to see any shadows lurking in the corners. After I opened the curtains and let sunlight pour in, I felt a little better. I lay across Dominique's bed.

Today had been a really crazy day, but Matt approaching me had to be the craziest. He seemed troubled by something. Everything about him seemed tense. Now that I had some quiet time to contemplate things, talking to him may not be a good idea. I am too afraid of what he might reveal. I remember when David had asked me to join him in the woods to talk, that didn't go over to well. That meeting only made things worse for him, especially since he was found with Dominique's scarf which she had on the night she went out him, which just happened to be the night she went missing.

Going to the creek is where I really wanted to be at the moment, but lately, I couldn't bring myself to go there. The last time I was there, Phillip was with me and something was not quite right with him. I never thought it was possible for those dark eyes to become even darker. Phillip had never frightened me before, but he did that day. There as something different about him and it terrified me.

Finally changing out of my good clothes, I headed for the kitchen to see if help was needed for dinner. My grandmother and Aunt Celestine were out back, while Mama was busy about in the kitchen.

"Do you need any help, Mama?" I asked as I head toward the sink to wash my hands.

She didn't reply.

"Mama," I said a little louder.

She jumped as if I had startled her.

"You okay?"

"Yeah baby, I didn't even hear you come in here," she replied. "I was apparently in my own little world."

"You need me to do anything in here?" I asked again.

She shook her head.

"No, we're having someth'n really simple tonight -- fish and fries. Nobody feels up to fix'n any big meals anyhow." She gave me a confused look, "Where is your brother?"

I shrugged, "I don't know. I didn't see him when I came in and he wasn't outside."

"Can you please go find that boy for me before he gets too dirty?" She asked. "I want to go ahead and check his lesson before dinner too."

I nodded and head off towards his room, which I seriously doubt he was in because of what happened last night. The door of his room was opened, but I still approached with caution.

"Xavier?" I called out from the doorway.

It was eerily dim in the room, as if the sun was afraid to let its rays take a peek inside. It appeared to be in the same condition we left it in last night. The unmade bed told me that no one had been inside of it today. Just as I was about to turn away, I caught sight of Xavier through his small bedroom window. He was walking towards Phillips back yard. I head outside quickly to see what he is up to. I raced down the front steps, hoping to catch him before Phillip saw him or me for that matter. By the time I got to the back of the house, I saw Xavier sitting down near the old garden behind Phillips house.

"Xavier, come on inside, Mama wants you," I said in a low tone, not wanting to be heard by no one but Xavier.

"Xavier," I said again, but he didn't budge. "What are you doing?"

His back was to me, so I couldn't see his face.

"I know you hear me talking to you," I said a little louder, as I bent down to grab his arm.

He snatched away from me and began clawing at the ground. He hands were moving so fast as he frantically dug into the earth as if he where in search of something. He was staring straight ahead, like he was in a trance, unaware of what he was doing. I picked him up quickly, but he didn't stop clawing. I could feel his nails digging deep into my back.

"Xavier, STOP!"

He didn't hear me. He just kept on digging. The stinging spread from my shoulders to my neck. I ran across the yard as fast as I could, trying to bare the pain. Blood was slowing trickling down my back as he continued to rake his nails across my exposed flesh.

"Daddy," I cried. "Daddy!"

Grandma and Aunt Celestine came running from the back porch. Mama and Daddy wasn't too far behind.

"Something's wrong with him!"

I quickly handed him to Daddy, but that didn't stop Xavier for giving me a few scratches across my face in the process. Daddy got a good grip on his arms so that he wouldn't attack him. We all followed closely behind him as he rushed inside the house with Xavier, who still looked as though he was daydreaming.

"Xavier, Xavier," Mama was trying as best she could to get him to snap out of it.

"Come on baby," she whispered as she stroked his cheek.

He started to blink, looking around at everyone obviously confused.

"Are you feeling ok?" Daddy asked, as he set Xavier down on the couch.

Xavier looked at him for a moment before finally answering, "I feel okay."

He looked down at his hands, seeing the dirt and specks of blood. He quickly ran them across his shirt repeatedly, trying to clean them. Mama appeared with a bowl of water and several other things. She handed Daddy a towel and the bowl of water, and she instructed me to sit on the other side of Xavier.

"Let me look at your back," she said, lifting my shirt in the back.

I heard her gasp.

"Is it bad Mama," I nervously asked, because if it looked anything like it felt, then I knew it was not a pretty sight.

"It's bad enough," she answered.

She cleaned the scratches on my back, as well as the ones on my face.

Xavier looked at me with a frown, "What happened to you?"

I stared at him for a moment. He honestly didn't remember a thing.

"Do you remember being in Phillips back yard?" Grandma asked him.

He shook his head.

"I wasn't over there. I was," he just stopped talking as a look of uncertainty spread across his face.

"What is the last thing you remember, baby?" Mama asked.

She pulled him onto her lap and hugged him close to her. He looked as though he was thinking very hard.

Then, he finally answered, "I don't know Mama."

He buried his face into her chest. She kissed the top of his head.

"It's okay."

She looked over at Aunt Celestine, who had said not one word this entire time.

"Let's get you out of these clothes," Daddy said, lifting him off of Mama's lap and signaling for her to follow him.

After my parents left the room, the rest of us sat at the kitchen table.

"What happened out there, Angelique?" Aunt Celestine whispered.

"Mama sent me to look for him and he was over there in the backyard at that old garden. I was talking to him and he acted as though he didn't hear me. And then, all of a sudden, he starts digging in the dirt. He was staring straight ahead the whole time, like he wasn't even in control of his own actions."

The sudden knock on the door caused us all to jump. That made Grandma chuckle.

"I'll get it," Grandma said, getting up from the table shaking her head.

Aunt Celestine rolled her eyes then leaned across the table and whispered, "There must be something mighty significant about that little garden. I bet my life that there is something there that ain't meant to be found."

"Angelique," Grandma called, "Phillip's here for you."

I don't know why, but at the sound of his name, my heart began to race but not like in the past when I would see him, think of him or when he touched me a certain way. Back then was when my heart would race with excitement. Now, it's racing with fear. I hesitantly made my way to the door and stepped out onto the porch.

"Hey, Phillip," I said without making eye contact.

"Hey," he said, taking a small step in my direction.

I waited for him to say more, but he didn't say another word. He just stared at me so intently that it caused me to look away. He was making me feel more uncomfortable than I already was.

"Everything okay?" I asked trying to ease some of the tension.

He smiled, "I was just 'bout to ask you the same thang."

Did he see us? This was the first thought that came to mind.

"Yes, everything's okay."

I tried to give him a genuine smile, but I'm not quite sure how that turned out from his point of view.

"Really?" He was squinting those dark eyes at me.

Both of his hands where shoved deep into his pockets as always, toying with the contents in one of them.

"I saw you and Xavier earlier coming from our yard. I hope he wasn't hurt, cause it's some dangerous junk back there," Phillip said.

I had to be sure to choose my words wisely.

"Oh, he is fine. He was just back there digging in that old garden and got a little," I stopped talking.

He frowned, "He has been back there a lot lately."

"Has he?" I seriously was surprised.

He nodded, "Yeah. He just s-s-sits there and looks at it."

"He is probably thinking of ways to bring some of that dirt over here for one of his many dirt ideas," I joked, trying to lighten the moment as well as change the subject.

He moved closer to me.

"I noticed you haven't been in the woods lately," he said, letting me know that he has been looking for me there.

"I know, but we have been having so much going on," I said, "I do miss it out there."

"Let's go," he said, holding his hand out for me to grab.

A few weeks ago, I would have reached out to him without a second thought, but something was different. The thought of walking in the woods with him now made me feel uneasy.

"Today is really not a good day, Phillip, I'm sorry."

He stared at me a moment before turning to make his way down the steps. He only turned back once and flashed me a smile that made my blood run cold. I quickly went back inside. When everything finally settled down, we all gathered together in the front room again with our pillows and covers, everyone except for Aunt Celestine. She said with all the empty beds in the house, she wasn't about to give up the chance to have a good night's sleep. Dad insisted that she take their room. I got into a comfortable position on the floor and fell asleep instantly.

Phillip and I were walking hand in hand through the woods. He brings my hand up to his lips and gave it a soft kiss.

"So many lies," he said.

I turn to look at him as he kissed my hand again.

"What?" I asked.

"So many lies," he repeated.

He stopped walking and turned to look at me. His face suddenly changed into Mr. Monroe's face.

"I will always protect my family," he said.

As his face changed to David's, "Why didn't you listen?"

He screamed at me as blood poured from his eyes and mouth. I tried to scream and pull away from him, but I couldn't. I watched as several faces shifted into another. Mr. Thomas is now in front of me.

"My sweet, sweet Pearl, I miss her so much," he said through quivering lips.

Now I see Claire's tear streaked face.

"My heart is broken beyond repair," she said before Mrs. Kirkland's face appeared.

"My Mama always told me I wasn't fit to raise a dog. I guess she was right after all," Mrs. Kirkland said spitefully.

Then, I see my Daddy's face. And just as his face was about to change into another, he closed his eyes and said, "NO," as if he had control of the transformation.

"NO, NO, NO," he screamed in defeat as Belinda's face appeared then, just as quickly, it shifted back to Daddy's again.

He brings both of my hands up to his chest and smiles at me.

After awaking the next morning, Daddy dropped me off at school a little earlier than usual. He said that Mr. Monroe wanted all the workers in early to complete some project. I didn't mind going in early, because it would give me a little time to catch up on some reading -- something

I haven't been able to do in quite some time. I took a seat on the steps after he dropped me off. I knew the doors would still be locked at this time.

Mrs. Vermont had sent over two more books a few weeks ago, *Little Women* and *The Age of Innocence.* She said that both books are good reads. I decided to read *Little Women* first because the cover of the book grabbed my attention. I'm not sure how long I had been reading before someone stepped in front of me, casting a shadow across the pages. I looked up and gasped.

I couldn't believe it. Her hair was short and unkempt, looking as though she took a pair of scissors and chopped it off herself. Those violet eyes were no longer brilliant, they were now dismal. The dark circles underneath them were very prominent. Her current appearance reminded me of him, of David. This is exactly what he looked like when I last saw him.

"Claire," I said dryly as I slammed my book close.

CHAPTER 22

I stood up, "I see you have finally decided to come out of hiding."

She folder her arms across her chest.

"I was neva in hiding," she sneered.

"So, what do you call it when you can't be found?" I asked sarcastically.

She rolled her eyes and ran her hand threw her short locks.

"Look, I don't have long before someone notices I am no longer home. We need to talk . . . NOW," she said with urgency.

"About what? Why does everybody want to talk to me all of a sudden? First, Matt, now you."

"Matt?" She asked. "Matt Reed?"

I nodded, "Yes."

She smirked and shook her head, "I am not surprised by that. I'm just shocked that it wasn't sooner. He was always the weak one."

A thought suddenly came to mind.

"Claire, how did you know I would be here? I am early today."

"I saw you leave your house this morning, my intention was to catch you before you went inside," she said, motioning toward the school doors. "Now, that is enough questions."

"No, it's just one of many," I said angrily. "I'm sure you heard that Dominique is dead and so is Belinda. She took her own life, but she left a message saying you know something."

"That's why I'm here. I do know something," she said loudly.

She took a quick look around.

"Now, if you would just shut up and let me talk before I change my mind."

My heart started racing.

"What do you know?" I embraced myself, "Do you know what happened to my sister?" I asked softly.

"I don't know what happened to Dominique," she said quickly looking around again to see if anyone was listening. "I know I wasn't always the nicest person, my mother's to blame for that, but I would never cause anybody no sorta harm. I'm not evil and I do care about you people's lives."

"You people?" I spat. "You mean us colored folk?"

Her eyes began to water, "Some of my closest, dearest friends are Negroes."

Tears were racing down her face now, "You don't know how hard it is to have to hide your friends, because they are different and unacceptable to your family. I have to lie so much about where I am going just so I can go spend time with them. So, regardless of what you think of me and what you may have heard me say, I don't see people as colors. I see people as people. I tried to tell my mother that once and the slap she gave me, I felt it well into the next week. That kind of talk is not welcomed in her presence."

I listened to her speak and I didn't know what to say to her. I would have never thought she was capable of being the person that she is describing.

"Claire, I'm not going to say that I understand what you are going through because I can't and I honestly don't care. All I care about is what happened to Dominique. You should tell me what it is that you know now, or I will beat it out of you. I swear I will!"

"Don't threaten me, Angelique. Like I told you, I don't know what happened to her," she said and took a seat on the step. "She ran into us in the woods that night. We would always hang out there, because we knew no one would ever look for us on that side of town. Her and David must have had some sort of fight. I could tell that much. All I can tell you is that she was alive when I saw her last her."

"David told us he didn't go too far into the woods."

"He lied to you," she said earnestly. "Someone did get hurt that night," she looked up at me, "but it wasn't Dominique."

Claire began to sob heavily. I sat down beside her. She continued.

"My best friend in this whole entire world and I let her down because I was afraid to tell what happened, but not anymore. My father will not."

Before she could finish her sentence, the front door of the school swung open. She stood up quickly and headed down the steps. I followed close behind her and grabbed her arm.

"What happened, Claire? Who got hurt? Was Dominique okay?"

She pulled away from me, "How many times do I have to tell you that nobody did anything to her. She left with that crazy lady who showed up with that gun."

"A lady? What Lady?"

Claire shrugged, "I don't know, but Dominique knew her."

The front of the school was starting to be filled with activity. Cars were beginning to line the street. Kids were making their way into the building.

"I have to go," Claire said.

She raced down the sidewalk toward her parked car, David's car. I caught up to her and grabbed her arms once again.

"Please, Claire, we are burying my sister in a few days. My family deserves to know something."

She stared at me for a long moment. I could see she was battling within herself, deciding whether or not to tell me anything else.

"Claire, please," I pleaded.

"The girl they pulled from Old George's Lake wasn't your sister, but she was someone special too."

She got into the car quickly, but I stepped in between her and the door to keep her from closing it.

"How do you know that, Claire?"

"Because the girl they found was my friend," she cried. "And they dumped her out there like she was nothing. We all had to remain quiet and it killed David to have to do that, and it's killing me too. And I hate them all for what they did. I hope they all die."

Every word she spoke was drenched in hatred. She shoved me out of the way and slammed the door. I was left standing in the street, paralyzed. I had to get my thoughts together, because my mind was all over the place. There was no way I was staying at school. I ran to get my things from the stairs and prepared myself for the walk home. Soon as I started down the sidewalk, I saw Matt getting out of a car. I rushed over to him, almost knocking another student over in the process.

"Matt, I need to talk to you."

He looked behind him to make sure his ride was long gone before talking to me.

"Okay," he said looking unnervingly perplexed, "When would?"

"Claire was just here," I said hastily in a rough whisper, cutting him off, "and she told me that the girl that they found was not my sister. Were you there that night? Is this what you wanted to talk to me about?"

"Shhhh," he said as he took me by the arm, "you are talking way too loud and we can't talk about this here."

I realized we now had a small audience. I pulled my arm from his tight grasp and I pointed my finger right in his face.

"I don't care how loud I am, and you better start talking before I get even louder!"

He grabbed me by the finger and pulled me away from the crowd.

"I will meet you after school," he began as he let go of my hand.

"No, this can't wait til then," I said furiously. "I am about to walk home now. My parents need to know about this."

He looked at me, "You're seriously gonna walk home from here?"

I knew he was referring to the distance. It would take me a little while to get home if I walked.

"Yes, and it doesn't matter how long it takes me to get there as long as I get there."

"Well, it should matter," he said. "Or did you forget that everyone around this part of town is white? So trust me when I tell you that you don't want to be caught walking round here by yourself."

His gaze went from my head to my feet.

"Especially not you."

I scowled at him.

"So you gonna walk me then?" I asked mockingly, knowing that he wouldn't.

Raising his brows, he shook his head, "No, but I will drive you."

"And just how do you plan on doing that?" I questioned.

"I will get Coach Dennis's car. He is my uncle and I'm sure he won't mind. I will just say I need to go to the store or something. Meet me at the parking lot behind the school in about 10 minutes," he said as he headed up the steps leading into the school.

I didn't trust him, but 1 really didn't want to walk either.

"Okay, but I have to tell my friend that you are taking me home."

"Sure," he smirked, "I will take you straight home if that's what you're worried about."

I spotted Cynthia standing near the door talking to Millicent Brody, a mousey little white girl who was actually one of the nicest people in this school but she was picked on because of her parents involvement with civil rights. They were just as nice as she was and were disliked by several local, because they fought for the blacks and attended many rallies on our behalf regardless of how they were treated.

"Cynthia," I called, interrupting her conversation. "Hi, Milli."

"Hey there, Angelique. How you been?" She placed her hand on my shoulder.

I placed my hands on top of hers, "Today is not one of my best days. I'm not feeling well and I am about to leave, that's why I need to speak with Cynthia for a second if you don't mind."

"Why sure. I hope you get to feeling better real soon," she said then gave my shoulder a gentle squeeze before heading inside the building.

"What's wrong?" Cynthia asked.

The look on her face told me that she was truly concerned for me.

"I just need to go lie down for a while," I faltered before continuing, "Matt has offered to take me home."

Cynthia's head snapped back in apparent shock.

"MATT?"

"Yes," I said, not intending on offering her any explanations. "I just wanted someone to know who I left with just in case."

"Just in case something happen?" She shook her head, "Why would you even go with him if you think something might happen? You know he is an awful person."

"Cynthia, I will be fine. I have to go, we will talk later."

I walked off quickly before she could say anything else. I made my way to the back parking lot where Matt was waiting for me.

"I thought you changed your mind," he said.

"I didn't," I muttered as we may our way to his uncle's car. "So Coach Dennis just let you have his car like this?"

"Yeah," he didn't offer any other answer besides this.

Once we got inside the car, I began to tell him how to get to my house. To my surprise, he said, "I know where you live."

He saw the look on my face and decided to explain, "David told us a while back when we were goofing off in the woods near there. Scoot down until we are out of sight of anyone around here."

I did as he asked, and we rode a little ways in silence, before he spoke again.

"You can get up now," he said. And by the way, David really liked you a lot."

"Yeah, he told me," I said getting up from the floor.

I remembered the conversation I had with him not too long after Dominique disappeared.

"So let's talk. You said you wanted to talk to me. Does it have anything to do with what Claire said?"

He pulled out a half smoked cigarette, not bothering to answer my question. He rolled down the window before lighting it.

"My uncle will kill me if he knew I was smoking."
He turned to look at me, "He really liked you."

"Your uncle?" I said with a bit of annoyance, because I knew he was evading my question.

He started to laugh, which turned into a cough because of the cigarette.

"No," he said throwing the stick out the window. "David."

I looked at him, "What does that have to do with anything?"

"It has everything to do with everything. David wouldn't hurt anybody, especially Dominique. Doing something to her would have been like doing something to you, and that's the last thing he would have wanted," he said in his friend's defense.

I shook my head, "Claire said the girl they found was not Dominique and that she left with a woman."

He was hanging on to my every word now. The expression on his face led me to believe that he didn't have any idea what I was talking about. He pulled off to the side of the road a couple blocks from my house.

"The girl died?" He asked as he rubbed both hands through his hair.

"Did you know her?"

"Look, I will tell you what happened while I was there, because I know David would want you to know the truth. But, you can't mention my name in any of this," he pleaded. "You have to swear it."

I nodded, "Okay, I swear."

I told him that, but I knew that was far from the truth. I would tell all that needed to be told to whoever needed to hear it.

"We would all meet up there sometimes just to get away. David and Claire found that spot a long time ago while out hunting with their Dad or something like that. It's well hidden and a perfect spot for teenagers who want to act a fool. So when I got there it was about five or six others there -- Claire, Connie and one of Claire's other friends."

"Claire told me that the girl they found was her friend, and I know it wasn't Connie. So is this the girl they found?"

"I honestly don't know, because I had to leave before everyone else did, because we were going out of town and my Dad wanted me home by a certain time. But from what I can gather, I would say yes," he answered.

"Who was she?" I asked.

"I don't know," he said, "Some half breed."

He looked at me as his entire face turned red, "I'm sorry. I meant to say she was a mixed girl from Jackson, I think. I can't think of her name right now, but she was still there when I left."

"Did David tell you anything about what happened? Anything at all?" I asked.

He thought a moment before answering, "Nothing was the same between us that night. He changed. I talk to him earlier that morning, the day he killed himself, he told me that he needed to talk to me, but he had to talk to you first, and that he would come by the house later. He never came. All the information I did get, it came from Clint, who was there that night also. All I know is that there was some sort of accident involving the girl, but I didn't know she died until you just told me. And I know that David didn't harm your sister in anyway, at least not physically at least?"

"What do you mean?"

"I know he told her how he felt about you and that's when they argued, so if he hurt her in any way, it was only emotionally."

For the very first time, I was really starting to believe that maybe David was innocent after all.

"I think you will be okay to walk from here," he said. "I need to be getting back to school."

He appeared to be in deep thought. I grabbed by books from the floor of the car.

"Thank you for telling me everything that you could," I said as I stepped out of the car, anxious to get home.

"Angelique," Matt called, "there is more to be told, a lot more, but it's not my story to tell."

He turned the car around in the middle of the street and sped off. When my house came into view, I made a run for it.

"Mama," I screamed as I burst through the door.

She came in from the back porch. Grandma and Aunt Celestine right on her heels.

"What are you doing here? What's wrong?" She asked with wide eyes.

"Mama, I have something to tell you."

CHAPTER 23

After I finished telling them about my conversation with both Claire and Matt, everyone began talking at once. I couldn't make sense of what anyone was saying. Mama jumped up and ran to the phone. I knew she was trying to get in touch with Daddy.

"We need to go see that body and we need to go right now," she said to Grandma.

Mama hung up the phone, "they will have William call me back." She begin pacing the floor; suddenly bursting into tears.

"There is no time to wait for him," Aunt Celestine said, "We can do this on our own."

As soon as she said that, the phone rang. It was Daddy calling back. Mama quickly explained to him what was going on. He instructed us not to leave the house until he made it home. When he finally did, we all rushed outside.

"I just came from talking to Mason," he said as he stepped out of the truck. "He said if wanna come down to the morgue, we have to come before 10, because that's when the other workers start to come in, so if we gonna go, we betta to go now."

"You all go on," Grandma demanded. "Enough time as been wasted."

Mama and Aunt Celestine climbed in with Daddy and I got into the truck bed. The funeral home wasn't too far from our house, so we made it there in no time. Mason Wiggins pulled in right behind us. He was obviously parked somewhere, waiting for us to arrive. He pulled up beside the driver door to talk Daddy.

"Pull 'round back," he instructed, then he pulled up to the side of the building and parked.

He looked around as he got out of the car. The building was situated far off the road, so no one would be able to really see us until they made their way down the long driveway. Mason opened up the back door for us. The first thing I noticed after stepping inside was the writing above several of the doorways; One read, "'Whereas you do not know what your life will be like tomorrow. For you are a mist that appears for a little while and then disappears.' James 4:14."

"I wanna help y'all out, but make this fast. JoAnn will have my head if I lose this job over this here, so be quick."

He led us down a dim lit hall that lead us to some stairs. As we headed down them, it suddenly went from being warm to cool. The smell changed as well. It almost smelled like rubbing alcohol, but much stronger. Mason flipped on the lights when we reached the bottom. There was no longer any carpet, only concrete. Long sheet like fabric that sectioned off each area, like a doctor's office, so you can't see the person who is on the other side of you. Mason rushed over to grab a clipboard that was hanging on the wall.

"Number four," he murmured to himself. "She's behind number four."

He pointed, "I will wait out here. Make it fast, Will."

"Angelique," Daddy said, "are you strong enough to do this, because I don't want her to do it." He looked at Mama.

"No, I want to see her," Mama said as she walked over to the curtain, she slowly moved it aside. It seemed to have gotten much colder now, as I stood looking at the silver freezer that I knew held the body inside.

"Lift the latch," Mason said from the stairway, "then you can slide her out."

Daddy gently moved Mama's to the side.

"I got it," he said.

He lifted the latch and opened the door. We could see the white sheet draping the remains. Daddy turn to look at us before pulling on the handle, bringing the long table forward. I don't know if already seeing this played a part in his bravery, but he didn't appear shaken like me and Mama did. Even Aunt Celestine seemed a little uneasy. When he reached forward to pull back the sheet, I closed my eyes and turned around, walking away from the table. I thought I was ready for this, but the truth is, I wasn't. I heard Mama's sharp intake of breath and the moaning started from deep within her.

"I need for you to look at her and tell me if this is truly your baby," I heard Aunt Celestine say behind me.

"Who could do this to someone? Who could do this?" Mama wailed.

Mama was falling apart and here I was with my back turned and my eyes closed. Facing that table isn't something I could bring myself to do. I opened my eyes and tried to find the courage to do what had to be done. Aunt Celestine came and stood in front of me.

"You and your Mama are the only ones that can tell me if this is Dominique or not. As her sister and her mother, you both would know her inside and out like nobody else does. Don't be afraid," she said.

"We need to be hurry'n up," Mason said from the stairway. "Everyone will be come'n in soon."

"We don't have much time," Aunt Celestine said as she grabbed my hands. "You can do this. We are all right here together."

I nodded as I allowed her to lead me back to the table. I then realized that I was not afraid of seeing the body, but of the possibility of this actually being Dominique and losing the memory of her being beautiful and vibrant, full of life, a source of pure energy. I didn't want those memories to be replaced with this one that would surely be embedded in my mind forever. But for the sake of my family, I would do this, no matter what affect it would have on me later.

Aunt Celestine placed her hand on Daddy's shoulders and he quickly stepped aside. I slowly allowed my eyes to look at the body on the table. The body was unrecognizable. Daddy's description was quite accurate. It was badly decomposed, gray in appearance. Bits of flesh was missing from her skin. And, her hair.

"Her hair," I said with a trembling voice, "Dominique's hair was never curly like this. It was always wavy, all the time. Even when she washed it, it never curled. This hair looks a lot like mine. It has the same curly pattern."

286

"Is there anything else?" Aunt Celestine asked urgently. "Look closely."

I moved the sheet down a little further revealing her naked body. Daddy turned away, showing the respect that was still deserved. I began to scan the body closely, waiting for something to jump out at me because this body was in really bad condition. It appeared to be swollen. The entire body was distorted. Then, I remembered something. Dominique slipped off the porch a few years back, receiving a really deep cut on the inside of her bottom lip caused by her teeth ripping into the soft tissue. It never healed completely.

"Daddy," I said uncovering the body again, "open her mouth."

"What?" He said, and looked at me in what I would call horror.

"Open her mouth," I repeated.

He hesitated a moment before doing what I asked. Opening her mouth wasn't as easy as I thought it would be. It took Daddy a little effort to do so. An almost unbearable cracking sound was made as he pried the mouth open, but when he did, my hands flew to my mouth in surprise. Her teeth were full of silver fillings. Dominique didn't have any fillings, none at all.

"This isn't her," I said loudly, "Mama, look in her mouth. All the teeth in the back are filled with silver."

Without hesitation, Mama peered inside, "OH, GOD," she screamed as she rambled off in French to Aunt Celestine, "This is not her! That's not her."

Mama pulled me into a tight embrace and we cried like we have never cried before and I felt that spark that I thought was long gone, but there it was. I was once again filled with hope. Daddy took a look inside the girl's mouth.

"My God," he whispered. "We got to go down to the station right now. If this isn't her, then she is still missing and somebody else got a child to bury. She must come from a well-off family because that type of mouth work cost a lot of money. Let's go."

We left the funeral home quickly and headed straight for the police station. The wind was whipping forcefully across my face as Daddy sped to down the road. I saw him keep turning around to see if I was okay. There was no need for him to worry about me, because I was hanging on for dear life. I just wanted him to get to the station as quick as he could.

The girl in the morgue was not Dominique, but someone went through the trouble of making everyone believe it was. She had on all of Dominique's clothes, right down to her ankle bracelet. My sister is still out there somewhere and I want her back. Even if she is no longer alive, I want her back.

We finally pulled into the parking lot of the station. None of us could get inside the building quick enough. Daddy headed to the desk where there sat this overweight white officer, who looked like he had washed in face in rouge he was so red. The name tag read "Halloway."

"How can I help you folks?" He asked politely before taking a sip of his coffee.

"We are the parents of Dominique James, and we would like to speak to Detective Daniels."

"The parents of who?" Halloway asked.

"Dominique James. The young lady that you supposedly found up on old man George's property a couple weeks back," Daddy responded.

I could tell Daddy was starting to get a little irritated.

"Oh yeah, I remember that case." He grabbed a sheet of paper from out of his desk and started to write something down, "You said, 'supposedly' found?"

"Yes, that girl is not our daughter," Daddy replied.

Halloway looked confused, "I thought we got a positive ID on her."

"Well, the body was in really bad shape and the only thang I could go by was the clothes she had on, which where Dominique's. But we checked something else."

"Mr. James?" Detective Daniels walks up.

"I will take it from here Chuck," he said to the red-faced officer.

I was grateful for him showing up when he did, because Chuck was no help at all and Daddy was about to explode.

"What brings you folks down today?" Detective Daniels inquired as he extended his hand to Daddy.

"We need to talk sir," Daddy answered as he gripped the detectives hand firmly. "Right now, if you have time."

Hearing the urgency in my father's voice, Detective Daniels asked, "Sure, is everything alright?"

"We have some information about Dominique. We are certain that the girl in the morgue isn't her," Daddy stated.

Detective Daniels looked at all of us as if we were the strangest group of folk he ever laid eyes on.

"Let's go to my office, because I am sure you have a really good story to tell me."

CHAPTER 24

Dominique's case was to be reopened. Detective Daniels assured us that he would do the best he could to get our case resolved and I believed him. I could tell he was a good man. His eyes were so gentle. I saw nothing but genuine kindness in them.

I sat in the truck a little while longer after we made it home. We were back at square one, and now I was consumed with guilt. Mama came to the side of the truck. Her eyes were so swollen from all the crying she had done. When would all of this end?

"Come on inside, Angelique. It's starting to get a little chilly out here," Mama said.

I looked over at her, "We stopped looking for her, Mama. We just gave up."

She reached out and grabbed my hand.

"We didn't know baby, but now we do, and we won't stop looking until we find her. Now come on inside," she said softly.

I went into my room and lay across Dominique's bed. I felt so helpless, so confused. *Please forgive us Dominique,* I thought. *We should have been 110% sure that you were gone.* I didn't even bother to wipe away my tears.

"Cynthia is here to see you," Mama informed me from the doorway.

"Cynthia?"

School wasn't out yet, not for another three hours at least. She was sitting at the kitchen table, about to have a cup of tea, courtesy of my Grandma. She kept looking over at Aunt Celestine. I'm sure she was entranced by her appearance. She did seem otherworldly.

"Hey," I said coming up behind her.

She turned around quickly when she heard my voice.

"Hey," she said. "Are you okay?" She asked getting up from the table.

I nodded, "Yes, I am fine. Did you leave school just to come here?"

"Yes, I called my mom and she came and picked me up. She let me use the car so I could come check on you. She knew how concerned I was."

The way she looked at me let me know that she was really concerned. I hugged her, which caught her off guard. It meant a lot to me that she was worried about me and wanted to make sure I was okay.

"Let's go outside," I said, grabbing her cup off the table and handing it to her.

"*Merci beaucoup,*" she said as she raised the cup in Grandma's direction.

This caused Grandma to smile.

"*Je t'en prie,*" she replied.

I smiled as well, knowing that she was taught a little French by Dominique.

"I really appreciate you coming over," I said, taking a seat on the top step.

Cynthia chose to sit in on of the old rusty chairs. We were both hushed for a instant, enjoying the shifting weather. The hot, humid summer was basically over. Fall was in the air and I would greet it with open arms.

"I don't like Matt," she said bluntly, catching me completely off guard. "He is not a nice person at all and I just couldn't rest knowing that you were alone, trapped in some car with him. And honestly, I am surprised you left with him. You know rumor has it that his family is part of the clan."

She got up from the chair and came to sit beside me, "So are you going to tell me what's really going on? There is something you're not telling."

I wasn't sure if I wanted to divulge any information to her, but I needed to talk to somebody.

"It's so much to tell, but if you got time to listen, I could definitely use a friend right now," I said.

She placed her arm round my neck, "Well, here I am."

She rested her chin upon my shoulder, and I told her everything. Cynthia was in tears after I told her what happened from the time I spoke with Claire. The thought of Dominique still being out there somewhere gave her a sense of hope as well. She grabbed my hand and pulled me up.

"I think we should go talk to Claire," she whispered, looking at the door to see if anyone was listening.

"Right now," she urged after taking note of my hesitation, "because if she was willing to tell you that much this morning, maybe she will be willing to tell you more. We need to catch her before he decides to leave town or something."

Now, it was my turn to look back at the door.

"Okay, but I will have to talk to her alone. I don't think she will talk to me with you being there," I murmured.

"I agree," she said nodding her head quickly.

"Let me go tell Mama I'm leaving," I headed for the door.

She grabbed my arm.

"You're gonna tell her where we goin?" She asked, sounding panicked.

I shook my head.

"No, I don't think that's the finest idea."

Mama was on the phone with Mrs. Vermont, when I came inside. I'm not sure if she even heard me or not when I told her I was leaving with Cynthia. She just nodded her head and kept talking. She was asking for more time off. I was grateful that she was on the phone, that way I didn't have to come up with some elaborate lie about where I was going.

As we passed Belinda's house, I could hear Tammy Terrell playing again. My heart went out to Mrs. Kirkland. I knew she had to be lonely. It had been only her and Belinda, every since Mr. Kirkland left. Now she barely came outside. It's as if she's trapped inside that house surrounded by memories that gave her comfort and those that haunted her as well. I would have to go check on her as soon as I could.

"Do you ever just sit back and think about the times we are living in?" Cynthia asked. "It's so sad that we live in a world where human life has absolutely no value at all to some people. We are looked at differently, treated differently simply because of the color of our skin. We are kidnapped, tortured, raped, murdered, because we are not considered a pure race. But no one ever stops to think about the fact that if God wanted us to be the same then he would have made us all the same from the beginning. We are meant to be different."

I gazed out the window.

"Sometimes I wish that he did make us all the same way," I told her. "Then maybe this world would be a better place."

As we turned onto the Monroe's street, I told Cynthia to park on the opposite side of the street, in the exact same spot that Belinda parked when we visited David.

"Be right back," I told her as I climbed out of the car.

I walked swiftly across the street. Hopefully Claire would be home and willing to talk to me. Before my feet even touched the front step, the front door swung open. Claire came charging out.

"What are you doing here?" Her tone was harsh.

I could tell she had been crying. She looked even worse than she did when I saw her earlier.

"Claire, we need to finish our talk," I told her. "Something has happened."

"No," she said. "We have nothing else to talk about. My folks will be home any minute and you don't need to be here when they do.

"Now leave," she ordered as she headed back inside.

"Dominique's case has been reopened," I blurted out before she could close the door.

That seemed to get her attention.

"The girl they found wasn't Dominique," I said quickly.

She gave me a knowing look.

"Claire, please, I am begging you to please tell me everything that you know. Because if there is a chance that my sister is still alive, we have to find her before it's too late."

She began to cry hysterically. I have never seen her this vulnerable. Under all that tough girl exterior, she was no different than any other teenage girl who was drowning in so many emotions. I took a step towards her, but she took a step back.

"We can't talk here," she said wiping her face.

"Okay, I can meet you somewhere. Anywhere you like," I offered.

I didn't want to miss this opportunity, because I may never get it again. She thought a moment.

"There is a park a few streets over," she said.

She told me how to get there and said she will meet me there in 10 minutes. I ran back to the car and told Cynthia what happened. We found the park without incident and waited for Claire to arrive, which she did shortly after.

She got out of the car and made her way over to one of the swings. I did the same. Sitting on the swing next to her, I stared at the ground. I had a very strong feeling that she was about to tell me something that would rip me apart.

"Do you know how we discovered that spot in the woods by your house?" She asked with a hint of a smile.

"No, I don't," I answered.

"I am going to tell you a story, and all I need you to do right now is listen," she said, her words softly spoken.

"When we were much younger," she began, "my father used to visit someone in the area near your house after our weekend outings. He would bring me and David along, but he would always make us stay outside in the car. This one time, David and I got tired of just sitting there waiting for him to be done with one of these long visits and we decided to explore the woods across the street. At that age, kids aren't afraid to explore anything."

She smiled at the memory.

"We walked and walked until we found that beautiful creek and each time we came with him, we would go there and sit for a while, because we knew Daddy wouldn't be right out like he always claimed he would."

She shook her head. Contemptuous is the word I would use to describe her expression.

"Then, David and I got curious and decided we wanted to know who he visited so much in this tiny house. So we crept around to the side of the house to get a peek inside a window or something. We couldn't see a thing at first, because all the curtains were drawn. But, then we found another window that was open at the very back of the house. When we looked inside, we saw our father on top of this colored woman and he was kissing her. I didn't truly understand what was going on back then, I was only 11 or so maybe. I remember the woman seeing us standing there. She told him to stop and pointed at us standing there at that window. David and I ran like hell to get out of there," she smiled and whispered, "David."

She covered her face quickly. I knew the memory of him was tugging at her heart. A feeling I knew all too well. She looked up at the sky as the tears rolled down the side of her face and continued.

"We jumped in the car, scared out of our minds. And when we looked up to see if he was coming, we noticed two pretty little girls sitting on the front steps. This was the first time we had seen them. I was a little confused at first though, because they looked like colored girls, but not quite. They were a little too light. I had never seen colored girls with skin like that, but I knew they weren't white. The older one looked about my age and we just stared at each other.

She came over to the car and said, "Hey, my name is Robyn, what's yours?"

The tears started to flow again.

"My father had been sleeping with this woman and he swore us to secrecy, because he didn't want to hurt our mother. He told us that she was just a friend that helped him with things concerning his business. He gave us whatever we wanted to make sure we stayed quiet. Eventually, Robyn and I became close, best friends, but no one could know. He said that no one would understand and they would want to hurt Robyn and her family. After a while, they eventually moved, but we stayed in touch, and hung out at the creek whenever we could."

She turned to look at me.

"We all decided to meet up that night, just to hang out for a little while. That was her first time meeting everybody, other than that, she only heard me talk about them. I told them I was bringing our cooks daughter along with me, because she was visiting for the weekend. By the time we got there, everybody was already drunk out of their minds and acting like fools. So, I had to play catch up so I could start acting a fool too. I had to show them I could hang with the best of them. But Robyn didn't want anything to drink. They kept trying to force her to drink something, but she kept refusing," Claire said.

"This only made the guys angry. They started teasing her and things started to get out of hand. I was too drunk to move, but I told them to leave her alone and the next thing I knew, they were all falling to the ground. Robyn was pinned beneath them, Clint, Mitchell and Joey. Everybody was laugh'n and howl'n like animals, then they all finally got up, everybody except her. Mitchell was pouring whiskey down her throat and I heard Joey say, 'You better not let that wench's spit get on my bottle, it will be contaminated.' I told them that was enough and finally they got up and left her alone. But she didn't move. Mitchell told her to get up from there and stop playing dead, but she still just lay there. He shook her, trying to make her get up. I went to her side and tried to get her up."

Claire buried her face in her hands and cried loudly.

"Her eyes were barely opened and there was blood pouring from the side of her head. I lifted her up and her head fell back as the gurgling sound came from her throat. There was this huge jagged rock that she must have fallen on, because it was covered in blood. Everyone begin to panic and I screamed for someone to help me get her to the car, but nobody was moving, and then Dominique showed up and David wasn't too far behind he. He saw me sitting there with Robyn in my arms, my clothing now covered in her blood. He asked what happened, but no one said anything. Mitchell started saying it was an accident and they didn't mean to hurt her."

Claire was in a daze now, allowing her feet to slightly rock her back and forth.

"David ran over to me and tried to take her from me, but I wouldn't let him touch her. I didn't want anyone to touch her. She was dead. David said we had to call somebody, but everybody started talking about what their parents would do if they found out what happened. They were all talking at once, and then that weird boy showed up," she paused to think a moment. "Phillip, I think is what Dominique called him."

My entire body went completely numb, "Phillip? Phillip Thomas?"

My hands gripped the chain of the swing. Phillip had been there for me every step of the way. I don't think I could have made it if some days if it wasn't for him. First, Belinda and now Phillip? Was there anybody that was truly on my side? Claire continued to talk, but it was it she was speaking to me from a distant place. *Phillip was there.*

Claire was still talking, not noticing that I was barely comprehending anything she was saying, I had to make myself tune back in to what she was saying, I needed every piece of this information.

"David asked Phillip if they had a phone that he could use, but he was so focused on Dominique, that I don't think the boy heard a word he said. Dominique said that he could come to her house to use the phone, but everyone started to panic again, and poor Connie was so upset that she just took off," Claire said as she got up from the swing and started to pace back and forth, arms folded over her breast. "Phillip told us all to leave and that he would call the police after we all left and tell them that he found her there. Dominique told him that wasn't a great idea and that if it was an accident then no one would get in trouble, but no one was listening to her. They liked Phillip's idea better, so everyone else got out of there. I didn't want to leave, but David made me.

"I was making my way through the woods when I heard a woman's voice. So I turned back around to see who it was. I peeked from behind one of the trees. I didn't recognize her, but it seemed that they knew her. She had a gun in her hand. I couldn't really make out what she was saying, but Phillip told her to take Dominique home and that he and David would handle the rest. So I finally got out of there as fast as I could. By the time I made it home, I was a mess. I felt so guilt leaving Robyn there. I loved her so much and I felt that I owed her, because she didn't want to come out that night, because she wasn't feeling the best, but I insisted and she relented. Then I did something that I will regret for the rest of my life, I immediately told my father what happened, and he left the house shortly after that. He was gone a very long time, but he returned with David."

She sat down on the swing once again.

"And then you and your father came to the house not too long after that and said that Dominique was missing. I heard the story that you were told and as crazy as it may have sounded to you at the time, David basically told you the truth, he did bring her home," she said. "What David told me later is what destroyed him; what our father made them do. We had trashed that spot pretty bad -- beer cans, food wrappers . . . they tried to clean up the area before calling the police, but father got there first. And the great Robert Monroe did what he felt he had to do, he covered it up. He had her tossed into that water, like she was nothing but a piece of trash to be thrown out."

She screamed through her tears, "I HATE HIM! How could he do that to his own flesh and blood? She was his daughter and he didn't even care."

I looked at her.

"Robyn was his daughter?" I asked bewildered.

Now it was my turn to stand up. This story was taking my mind in too many directions. *Robin Tucker. Why does that name sound so familiar to me?* I think to myself, and then I suddenly remembered. I saw a missing poster of her in downtown Jackson along with several other missing persons around the area. Hers stood out to me the most, because of her mixed race. She is the sister of Raven Tucker.

"Raven Tucker. Is she your sister?"

She nodded.

"Yes, she is. He doesn't even know that we are aware of that. He has been messing with that woman for as long as he has been married to my mother. All five of the Tucker children belong to him and I know that he does love them, because I heard about all the things he would do for them. He makes sure they have what they need and more. They live a good life. But he doesn't love them like he loves us, his legitimate, precious white children. He will protect us and his reputation no matter the cost," she said, then looked at me. "All I know for certain is that Dominique was alive when we left and she was alive when David made it home, but that can only be assumed. You can tell the police everything I told you, including the fact that I am the one who called them about the body being at George's place. Now my conscience is clear. I don't care anymore what happens to my father. But David is innocent in all of this. He only did what he was told to do."

Her voice was drenched in melancholy, "You need to speak with Phillip and that woman."

She stood up and began to head for her car.

"Thank you Claire," I said to her, "but I have just one more question."

This question had been eating away at me for a while now and I had to know the truth.

"What is it?"

"How did Belinda know that you knew what happened?"

She shrugged, "I honestly don't know. I never talked to her, barely saw her."

A strange look came across her face.

"Oh my God," she said recalling something.

"What?" I asked. "What is it?"

Her eyes expanded as he ran her fingers through her hair, "That woman!"

"Do you remember who she is?" I asked eagerly.

"Yes," she answered, "I think I do. It was Belinda's mother."

"Mrs. Kirkland?"

She had to be mistaken. *Mrs. Kirkland?* My heart began to pound rapidly.

"Are you sure?" I asked.

I hoped that she wasn't. Mrs. Kirkland was one of my Mama's best friends, just as Belinda had been ours. I was beginning to feel dizzy. I had to brace myself up against the car.

"That's who it was in the woods that night. I remember seeing her and Belinda in town a couple times before and once I heard Belinda called her Mama. That's who it was that night. She was supposed to take Dominique home."

CHAPTER 25

I gave Cynthia the latest details as she drove us back to my house. She was still quite emotional when we finally pulled into the yard. I didn't allow the car to come to a complete stop before jumping out.

"Thank you so much for today. I really appreciate it," I told her before heading across the yard.

"Please keep me updated on everything," Cynthia shouted behind me and I promised her that I would.

"Hey there Angelique," I heard someone say.

Mrs. Kirkland was sitting on her porch. She waved at me, but I didn't say a word, nor did I bother to give her the courtesy of waving back. Just before I made it to the door, I caught sight of Phillip leaning against the side of his house with his head leaning up against the wood. Everything inside me screamed at me to go on inside and let everyone know what had happened. But, the rage I felt had a firm grasp on me and would not let me refrain from speaking out.

Phillip was part of all of this from the start. I thought he was my friend too, but it's becoming pretty obvious that those I considered my friend, didn't label me as such. But today, he was going to tell me everything. I jumped off the porch and headed in his direction. He walked toward the back of his house and I followed him.

"PHILLIP," I shouted in his direction.

He looked back at me, letting me know that he heard me calling out to him, but he didn't reply as he continued to head into the woods. He looked back again and I started to follow. I saw a red stain on the back of his shirt. That voice inside me screamed even louder to stop. This time I listened and headed for home, but not before I noticed that the old garden behind his house was no longer recognizable. It was now covered with debris.

I ran to the back of my house, but the screen door was latched, and the kitchen door was closed. I headed for the front, noticing Phillip standing among the trees, not moving, just watching. Quickly making my way around the house, I see Xavier standing in our yard near the street.

"Xavier," I called, but he didn't answer.

I walked over to him thinking about how I didn't have time for any of this right now. I looked back quickly to see if Phillip had emerged, relieved that he had not, I focused on Xavier. As I got closer to him, the temperature seemed to drop.

"Xavier!"

I took hold of his shoulders. He was staring at Mrs. Kirkland, who was now sitting with her back turned to us. It was if she could feel someone staring at her. She turned around to see us glaring obtrusively in her direction, and gave a wave before retreating inside. The last time Xavier did this, he saw Belinda standing on the porch.

"Do you see something?" I whispered.

"Go talk to her," he commanded in a voice that didn't sound like his own.

His kept his eyes on that house, as if there was nothing else in the world mattered, nothing except for that house. He reached up and grabbed my arm, his hands were freezing cold.

"Go talk to her now."

"About what?" I asked. "We need to go inside right now, I will talk to her later."

I tried to lead him into the house, but he wouldn't move. He looked up and stared at me. His eyes were hypnotizing, as if he was peering deep into my very being.

"You already know," he said.

His cold fingers wrapped tighter around my arm as he gave me a smirk. There was something wrong with his eyes. It was as if a thin white coating had been placed over them. It seemed to be getting colder. I could see his breath when he spoke. *Impossible!* Something was wrong. I knew without a doubt in my mind, that this was not my little brother.

Fear filled me. I tried to pull away from him, but I couldn't. His strength was unbelievably magnified. I opened my mouth to scream for my parents, but before I could, he said, "Don't be afraid, Angelique. You may never get the chance again. Please go now. No more innocent lives shall be taken."

Finally releasing his grip on my arm, Xavier turned around and headed for the house -- taking the cold air with him, that sweet smell trailing behind him. He took a seat on the bottom step. I watched him watch me before finally heading across the street. The light breeze of air danced around me as I approached Mrs. Kirkland's house. I felt it tug at my arms then my legs as if it were trying to prevent me from taking another step, warning me about the danger that was preceded me. Aunt Celestine's words sprang quickly into my mind. *She smells of dead things.*

I tapped on the door only once before she opened it, as if she saw me approaching. She opened the screen door and stepped aside. I noticed that she looked really nice in her strapless dress that fell to the floor, and her hair was piled high on her head -- which seemed to make her appear much taller than she actually was. Her eyes, there was something different about them, but I could figure out what that difference was.

"Did I come at a bad time?" I asked her because she appeared as though she was about to leave.

"No, you're fine. Come on in," she said as she motioned for me to come inside.

But I was hesitant, which she quickly took note of and frowned.

"Angelique?" She asked suspiciously. "You okay?"

I looked at her as if I was seeing her for the first time in a new light. Again, something inside me was telling me to turn around and go home, and again I didn't listen. I nodded and smiled.

"Everything is fine."

I stepped inside, not realizing I was about to find out the consequences of not listening to that inner voice.

"So what brings you by?" She asked without taking a seat or offering me one. The look on her face was so strange.

"Um," I began, staring at the floor not sure what to say exactly.

So, the truth will have to do.

"Mrs. Kirkland, did you see Dominique the night she went missing?" I asked, then held my breath.

She answered with a straight face, "No, I didn't. You know that Angelique."

She took a seat, crossing her legs at the ankle as she smoothed out her dress.

"Why would you ask me that?"

I chose my words carefully so I didn't sound as if I was calling her a liar or sound accusatory. Even though my mind was made up that she was one of many accomplices.

"Well, someone told me that they saw you in the woods that night. That you left with Dominique and was supposed to be walking her home."

Her cool manner was quickly changing.

"You know I would have told you that if that was the case, but it's not. Don't believe everything you hear now. That makes you seem a little naive."

She began shaking her feet quickly and couldn't seem to keep her hands still. I smiled at her politely.

"Yes, I know. But the person who told me seemed to be pretty sure that it was you," I added. "They were certain."

She was going to have to tell me something more believable, because I didn't accept what she was saying as the truth. She shifted her position.

"That's not true!" Her tone quickly changed from sugar to salt. "Who told you that Angelique?"

She got up from her seat and took a step towards me.

"You keep saying 'the person said this, the person said that.' I want to know who is spreading these lies," she said as she grabbed me, catching me by surprise.

I tried to pull away from her, but she slung me around, causing me to stumble into one of the end tables. She slammed the front door shut, making sure I could not leave. Her demeanor had changed completely now. This was not the Mrs. Kirkland I knew and loved.

"Who else have you told this to?"

She was blocking the door. It was obvious she had no intention of letting me leave anytime soon. I took a small step in her direction.

"Mrs. Kirkland," I said softly, trying to calm her down, "I just asked a question?"

She glared at me and shook her head slowly, "You're lying, and you not leave'n this house until you tell me who told you that."

I could see the sweat starting to form on her face. Her chest was rising and falling rapidly as if breathing had become an instant struggle.

"WHO TOLD YOU THAT?" She asked loudly, as her body began to tremble with anger.

I held both my hands up, palms facing her, trying to signal that I didn't come over to cause no kind of trouble.

"Mrs. Kirkland."

She walked towards me.

"Did he tell you something?" She questioned. "Have you been talking to Phillip?"

She took another step toward me as she began scratching the side of her leg nervously.

"Phillip?" I asked softly.

She pretty much told me what I needed to know by asking me that. I gazed at her a moment, challenging her.

"Why would Phillip tell me something like that?" I squinted.

She suddenly took a step back, stepping off to my left slightly. Something behind me suddenly held her attention.

Pointing her finger, she angrily said, "I think that crazy son of yours has been running his damn mouth."

Before I could turn around, there was a sharp pain that began at the back my head and ran to the base of my neck that brought me to my knees instantly. I tumbled over to the floor, slowly rolling over. I looked up to see Mr.

Thomas standing above me holding what looked like a stick of some sort in his hand.

I heard Mrs. Kirkland say, "You crazy fool. Why did you even come in here? That wasn't necessary. Now look at this! We got a bigger mess to clean up now."

I heard the lock on the door click. That sound sent waves of fear through me so profound that the only thing I could do was start praying. Here I was, locked inside this house with two obviously unhinged adults who I knew, without reservation, didn't have any plans on letting me leave this house alive. What were they going to do to me? Mr. Thomas kneeled down beside me as I felt what I knew to be blood sliding down my neck.

Gently moving my hair aside as he said, "I am so sorry, sweet Angelique. You don't deserve any of this. Neither one of you did."

I could hear Mrs. Kirkland chuckle, as If there was something amusing about him talking to me.

"Why you talking to her dammit? You're as stupid as your crazy son."

Mr. Thomas ignored her as he gave me the oddest smile.

"I'm gonna take ya someplace," he said in a ragged whisper.

"You ain't taking her out of this house alive, and you gone make sho of that. I already got one kill'n under my belt, now it's yo turn to play the reaper," she said as she took out a cigarette, placed it in her mouth, and quickly took it out again.

"Do you know how much I hate you?" She asked, pointing her cigarette at me. "I hate yo whole got damn family."

She chuckled as she took out a match box.

"Every thang was fine until y'all showed up. Shoulda stayed down there in the swamps of Louisiana where you belong, come'n up here taking what don't belong to you."

Mr. Thomas, with that strange smile still plastered across his face, leaned a little closer to me.

"I'm gonna take ya to see somebody real special to ya. Close yo eyes for a few minutes, this won't take long."

He stood up, covering the distance between him and Mrs. Kirkland almost instantly. A small knife suddenly appeared in his hand as he grabbed a handful of her hair, forcing her head to the side. She didn't have a chance to even think about fighting back. I watched in horror as that knife was plunged into her throat repeatedly. I could see the muscles in his arms protrude as he attacked with so much force, it appeared as though her head was being

317

detached from her shoulders. I tried to call out, but I couldn't. I could feel myself slipping away into unconsciousness just as Martha Kirkland's body hit the floor. Those sinister black eyes fixed on nothing. My last thought before darkness overtook me was, *Mr. Kirkland's eyes are brown.*

I slowly opened my eyes to find myself in a reeking, dimly lit room. Everything was out of focus and I'm sure my injury played a part in that. The pounding in my head was so severe, that I hesitated a moment before attempting to move; quickly realizing that I couldn't. My hands and legs were strategically bound, my mouth covered. I shut my eyes tightly, trying not to panic, so I could think of way out of this predicament. But panic did set in as I thought of how the inevitable was going to happen sooner later. My fate was going to be the same as Mrs. Kirkland's. I'm going to die. I began to cry uncontrollably.

Everything flashed in my head at once. I thought of all the people that I had trusted -- each one of them, a part of some camorra that had, without hesitation, betrayed my family in the worst conceivable way. Mrs. Kirkland watched us grow up. I thought she loved us. Now I know that was all an act. What did we do to her to cause her to hate us so much? We never showed her anything but kindness and respect.

And Phillip, I had been right about him all along. I always said something was off about him, but I tried to overlook that and allow him to be my friend, all the while he was hiding a precious secret. He made a fool of me, all of them did -- Mr. Monroe, Claire, Belinda, David, and (most shocking of all) the quiet, meek Mr. Thomas. All of them were pieces of this complicated puzzle that would never be solved. My poor Mama. She wouldn't survive this. Losing both of her daughters this way would kill her.

I didn't think I could cry any harder, but I did. I wanted to be home. I wanted to be in my Mama's arms. But, I would never see her again. I wouldn't see any of them again. I heard something move near me. Imaging all sorts of rodents sharing this space with me, I tried once again to sit up. The heaviness in my head seemed to weigh me down, but after a bit of a struggle, I managed to sit up. I could feel the wall behind me, so I leaned back against it and listened.

The pain in my head was starting to get worse. I needed a doctor and soon. My vision was getting worse as well. Now, I'm not so sure if sitting up was the best idea. I could feel myself on the verge of passing out again. I opened my eyes wider in hopes of preventing that from happening, but that seemed to make the room spin even faster. I silently prayed to God, letting him know that I didn't want to die in this place, not like this and not alone.

Something brushed up against my leg causing me to shift my weight quickly. Suddenly my stomach started to turn. I kept telling myself that I couldn't vomit. *Not now. Not with my mouth covered like this.* But this was something that couldn't be controlled. Vomit poured from my nose and came through whatever covered my mouth, but a great deal of it remained trapped inside. I fell over on my side as another batch of fluid made it way up again. I was starting to choke. I couldn't breathe. It was as though I was being held under water. I could feel someone's hands on me, tugging at the covering on my mouth. *Was it Mr. Thomas? Where did he come from?*

My mouth was suddenly freed, allowing all of the fluid to pour out freely onto the floor. I coughed loudly as I was pulled back into sitting position. My back was being patted gently, just like Mama did whenever we got sick. I lay back down again, because I didn't have the energy to sit up any longer. A wave of drowsiness swept over me. I closed my eyes. I wasn't sure if this was real or not, but I could feel my face being stroked as someone cried softly. No, this was not Mr. Thomas. These hands were far too delicate.

"Who are you?"

It was a struggle for me to get out these simple words.

"Angie?" The familiar voice inquired urgently.

She was so close to me, but sounded so far away.

"Angie, is it really you this time?" I heard her say as she touched my bound hands with hers.

She quickly pulled me up again and embraced me, "Please, please let this be real, Let this be real! Don't let this be a dream."

She was still weeping as she removed the tape from my hands and feet. *I am the one dreaming*, I thought. *I know this isn't real.*

"Open your eyes, Angie. Please," she begged as she gently rocked me.

I wanted to see her face.

"Open your eyes," she commanded loudly.

Why did she sound so far away? This had to be one of those lucid dreams I've heard people speak of, the ones that seem so real. She couldn't really be here with me. I felt something cold being poured on my face.

"Come on, Angie. Open your eyes. Don't leave me here," she sobbed.

It took all the strength I could muster, but I slowly opened my eyes, trying to prove to myself that this wasn't real. I was still unable to see her, but I touched her. Her face, her hair. *How am I able to touch her?* Was I able to pull her from my dream? I guess there's a lot Aunt Celestine forgot to tell me.

"Dominique," I said in a low voice, "Dominique?"

She sobbed even louder, "Yes, Yes it's me."

Her tears fell on my cheek and slid down to my chin. Did she come to make sure I didn't die alone? Did God hear my prayer and send her to keep me company? I smiled. Peace had finally embodied me. Here I was with my sister's arms around me, ever so tightly. The dubiety of this moment was not a concern any longer. I was okay and now I would welcome death fearlessly.

CHAPTER 26

I could feel the refreshing coolness on my face as someone sang softly to me. The pain in my head had subsided tremendously. Only a dull ache remained. I was diffident about opening my eyes, not sure if I could handle what I might see, or who I might see. But I had to, and so I did. Even in the weakly lit room, the first thing I saw was her. She was as clear as the moon was bright. She stopped cleaning my face when I opened my eyes. We just stared at each other, neither one of us blinking for fear that the other would disappear.

"Dominique," my voice was barely audible.

The dryness I felt in my throat made it almost impossible to speak. She nodded her head swiftly as the tears fell to her cheeks. I wasn't able to see her before, and I wished I couldn't see her now. She looked older than her 17 years. She looked so frail. Her gray eyes were dull and sunken in the middle of dark rims. She was covered in dirt, just like the thin gown she wore. It was so filthy that I couldn't make out its true color.

Her beautiful, wavy hair was just as grubby from being unwashed, but it was as red as hot coals. She noticed that I was trying to sit up, and moved quickly to assist me, and that's when I noticed them. Bruises seemed to cover every inch of her body. I closed my eyes trying to fight back the tears has my heart broke at the thought of how much she must have suffered.

"You've been out cold for two days," she told me as she brought a cup of water to my lips.

I gulped it down quickly.

"I thought you were going to die, Angie. You looked so bad, but I prayed and I prayed. Then Mr. Thomas brought in medicines and bandages to fix you up."

I just looked her for the longest time. I never thought I would be able to lay eyes on her again, but there she was.

"We gotta get you better, so we can get out of here. Together, I know we can do it," she said quietly, making sure that no one could overhear.

I brought both of my hands up to her face, bringing her forehead up against mine.

"What happened to you?" I asked. "We looked for you for so long, day and night. But when they found that body, we thought you were dead. What happened?"

The sound of a door opening and closing silenced me. Dominique sat down beside me, wrapping her arms around me tightly, shielding me from whoever was coming through the wood door that stood before us. That door caused me to take in my surroundings. We were in a small room that was about the size of our room at home. Several lit kerosene lamps were near the wall. Bandages and different types of medicines lined the dirt floor which was covered in remnants of grass and hay. There was only one wide window that was so high up, making it impossible to reach. The light coming threw it shined on one spot only. A barn of some sort is the first thing that came to my mind.

That wood door swung open and there stood Mr. Thomas. He had a big brown paper bag with him.

"I brought you girls some food. Some soup for you," he said in my direction.

"Are y'all gonna drug her too, after you already tried to kill her?" Dominique asked angrily.

Mr. Thomas turned on a flash light and aimed it at Dominique, causing her to shield her face from the blinding brightness.

"If I wanted her dead, she'd be dead."

He sat the bag down in front of us. I remembered what he did to Mrs. Kirkland.

"He killed her, Mrs. Kirkland. She's dead."

Dominique looked at me, obviously shocked by the information.

She turned to him, "I thought dogs never turned on their masters."

This angered him.

"I AIN'T NOBODY'S PET," he yelled as he threw the flashlight in our direction.

Dominique threw her arm up just in time to keep it from hitting her in the face. She glared at him as she rubbed the spot on her arm that was now turning red.

"She used to be so beautiful didn't she?" He said as he walked near us to retrieve his flashlight and drop the bag of food at our feet.

He pointed the light at us once again.

"I can actually tell you apart now," he said as he moved the light from Dominique to me. "I couldn't before, but my boy always could."

Just the mention of Phillip made my stomach ball up in knots.

"I thought he was my friend, but he was helping you and Mrs. Kirkland, wasn't he?"

He kept right on talking as if I didn't utter a single word, "He said you were the worse of the two, Angelique. The rude one is what he called you. A real firework."

I shook my head, "I wonder why your eyes aren't as dark as your son's, with a spirit as tainted as yours, they should be."

326

"And I wonder why you're dumb as hell. You don't even know your basic colors. Phillip has his mother's eyes. Pearl's eyes were a pretty shade of brown, like milk chocolate," he let his thoughts wonder to a time long ago, a happier time.

His smile was so broad that it reached his eyes. Dominique was still slightly in front of me. I tried to move from behind her, but she grabbed my arm and whispered, "Stop talking to him, Angelique. You're only going to make him angry."

She warned, "I didn't get all these scars for good behavior."

I don't know what came over me in that instance, but the thought of him hurting her made me want to hurt him just as bad.

"YOU SICK FREAK," I screamed as loud as I could. "You like abusing kids, don't you? You beat your own son, you beat my sister! I guess I'm next, huh?" I asked.

I should have left it at that, but I didn't, "Is that what happened to your wife? Did you beat her and that's why she wanted to leave you?"

Before I could think of any more unsympathetic slander to heave in his direction, he came across the room, shoving Dominique aside and slapped me hard across the face. I could taste the blood inside my cheek. My head quickly started to hurt again, so I lay back against the wall and closed my eyes. He hovered over me a while. I could hear him breathing heavily. I opened my eyes and glared at him. My eyes told him that I wasn't afraid.

"Y'all better eat while it's still hot," he turned to look at Dominique, "and don't worry. Drugging you was never my thang."

He paced the floor for a few minutes as Dominique rushed back to my side trying to make sure I was okay.

"Angie, you fool. I told you to be quiet. Here, take these," she said handing me some pills, which I was grateful for. "Please be quiet."

She glanced up at Mr. Thomas as she grabbed the bowl of soup from the bag and sniffed it. She took a spoonful for herself first and waited a moment before giving some to me. Mr. Thomas stopped pacing the floor and sat down across from us. There were tears in his eyes.

"I am not a monster. I didn't do all that to her," he alleged as he pointed at Dominique. "I don't beat my son and I have never hit my wife. I loved them more than life, more than anything in this world. I am still good to that boy. All I ever tried to do was help him."

He covered his eyes a moment.

"Every since he was a little boy, he was different. He had some serious issues, but Pearline and me, we did our best to help him. But, that wasn't good enough."

Me and Dominique glanced at one another, not sure where he was going with this story or why he was even divulging this information to us. But, we knew better than to interrupt him.

"Pearline thought he needed some special type of attention," he continued. "The type of attention that only the doctors could give, but I didn't listen to her."

He pounded himself hard across the head with his flashlight. He stopped suddenly and shined the light on us once again.

Sitting forward, he said, "All of this mess started the moment yo Mama came to town."

"Mama?" I asked. "What does my Mama have to do with any of this?"

He looked at Dominique and smirked, "Do you wanna tell her sweet Dominique or should I?"

"I won't grant you the satisfaction by repeating your lies."

He leaned back against the wall again, "Well I don't mind telling her, and they are not lies. I was there from the beginning and I saw it all unfold."

He moved a little closer to us.

"How bout, I start from the beginning?" He said. "Before your Mama and grandma came here, things were okay on our little street. Not the best, but okay. You see, your Daddy, well the man y'all call Daddy, was involved with Martha for many years. But when your Mama moved to town, that all changed. Ole Will just had to have her. It didn't matter to him that he had someone who loved him."

"What?"

"Don't listen to him, Angie," Dominique told me. "He is lying."

"Oh, believe me it's the truth," he replied with a smirk. "Will wanted that girl from Louisiana and he eventually got her. And you know what happened next? Well, Martha tries to find out all she could about your Mama, even going so far as to move across the street from her to irritate the hell out of Will. I use to love how they would be talking to each other with smiles on their faces, so everybody thought they were being friendly, but they was actually ripping each other to shreds with they words."

He bellowed with laughter.

"I don't believe you," I stated, unconvinced that he was speaking the truth. "Mama and Mrs. Kirkland were friends for years. There is no way Mama wouldn't have known that."

330

"Really? Well y'all was friends with Belinda for all these years and didn't even know she was your sister, well your step-sister."

He waited for my reaction, but I didn't give him one. Even though my thoughts were racing at one hundred miles per hour, I refused to let him witness his words affecting me in any way.

"And the thing is, he knew that Belinda was his and he chose not to acknowledge her. But he claimed you two, treated you like his own flesh and blood while another man raised his child right across the road. Now just how do you thank that made Martha feel?" Mr. Thomas asked.

"Mrs. Kirkland has always been very straightforward. I can't imagine her not saying anything about something like this," Dominique answered. "She said that Daddy told her that if she truly loved him she wouldn't say anything and that he would work it out so that they could be together again, but that never happened."

"And that's why we're all sitting here today" Mr. Thomas said as he spread his arms wide, "because that never happened.

"But you know," he continued as he wagged his finger at us, "she tried to move on. She married Amos and after that failed, she allowed me to keep her bed warm. And I thought she was finally okay."

He was speaking to us as if he were speaking to his closest confidants.

He sighed heavily, "I was actually begin'n to like that woman. Can you believe that?"

He giggled in a childlike manner.

"I didn't think I could like anybody like that after losing my Pearl. But you know, I thought we was starting to build a good strong relationship of some sort. We even discussed move'n away together. But for some reason, she still was hung up on Will. She knew how much he loved his family -- you girls, his son, that pretty wife of his. She couldn't stand it and she finally snapped. When she finally got the opportunity to hurt him, to hurt yo mama, she did just that. Yo mama took from her what she loved the most, so she did the same to them."

I shook my head at him, "And you helped her because it was such a good idea? But you say you're not a monster? You're an evil man, Mr. Thomas."

I braced myself, expecting to be slapped again at any second. He smiled at me.

"No, I'm not. I'm not evil. I just don't care about anything or anyone anymore. I realize now that my heart turned to dust a long time ago when my Pearl was taken away from me," he said.

"Mr. Thomas please," Dominique pleaded, "Let us go home, Angie needs a doctor. I need a doctor. Neither one of us are well. Mrs. Kirkland is no longer here to care what happens to us. You say you are not a monster, then prove it."

He took several deep breaths.

"They are looking for you now, Angelique. I guess letting you go is the right thing to do. But as you can see, I'm not good at doing the right thang these days."

"Mr. Thomas, please," Dominique begged.

"I realize that I have done some very bad thangs. I am disappointed in myself because this is not who I am. When my Pearl was taken from me, that changed me forever."

I noticed that he kept saying she was taken away. What did he mean by that? I know I needed to keep quiet and not get him irritated, but it was as if a voice in my head was telling me to make him talk, because there was more we needed to know.

"Why do you keep saying she was taken away? She didn't leave voluntarily? Everyone said she run off," I told him.

Dominique gave me a look that screamed, "Shut up right now!"

He looked at me in such a way that made every inch of my body stiffen.

"That's a lie that I started. And I had to do that to protect my boy."

Dominique and I looked at one another.

"Why would you have to protect Phillip?" I asked.

"Phillip is sick," he replied, bringing his hand up to his head, "in here."

He paused a moment before continuing.

"He has always been violent, even when he was a little boy. Pearline and I would stay bruised up from his fits of rage. Like I said, we did the best we could for him. I knew he needed professional help like Pearl said. He did," his tone begin to change, he was getting angry again. "But I didn't want nobody knowing what went on up in my house. A man's business is his own, especially when it comes to his family."

He got up from the ground and started to pace the floor again. "She would be alive today if I had listened to her."

He began pounding on his chest with a closed fist. I knew I was taking a risk by asking him another question, but I asked anyway.

"What really happened to Pearline?"

Dominique looked at me again, but I knew she wanted to know the answer to that question as well. He was silent for so long that I begin to think that he was done talking, but he finally stopped pacing and sat down again.

"She had come in from messing around in her garden one afternoon. She loved her garden. she'd stay out there all day if she could. Y'all don't remember her do you?" He asked us.

"Probably not," he answered before we could offer a response.

He was losing it, he was starting to get this wild look in his eyes.

"Y'all were too young to remember her, but anyways," he said before starting again, "she came in and fell asleep on the sofa. I said she must be some kind'a tired, because she slept the day away. Which really didn't surprise me that much, because we had just found out that she was expecting again. So, I ran her a bath, woke her up to bathe, and get ready for bed. I always ran her bath."

He smiled, "She said the water always felt better when I ran it for her."

He looked up at us with that broad smile plastered across his face.

"So I ran her bath every day," he said before he paused a moment to wipe the tears from his cheeks. "I could hear her start the music once she got in the tub. Billie Holliday, that's who was playing, Billie Holliday, 'Strange Fruit.'"

Then he started singing.

> *Southern trees bear strange fruit*
> *Blood on the leaves and blood at the root*
> *Black bodies swinging in the southern breeze*
> *Strange fruit hanging from the poplar trees*
> *Pastoral scene of the gallant south*
> *The bulging eyes and the twisted mouth*
> *Scent of magnolias, sweet and fresh*
> *Then the sudden smell of burning flesh*

He was quiet for a moment. I looked at Dominique, wondering if she had the same thought that I did. *This man has gone crazy and there is no one around to help us.* He let out a heavy sigh.

"I rememb'a think'n, what a perfect song for imperfect times. Then the music stopped and all the power shut off. I called out to her while I went looking for Phillip, but I couldn't find him. I went on to the bathroom think'n

336

that he may have gone in the bathroom with his Mama, because he did that sometimes. And I was right."

He wept loudly this time, not bothering to wipe away the tears.

"I opened that door and there he was sitting on the bathroom floor. And Pearl, I could see her head under the water, and her arm was hanging on the outside of the tub. The radio was floating in the tub. She had been electrocuted. And Phillip, when he saw me, he started clapping and said 'I gave the radio a bath too Daddy and Mama started dance'n,' and he just laughed and laughed as if that was the funniest thang. He was only three or four maybe.

"In that moment, I wanted to strangle the life out of him, but I knew I couldn't do that. I looked at him and he gave me the strangest look that said you're next. That was when I realized just how sick he truly was and that I had to watch him, to protect him. So I buried her in her garden, her favorite place in the world to be. Phillip watched me bury her from his bedroom window. From that moment on I hated him, but I still protected him in many ways and I tried to love him, but after what he did to our good friends."

He put both of his hands on his head and stared at the ground a moment, "They were so good to him, gave him whatever he asked for and he did that to them. Ole Sam and Daisy were the nicest people you'd ever meet."

Dominique looked at me.

"Sam & Daisy?" She whispered.

I could see she was searching her memory.

"The Shine's?" She asked Mr. Thomas. "Shine's Corner Store?"

Shine's was destroyed in a fire, killing the owners, Sam and Daisy Shine.

"Did Phillip start that fire that killed them?" I asked.

"Yes he did, but the fire didn't kill them."

"Phillip? Phillip killed them?"

That was a question he chose not to answer.

"Just because he wanted more treats and they told him no," he shook his head. "Phillip didn't think no one had seen him that night, but he was wrong. The night in the woods, Robert Monroe let him know that he had seen everything so that Phillip wouldn't say a word about what went down there. I wonder what that old money bag was doing in this part of town that late at night. I had to help him clean up that mess, which was nothing compared to having to dress a dead girl. Martha wanted to make sure that the search for Dominique did not continue."

"That's why she took my clothes," Dominque whispered as she shook her head in disgust.

It was all starting to come together now and everything that Claire had told me as proving to be true. She had no idea how much deeper the story went.

"I never would have imagined that the day would come where I wanted to hurt my own child, but it did," Mr. Thomas said as he started pounding his fist up against his head. "I wanted to kill him, but I couldn't. I couldn't kill my own son. What parent could do that? But Martha showed me that it was it was pretty easy to do. She killed her own daughter without batting an eye, letting me know that all it took was just having a huge pair of balls to get it done."

My chest felt so heavy at that moment. How could she do that to her own daughter?

"She loved Belinda. I know she did. And I saw Belinda's body, she slit her wrist," I said.

I just didn't want to believe what I was hearing, but deep in my heart of hearts, after all that had happened, I knew it was probably true.

"WHAT?" Dominique asked. "What are you talking about?"

She hadn't heard about Belinda's death? They didn't tell her.

"Belinda died a couple weeks ago," I said softly. "We thought it was a suicide, but that's not the case apparently."

I looked at Mr. Thomas.

"Without batting an eye," he repeated.

Tears soaked my cheeks.

"Why? Why would she? I know she loved her. We saw that love displayed many times," I cried.

"She did love her. But Belinda discovered what Martha had done. We thought that she was still at your house that night. Martha saw her head over there, but she didn't see her come back, and she overheard our conversation regarding that Monroe girl, Claire. She told me that they saw her that evening while she was out with Belinda shopping, and that the girl just stared at her. She was worried that she recognized her from being out in the woods that night. Belinda heard it all, and was coming back to tell you everything. Martha could have that. But I knew that she figured something out way before then, because of something Phillip told me when he was having one of his good days," Mr. Thomas said.

He began pacing the floor again tapping the flashlight up against his temple.

"Did you know that Phillip and Belinda had a thing going for a while?" He asked me suddenly.

I shook my head, "I don't believe that. Belinda would have told me that."

He just laughed at my reply.

340

"Well, apparently, she didn't. Especially after that big fight the both of you had after finding that jewelry. Jewelry I'm surprised you didn't recognize."

"My jewelry set?" Dominque asked. "So she did give it to Belinda?"

I looked at the both of them, "I thought she bought that necklace when she was visiting her Daddy."

"I'm really starting to see that you are as dumb as they come. How did you not see that it was Dominque's? I couldn't believe you fell for that lie," he said and laughed loudly. "Oh, and don't blame Belinda either because, you see, that's when everything started to fall apart. Martha told her that Amos bought it for her as a gift when she went to visit, but he forgot to give it to her so he mailed it."

Mr. Thomas started to chuckle, "But, for some reason, Belinda didn't believe her and when you confronted her about it, she told you she bought it and Martha went along with it. But Martha couldn't figure out why Belinda told you that when she had already told her that Amos sent it. But see, Belinda was real smart. She felt that her mother was lying about it and that's why she questioned her from the start. Once she talked to Amos and he had no idea what she was talking about, she started to suspect something more was going on."

He came and stooped down in front of us, "See, she confided all this in Phillip, but not in you.
Didn't he, at one time or another, tell you not to trust her?"

He continued to talk but my ears seem to have blocked out all sounds. I couldn't believe it. I thought back to those times I had seen Phillip coming from Belinda's house and when he told me not to trust her I brushed it all off, thinking it was nothing to really be concerned about. I didn't want to hear anymore of Mr. Thomas's babbling, even if what he said was the truth.

But, he continued to talk about how Mrs. Kirkland fought with Belinda after being confronted and later injected her with a drug filled syringe that rendered her helpless before she placed her daughter in the tub, slit her wrist to make it appear as a suicide, and walked out of the bathroom without looking back. At that moment, I realized that, in Belinda's final moment, she could have told who had did that to her but her last thoughts were of Dominique. And with what had to be her last ounce of strength, taking in her last breaths of life, she tried to help us by pointing us in the right direction to find the answers that we urgently desired. I turned to Dominique. I could see the emotions start to swell up inside of her.

"She's dead? Is she really dead?" She asked as her shoulders started to tremble.

I nodded as the tears blurred my vision. Then, I wrapped my arms around my sister as she mourned the loss of our friend. She kept saying Belinda's name over and over, as if saying it would make her re-emerge. *If only it were that easy.*

"I loved her so much," she whispered as our bodies rocked together from side to side.

"She loved you too," I said, "and you have no idea how much."

"Now they all together," Mr. Thomas said in a low voice, speaking more to himself than to us. "Mother and daughter, mother and son, so I think I am the hero here. I put an end to it all and got rid of the crazies."

I looked up at him.

"What did you do?" I asked him. "Did you do something to Phillip?"

At that moment, Dominique begin to tremble fiercely in my arm. Her breathing suddenly changed, it became rapid. Her body suddenly stiffened and as it became instantly cold.

"Angelique," she called out.

I pulled back so that I could look at her.

"Something's wrong," she said in a quavering voice.

I could see vapor coming from her mouth as if she was outside in the dead of winter. The hair on my arms began to stand as the vapor began to pour from my mouth as well. Mr. Thomas looked at us. A look of confusion spread across his face as he stood up. Beside him, I could see something, "something shimmering" as Mama called it. Then, I understood what was happening.

"No, nothing's wrong. I think we have a visitor," I said.

They both looked at me simultaneously, not quite understanding my meaning. The shimmer came closer to me and I wasn't afraid. I knew she didn't mean me any harm. My ears turned cold as I heard her whisper.

"Hey, there, Papa."

I looked to see if they had heard it too, but apparently they did not.

Mr. Thomas began to look around the room. He rubbed his arms briskly, trying to fight off the unexplained chill in the air.

"Do y'all smell that?" He asked. "Y'all smell those . . . flowers?"

"Hey there, Papa?" I said with a bit of uncertainty, but hearing it still caused Mr. Thomas to give me a sharp gaze.

"What? What did you just say to me?" He took a step towards me.

"I just repeated what I heard, 'Papa.'"

"What?" He asked, coming closer to me. "How do you know she used to call me that? What you playing at girl?"

My ears started to turn cold again as she whispered in my ear.

"This has to end," she said over and over.

Dominique turned to look at Mr. Thomas, "Someone wants to say hello."

Her voice was coated with scorn.

"Close your eyes, Angie," she said as she grabbed my hand. "Close your eyes now, and keep them closed. There are some things we ain't meant to see."

I looked over at Mr. Thomas, who didn't know what to make of our behavior. I closed my eyes. It sounded as if a million voices begun speaking at once. I wanted to open my eyes, but my intuition told me that was not an option.

"What the hell are y'all playing at?" He yelled with agitation, but neither of us answered him.

"Oh . . . my," Mr. Thomas cried, then he let out a loud wail.

I could hear the terror in his voice. I could hear him stumbling across the room.

"HELP ME," he screamed. "PLEASE!"

Then, I heard a voice. It was an icy tone filled with bitterness and condemnation.

"No . . . more . . . innocent . . . lives . . . shall be taken."

The temperature seemed to have dropped even lower as the aroma of flowers loitered in the air.

"Don't open your eyes," Dominique commanded right before Mr. Thomas let out another horrifying scream.

Then, there was a loud crack that caused my eyes to instantly open. Dominique's were opened as well. She helped me stand and we made our way to the only window in the room. Under that single window, in the only natural light in the room, lay Mr. Thomas, barely identifiable. There was a gun in his hand, his hair had gone completely white, and his skin had taken on an ashy appearance. I thought at first that he had taken his own life, but that was not the case. There wasn't a wound on him. Dominique squeezed my hand.

"Look. Do you see that?" She whispered.

In the corner, out of the light, we saw her. Not the shimmer, but her. Crouched low to the ground was Pearline Thomas. As she got a little closer to Mr. Thomas, I realized she looked exactly how I remember seeing her in my vision. She was frightening, but we weren't truly afraid of her. It was the moment in itself that brought about the fear.

We watched as she slowly crept into the light. And once she was fully embraced in the pouring beam, those grotesque features began to fade away, revealing both her loveliness and her sorrow. She placed her hand on Mr. Thomas's face as she laid her head upon his chest. The door behind us unexpectedly swung open with a thud. We stood there, shaking, waiting for someone to walk through that door but no one did. We turned back around, and there was Pearl, standing directly behind us, which caused Dominique and I scream in surprise. She stared at for a moment before a poignant smile spread across her face. She pointed to the open door. This was her way of telling us that we were free to go now.

We didn't wait around to see if anything else was about to happen. We ran for the door and didn't look back. Another door flew open with a crashing sound, leading us out to a huge field that was surrounded by trees. My head was starting to pound again as I looked around, trying to figure out where we were. We were kept in a barn of some kind. Ahead of us stood a large house.

"Come on, Angie," Dominque said, pulling me by the hand.

I noticed how well maintained the surroundings were, which led me to wonder how they were able to keep Dominique here for so long without being noticed. Once we made it to the back of the house, everything in front of me started to sway. I quickly took a seat on the bottom step. Dominique took one look at me and automatically knew what ailed me. She continued up the steps and banged on the door and called out several times, but no one came.

"We need to try the front," she said. "Stay there. I will be back."

"NO," I said a little too loudly. "We are not separating. We have been apart long enough."

I stood up slowly. She grabbed my arm to steady me. But, before we could head to the front, the back door opened slightly.

"Anybody there?" Dominique asked, "We need some help! PLEASE!"

There was no answer back, but the door opened a little wider. The sweet scent of flowers filled my nostrils.

"I think Pearl is still helping us," I whispered.

We cautiously made our way up the steps.

"Hello?" Dominique said as she pushed the door open slightly and stuck her head inside. "I don't think anyone is here."

We ventured further into the house and it appeared to be unlived in. The curtains were drawn, furniture was covered, boxes lined the floors, and several pictures sat on top on of the boxes.

"There's a phone," Dominique said, rushing over to the counter where it sat and quickly picking it up.

"It works," she said with relief.

The first call she made was to the police. When they asked for our location, we had to dig around. I went back to the room where I saw the box of photos and as I dug through them, one caught my eye. It was a picture of Mr. Fuller. He was a littler younger, but it was definitely him. He was on several pictures with what had to me his parents and a younger boy who appeared to be no more than 10. I assumed this was his brother due to the remarkable resemblance.

"Did you find something?" Dominque yelled out from the kitchen.

Forgetting my original purpose, I quickly started to look around and noticed a box full of papers and unopened letters which had the address on them. After giving them the address and answering what seemed like a million questions, Dominique handed me the phone.

"I think the next call should be yours to make," she said.

CHAPTER 27

We sat near the end of the driveway and waited for help to come. I held Dominique in my arms as she cried. She was inconsolable. She kept saying, "Please be real," over and over. No matter how many times I told her it was, that she was truly free, she wasn't convinced. She had dreamed of this moment so often but that's all they were, dreams. Two police cars pulled into the yard. The first car's back door swung opened and out jumped Mr. Fuller. He headed towards us and stopped in his tracks when he saw me and Dominique.

"Are you girls ok? What the hell happened here?" He looked at me intently. "Your name is Angelique right?"

I nodded. He stared at Dominique a long moment.

"Are you Dominique?"

"Yes," she said as tears slid down her face.

He stared at her a long moment. I know he must've heard what happened to her if he knew who we were.

"I've heard so much about the both of you from other teachers, good things. Can you girls tell me how you ended up here at my grandparent's home?" He asked us just as two of the officers approached while another two went inside the house.

It was Dominique who spoke, "Should I start from the beginning?"

"Yes," one of the officers said. "That would be the best place to start."

I listened as she told the events that lead to her being kidnapped. She filled in all the missing pieces of that night. Much of what she said collaborated with Claire's story, picking up basically where Claire's ended. She talked about the girl that was unconscious on the ground, about what happened with David, and about her unending abuse at the hands of Martha Kirkland and Mr. Thomas -- who really didn't want to have a part in any of it at first but something changed in him and he became merciless like Mrs. Kirkland, who coerced Phillip's father into doing awful things to Dominique because Mrs. Kirkland seemed to get a thrill out of watching Dominique being tormented. She was beaten and starved more times than she could remember.

"But there is one thing that stands out among the others," she said. "Mrs. Kirkland said to me not too long after she had taken me, 'Your innocence is sickening.' She wanted to see my 'innocence' snatched away in the most vicious way conceivable. No woman should have that taken away from her! Not like that!"

The officer stopped writing and looked at her.

"Where you raped?" He asked.

Dominique nodded and I gasped loudly.

"But not by Mr. Thomas," she said.

He looked at her strangely, obviously confused and so was I.

"You have to give me a little more detail than that," he said.

She shook her head.

"Not really sir," she said.

"What does it matter now that they're both dead. So, who will pay for what happened to me? To my sister?" She asked through her tears. "Nobody. So what's the point of me telling you every single detail of what I been through? It's over. They both got what they earned, and I don't want to talk about it anymore."

The officer could only look at her a short moment before writing something on his pad.

"I will have to get a little more info from the both of you, but we can do that a little later," he said.

He looked at Dominique again, his expression clearing saying, *I'm sorry.* He then headed towards the house. I wrapped my arms around Dominique even tighter. She rested her head against mine and cried softly.

The familiar grumble of Daddy's truck was like a sweet melody to my ears. Dominque raised her head and stood quickly to her feet, pulling me up with her. The truck came to a screeching stop in the middle of the street. The passenger door swung open, but Mama didn't get out until Daddy came around to her. We could hear him talking.

"It's ok, baby," he told Mama. "There they are, and they both ok. It's over."

Dominque didn't give them a chance to make it over to us. She released my hand and walked slowly towards them as she cried loudly. Suddenly, she ran to them. Daddy caught her up in his massive arms, lifting her off the ground. Mama just stood back and observed for a moment, letting them have their moment. She looked at me. I smiled and nodded, and motioned towards Dominque -- letting her know that I was okay and it was Dominique who was so in need of what they were offering at the moment, that feeling of pure love and security that can be felt in the arms of those who truly love you.

She allowed her hands to glide over Dominique's matted mane, while Daddy still held her. Dominique put her other arm around Mama's neck as she was finally lowered to the ground. Mama pulled back to look at her more intently. First, she took in her frail dirt-covered body. She studied her hands that were now scarred and bruised. Then, she looked into her eyes.

I knew, without a doubt, that she no longer saw that light that used to shine there. It had grown dim behind the sunken shadows that now circled them. Mama suddenly dropped to her knees, grabbing Dominique around her waist as she screamed into her belly.

"I am so sorry we didn't find you! We tried, baby. We tried so hard to find you," Mama sobbed.

"I know you did, Mama," Dominique pulled Mama up and held her once again.

How is it that the one that needed consoling the most had the strength to console us as well? Daddy came and took me in his arms.

"I love you so much," he said to me. "I don't know why you did what you did, but thank you for doing it because, if you hadn't, this reunion may have never happened."

I looked up at this big powerful man standing in front of me, and I couldn't help but think about what Mr. Thomas had told us about him. I couldn't, not even for a second, fathom how this man that I have loved for basically my entire life could ever be capable of doing something that he knew would only cause pain and heartache. Deny his own flesh and blood? No.

"I love you too, Daddy."

I saw Mama extending her arm, motioning for me and Daddy to join her and Dominique in this loving embrace that signaled answered prayers and new beginnings. And, so we did.

EPILOGUE
7 months later

I remember my Grandma saying to me once that sometimes evil takes root so deep inside a person's heart that it cannot be pruned out. And that, occasionally, the only way for those individuals to be saved was for them to be removed from the world altogether. I really didn't understand what she meant by that before, but I fully comprehend what she was saying now.

Evil is just the true nature of some people. And no matter how much help they receive, they would never fully be able to submerge the darkness permanently because the evil inside of them has encompassed their entire being and its hold on them will never slacken. Sadly, the life of one must sometimes be taken to save the lives of many.

Mrs. Kirkland was one such person. I can't understand the reason behind a mother mercilessly taking the life of her child. Any reason would be beyond my comprehension. There is no justification for such an act. She killed Belinda without a second thought and I'm certain that she would have taken my life as well. I saw it in her eyes -- the coldness, the darkness. Mr. Thomas saved my life after taking the life of his own son. I now questioned if that was an act of redemption of some sort for what he had done, or if it was something he wanted to do all along.

Phillip's body was found underneath the piles of rubble that was suddenly covering their old garden. Multiple stab wounds was the official cause of death. It appears as though he was killed while he slept, due to the fact that his bed was covered in blood and he was still wearing his pajamas. Found in his room, inside one of the pant pockets, was a silver ribbon. Now I knew why he used to fiddle around in his pocket so much. And surprisingly to some, but not to us, Pearline Thomas's body was found buried in that same garden.

The word around town was that Claire left Mississippi shortly after my last visit with her, but not before telling the police all that she knew regarding the night Robin Tucker and Dominque went missing. Of course, Mr. Monroe was questioned and released -- claiming that Claire had become mentally unstable after the death of David, she blamed him for it, and vowed to make him pay. He even said that he had never heard of Robin Tucker. The police said they would investigate it further but, of course, we all knew that wasn't going to happen. There would be no justice for Robin. Mr. Monroe made sure of that. Lives were destroyed, people are dead, and his life remains intact.

The color of his skin and his abundance of wealth has afforded him the luxury of escaping punishment for his contribution to the events. But, I will admit that even though he had a part to play in it all, this rich and powerful white man wasn't the cause of all our problems. It was some of our own kind that set out to destroy us because of jealousy and unrelenting hatred.

Grandma said it best, "Just because we all face the same struggles, doesn't mean we are all on the same team."

On my last day of school, I got to talk with Mr. Fuller. He apologized for what happened at his grandparents' house. Mrs. Kirkland had been hired to keep the house in order and he had no idea what she and Mr. Thomas had been up to because he didn't visit the property often. He told me how that house held a lot of fond memories for him and how he spent every summer there, him and his little brother, Jacob. His grandparents' home was Jacob's favorite place in the entire world to be.

He even claimed a room in the house as his own, making a sign for the room that said, "This room belongs to Jacob B. If you want to come in, knock." The B stood for Brian. He said he always felt closer to Jacob whenever he was in Mississippi, and that his little brother was buried here in a cemetery not too far from where Belinda and her mother are buried. I didn't know how to tell him that his brother spent a lot of time at my house.

We were heading back to Louisiana for a new beginning. Aunt Celestine had convinced Mama and Grandma to move back and face those demons that they were running from so that everyone could finally move forward and embrace who we truly are. I even learned that the reason I was seeing certain people with dark eyes was because I could somehow tap into their true nature. I remember being told that the eyes are a way to see into a person's soul. I always thought it was just a figure of speech, but apparently not.

The reason why I didn't see Mr. Thomas's eyes that way was because he really was a good, decent man although circumstances clouded his judgement and he made some life-altering decisions. She also told me that, with the proper teaching, I would be able to tell the good from the bad -- no matter the color of their eyes, but based on the aura that surrounds each and every one of us.

Daddy wasn't quite himself lately. I had the opportunity to speak with him alone, and I told him everything that Mr. Thomas had said. He didn't deny or confirm anything. Sometimes, I would see him sitting outside in his truck when he thought everyone else was asleep. I could sense his sadness and pain. And, for me, that was an unstated confirmation of guilt. I knew he felt responsible for all that had happened, and it was tearing him apart.

We decided against telling Mama. Now wasn't the time to mention anything about it, not while everyone was just beginning to mend fragmented emotions. If we told, our family would certainly be ripped apart once again. We didn't want or need that. Our shoulders couldn't carry the weight of any more heavy loads. I told him that the truth was owed to Mama, but it was his truth to tell and that our love for him would never cease regardless of the outcome. For now, he would have to deal with his guilty burden alone.

Cynthia came by a few times to help us pack. She was so excited to see her best friend again and heartbroken that she was losing her all over again. The day before we left Mississippi, Dominique and I decided to take that familiar path to Willows Creek one last time. She told me she dreamt of me running from someone in the woods and she warned me to keep running and she dreamed of speaking with Xavier in the woods, offering him comfort. I told her that those things were dreams to her, but they actually happened to us and that we heard her. This wasn't a surprise to either of us now that we knew a great deal about our family history.

The bench that Phillip made for me was still there. It had become a little weathered, but it was still strong. Part of me wanted to bring it along to Louisiana, but in my heart, I knew that it belonged here. We sat down and talked for a long time about all the fun we had there once upon a time. There were so many good memories. She stood up and made her way over to the creek. I sat there and watched her as she put her bare foot into the cool water, thankful that she was returned to me.

Her nightmares drove her to my bed almost every night, but I welcomed her with opened arms. I gave her the comfort she needed day after day as she mourned for those that I mourned for long ago -- Belinda, David and now there was Phillip. They were young, vibrant and each faced a fate that was undeserved.

I noticed the color had return to Dominique's cheeks and some of the lost weight was now returning. Her eyes and hair shined brilliantly once again. Even though this wasn't the same girl that I remembered, our bond was stronger than ever before. She turned and looked at me.

"Je'taime, Angie."

I smiled at her and got up from the bench.

"Je'Taime," I said in return.

She displayed a beaming smile that warmed the innermost part of my spirit. I realized, in that moment, just how important it was to let those we love know just that. I will never let another day go by without telling my family what they mean to me because tomorrow isn't promised to any of us. That's one thing that will always stick with the people close to us. Those three small, but powerful, words spoken to them – "I love you."

"Well, let's take our final walk along the creek," Dominique said, holding her hand out to me as her crimson hair danced like a flame against the wind.

ACKNOWLEDGEMENTS

I am grateful for the encouragement I have received from people like you throughout my lifetime. I especially want to take time to express gratitude to my family. The support you each have shown me over years meant more to me than you could imagine. Without you, I wouldn't be.

THE ART & ARTIST

THE BOOK

Published with assistance from BePublished.Org in January 2018, **THE DARKEST NIGHT: WINGS OF DAWN** by A. LaQuette is the author's third release comprising THE DARKEST NIGHT trilogy. Volume 3 answers readers' long-lingering questions about the mixed-race Southern twins and the fate of the missing twin, Dominique. Navigated by Angelique, readers canvass through the accusations, confessions, revelations and determinations to arrive at the  twisted conclusion that uncovers secrets in the small community that toy with truth and trust. From bloody hands to battered bonds, what resolution can be found for a family suffering through nights in desperate need of answers? When new days dawn, will they be able to heal and blissfully move forward again?

Ideal for teen and adult audiences, the book is available for order worldwide via **ALaQuette.org** as an e-book, softcover and hardback. This work may also be ordered from bricks-and-mortar and online book retailers including Barnes & Noble, your local bookstore, Kindle and Amazon.Com.

THE AUTHOR

One who strongly trusts in God, A. LaQuette is a Mississippi native, loving wife, and proud mother of three. Her debut release of THE DARKEST NIGHT series was THE DARKEST NIGHT - "Gemini" published in February 2013. Its sequel, THE DARKEST NIGHT – "Darkest Hour" was released in May 2013. With the January 2018 release **of THE DARKEST NIGHT – "Wings Of Dawn,"** audiences worldwide received the final installment of THE DARKEST NIGHT trilogy just weeks after the author decided to begin work scripting the series for filming and release as a full-length movie.

ALaQuette.org

CPSIA information can be obtained
at www.ICGtesting.com
Printed in the USA
LVHW011541121119
637136LV00011B/750/P

9 781983 546778